Go to the Hill

a novel by
Stevie Platt

American Literary Press, Inc.
Five Star Special Edition
Baltimore, Maryland

Go to the Hill

Library of Congress
Cataloging-in-Publication Data
ISBN 1-56167-771-X

Library of Congress Card Catalog Number:
2002094132

Published by

American Literary Press, Inc.
Five Star Special Edition
8019 Belair Road, Suite 10
Baltimore, Maryland 21236

Manufactured in the United States of America

To my family, relatives, and friends
I hope you like my first book, *Go to the Hill*.
I am planning a second book. Thanks, and I love you.
Stevie

Chapter 1

The sun came though the dark green shade, and its light touched Jeffery Johnson's face in bed. He started to wake up slowly and look at the ceiling toward the shade. He tried to stand up and knew that it was too late to show up for graduation in the gym. He got out of bed and shook his roommate Greg McLean. He looked at Jeff with a sleepy head.

"What do you want?" Greg said sleepily.

"Look," Jeff pointed to the window. "Better get up and shower right away for graduation!"

"What are you talking about?" Greg asked.

Jeff walked to the window and pulled the shade down, dropped it, and let the shade roll up. The room became bright from the sun.

"Okay! I'll get out of bed now!" Greg awoke.

He jumped out of his bed, grabbed a white cotton towel and small bag, and ran to the hall toward the bathroom. Jeff laughed and took a small leather brown bag and towel with him. He went out of his room and walked to the bathroom in the hall. It was quiet, and no one was around the building. He knew that they were late. Jeff started to run to the bathroom and started to shave and shower quickly. He came back to his room and put on a nice suit.

Greg and Jeff ran though the hall to go downstairs, but they forgot to get their caps and gowns. They went back to their room, grabbed them, then went back downstairs, skipping steps to save time until they arrived on the first floor from the fourth floor. They pushed the door open hard to get out of the building and ran though the Yale College campus to the gym.

Jeff's parents were standing and waiting for him in front of the gym. His father kept looking at his watch, which was a little late, and his mother was kind of worried because she did not want to miss Jeff's graduation. The moment his mother saw Jeff and Greg, they were running with their caps and gowns across the street.

"The boys are coming now!" Mrs. Johnson pointed.

"They're supposed to be at the graduation early." Mr. Johnson sighed.

Jeff and Greg were sweaty and breathing heavily from running all the way to the gym from the dorm.

"Dad and Mom," Jeff breathed, "I'm sorry that we got up late this morning..."

Greg nodded to Jeff's parents. Mrs. Johnson looked worriedly at her husband, Mr. Johnson. He had a hard time accepting Jeff's words.

"All right," Mr. Johnson sighed. "Better put your cap and gown on before you go to the gym."

Jeff and Greg nodded, put on their caps and gowns, and ran to the doors to look for their seats. The Johnson's looked at them in the gym. Mr. Johnson thought that was so funny and came to the doors. He looked at his wife standing there and wondered what was on her mind.

"Yes, Nancy?" he asked.

"Well, Jerry," Mrs. Johnson said softly, "they embarrassed us!"

"Come on!" Jerry chuckled.

Nancy could not accept that Jeff arrived at the gym late. She tried to forget about it and went with her husband into the gym.

After graduation, Jeff got his degree from the Medical School at Yale College in New Haven, Connecticut. For a graduation gift, his parents gave Jeff a new 1925 Duesenberg Model A Roadster with a straight-eight engine of 4.2 liters and 90bhp. He became a doctor at a hospital in Boston, Massachusetts.

A few months later, Jeff was very busy with patients. Sometimes he was so tired, he would sleep at his desk in the office. His co-worker, Mike, came into the office.

"Are you giving up your job?" Mike chuckled.

"No, I am not!" Jeff slapped himself in the face. "I am so damn tired!"

Mike started to laugh and sat on a leather chair next to Jeff's desk. Then he stopped laughing and looked at Jeff's eyes. Jeff was puzzled as to why Mike was staring at him. " "Excuse me," Jeff muttered. "Do you want to say something to me?"

David nodded and stood up from the chair slowly. Jeff looked at his face.

"I would like to ask you something," Mike stated. "I would like to invite you to a party at my house this Saturday."

Jeff was surprised that Mike asked him. He heard a lot about Mike, who was always having parties at his house, but was never invited.

"Yes, I would like to go there this Saturday." Jeff nodded.

"Good, then I'll see you Saturday!" Mike smiled.

He left the office, but came back because he forgot to say something to Jeff.

"There are still single women," Mike said. "You can pick a good woman if you have a good heart."

"Sounds good to me!" Jeff laughed.

Mike laughed at Jeff and left the office. Jeff sat back in the chair and felt so weird that Mike asked him to meet some women. He did want to get married.

In the morning, Jeff picked a nice suit for the party at Mike's house. He found a navy blue vest with pants and a white shirt with light blue stripes. He put them on and left the apartment a little late.

He got to Mike's house in a few minutes. Jeff stopped by the front gate and told the host that Mike invited him to a party that day. The host asked Jeff for his name to check Mike's list. The host looked on the book, found Jeff's name on it, and told him to come in and park his car. The host pointed Jeff toward the cars parked on the grass. Jeff drove across the grass slowly and parked his car next another car. He came out and looked at the house, which was English Tudor. He was nervous because this was his first time at meeting some single women there. He went to the front door, which was already opened, walked in and looked around the foyer. It was a long foyer with black and white tiles on the floor that reached from the front door to the back. He saw people in the living room, including his friend, Mike, who was talking with other friends.

He saw Jeff and smiled. "Thank you for coming here!"

"Sure, but I'm very nervous," Jeff chucked.

The people laughed at Jeff's good sense of humor. Mike introduced his friends to Jeff. They had a good talk with Jeff. More people came into Mike's house. Jeff met many people, most of whom were doctors and lawyers. Jeff needed to go outside for fresh air. He went outside and looked at the yard with surrounding woods and a swimming pool with bathhouse. He saw a few people. There were three women and two men who sat under the saddletree. Jeff thought that he should join them. He went to the tree and introduced himself to the people. In a moment, Jeff noticed a short woman with light brown hair. She noticed Jeff staring at her. Megan knew that Jeff already fell in love with her. She tried to talk to him, but Jeff did not say anything to her. She waved at Jeff's face, which made him stop and stare at her face. Other people noticed Jeff's behavior was strange. Jeff was already embarrassed because they saw he was staring at Megan.

"Are you all right?" Megan laughed.

"Yes, I'm fine," Jeff chuckled.

Jeff looked at the people; he knew they were not that stupid. Good thing they understood that Jeff liked Megan. She asked Jeff to walk with her around the backyard. He wanted to go with Megan, so they left the people alone and walked another place. She saw a wood bench near the roses.

"I'd like to sit there with you" Megan pointed.

"Yes, that's a good idea!" Jeff smiled.

They went and sat on the bench and talked to each other for a few hours. The dinner service started, and Mike looked for Jeff to come to his table. He noticed the couple together outside. Mike came over them. Jeff and Megan laughed something funny. She saw Mike on the way to there.

"Mike's coming now." Megan whistled.

Jeff looked at Mike; he was right there.

"I'm glad that you're still here," Mike said. "Dinner is ready. Will you join us at the table?"

"Sure," Jeff nodded, "but I would like to spend time with Megan at the same table."

"Oh that's nice of you," said Megan surprised. "You didn't have to worry about me. I have my friends that I can join. Thanks."

"You can sit with Jeff if you want do," Mike suggested. "There's a seat for you with him. OK?"

"Oh, that's fine with me." Megan nodded.

Jeff was surprised that Mike did not mind Megan joining the table with all the men. They went in the house and followed Mike to his table. Jeff and Megan joined Mike's friends. It was all men at the round table, except one woman. They had good conversation.

The party was over by 11:30 p.m. The people started to leave the house. Jeff was thinking of asking Megan if she would like to see him again. Megan's friends had to leave the party. They went outside to her friend's car. Jeff ran and looked for Megan at the parking area. He saw Megan while she came to the car.

"Megan!" Jeff called.

Megan heard Jeff's voice and looked toward the direction where Jeff was calling her name. Jeff came over to Megan. She felt that he might to tell her something that he wanted to say.

"Can I see you again?" Jeff muttered.

"Yes, sure," Megan smiled. "It's easy to remember my phone number. It's 1234. You can call me any time. My roommate will give me the message from you. OK?"

Megan kissed Jeff's cheek and went in the car. Jeff's heart beat so fast. He felt so good that Megan already liked him. Megan looked at Jeff while the car went to the street. He waved at Megan and went to his car.

Two years later, Jeff and Megan got married and honeymooned in South America for three weeks. Jeff had not been happy with his job at hospital for several years, so he decided to move to another state. He wanted to be a family doctor in a small town that had no doctor. He was planning to travel with his wife, Megan, to North Carolina. They traveled on Route 1 South for two days, but they stopped in the middle of Virginia, because they were tired of traveling while Megan was four months pregnant. They decided to stay at a motel for one night. Early in the morning, they would visit the Blue Ridge Mountains.

They drove west of Virginia for an hour. Jeff tried to drive across the mountain, but his car seemed unable to drive up the mountain. He had given up the struggle to drive up the high hill. Megan saw a sign that said "Culpeper". It was about twenty miles away. She thought that it might be interesting to visit the small town.

"I want to see the town," Megan pointed. Jeff looked at her point toward the sign.

"Culpeper?" Jeff wondered.

"Umm, why not visit there?" Megan asked. "Never know, maybe we'd like to live there."

"Sure, let's go for it!" Jeff agreed.

They drove to Culpeper in a half-hour. They arrived at town and looked around. It was small and had friendly people in the community. They stayed in the hotel for a few days while they looked for the house. Megan saw a house with a long porch, which was on sale.

"I want to look inside the house," said Megan curiously. Jeff nodded, went to the door and knocked. A widow opened the door.

"Hello, what do you want?" the woman asked.

"Can we look in this house?" Jeff asked.

At first, the woman would not allow Jeff and Megan to come into the house because she didn't realize that they could buy her house.

"Are you planning to buy my house?" the woman wondered.

"Maybe, but can we please see inside first?" Megan begged.

"Sure, you can look around," answered the woman.

They came in the house. The first floor had a large living room with shelves, formal dining room with a bay, a long narrow kitchen with breakfast room and a room for office. Then they went upstairs to the second floor. It had four large bedrooms and a full bathroom. The third floor had a big attic with fully finished room. They fell in love with the house and bought it right away. After the house was sold, they went back to Boston in two days.

Go to the Hill

A month later, Jeff and his wife, Mrs. Megan Johnson, moved to Culpeper, VA, from Boston, MA. They followed a moving van to their new home. Jeff started to set aside a room to work as a family doctor out of his house. Dr. Jeffery Johnson was the only Doctor in the small town. He worked out of his own office at his house and visited the sick at other families' houses to give them medical attention.

A few months later, Megan was in the kitchen pushing the table against another wall when, suddenly, her water broke. She felt something wet on her legs. She checked her legs, but it was coming from the water bag that broke. She knew that the baby would come out any time.

"Jeff, my water broke!" Megan yelled.

Jeff was in the office and heard Megan's voice. He ran to the kitchen and looked at Megan, who stood with her wet dress. He took Megan upstairs to their bedroom and ran downstairs to call the hospital, but it was far from this town. The doctor was on the way to Jeff's house an hour from Warrenton, VA. Jeff went upstairs and helped with Megan's labor in their bedroom. A neighbor came in Jeff's house to help with Megan. A few hours later, the doctor and nurse arrived at the house. They helped with Megan's labor. She tried to push the baby out for almost twenty-three hours. Two women from the neighborhood and one nurse were helping to change the bed sheets and give Megan some water and light food. Finally, the baby's head was coming out. The doctor pulled the head out of Megan's womb and held the baby's legs.

"It's a girl!" The doctor smiled.

They were happy that the baby was born safely at the house. They named the girl Jeanette Joyce Johnson. She was the first born in the house.

Megan wanted to become a housewife and take care of her new baby. For a year, Megan had a hard time calling Jeanette's name, because she did not hear her mother's voice. Megan gave up and left Jeanette alone. She found out later that Jeanette was deaf when the baby didn't react to a fire truck passing the house. Megan was shocked and upset about Jeanette. She became an alcoholic. She did not care what other people were talking about in relation to her own daughter and felt ashamed that Jeanette was deaf. She felt that she might have to take care of Jeanette her whole life. But Jeanette's father accepted his daughter no matter what. He felt it was better to not have hearing than to not have sight, for it life would be more difficult if she were blind.

Norman and Shelly Wilson lived upstairs in an apartment, and Shelly owned the Beauty Salon downstairs. They had a daughter named Maria Wilson. When Shelly was pregnant, she had the flu with a high fever. It would have killed both of them, but the medicine made her fever go down. When Maria was two years old, her mother tried to call Maria's name, but she could not hear her voice. Shelly came in the kitchen and sat on a chair. Mr. Norman Wilson was an English teacher at Culpeper High School. When he come home, he looked at Shelly's sad face.

"What's the matter?" Norman asked.

"Maria did not listen me at all," Shelly complained. "I give up on her."

Norman felt that Maria might be deaf like Dr. Johnson's daughter.

"Shelly," Norman said, "I think that you should go to Dr. Johnson's office, which is across the street from my school. You can walk there in a few minutes."

"OK, that sounds like a good idea." Shelly nodded.

The next day, Shelly decided to take Maria to Dr. Johnson's office at his house. Shelly held Maria's hand because Maria was stubborn and often did not pay attention to the road. She could not hear the cars coming.

When they arrived at the house, Shelly looked through the window of the front door. She could see wood railings with stairs. She walked to another door where the family doctor worked. She came in the office with Maria. Dr. Jeff Johnson was doing paperwork at his desk. He looked at Maria, who looked at the basket full of toys and books. Shelly sat down the chair.

"Hello, can you tell me what the problem is?" Jeff questioned.

"Yes," Shelly explained, "my daughter, Maria, has some problem with her brain. Sometimes she has a rough time understanding me, and she doesn't listen when I try to call her name."

Go to the Hill

He felt that Maria might be deaf like his daughter. Dr. Johnson took out some toys for Maria and put them on his desk. Shelly was puzzled at what Jeff was doing with Maria. Jeff walked behind her back and started to clap his hands a few times, but Maria did not look back to him. He did the right thing to test Maria's ears. She was deaf.

"She is deaf," Jeff said.

Shelly was shocked and upset that her own daughter was deaf. She started to cry. Jeff came over to Shelly and wanted to introduce her to his wife and daughter.

"What was your name?" Jeff asked.

"I'm Shelly Wilson," Shelly muttered.

"What's your daughter's name?" Jeff pointed.

"Maria Wilson. She is two years old." Shelly said.

"Will you come with me to see my family?" Jeff said.

Shelly nodded and stood up. Jeff took Maria and opened another door inside the house. They walked through the hall to living room. Shelly felt awed by the hall there with a fancy lamp on the ceiling, which she didn't see before. They came in living room. Shelly looked around the living room. There was bright jet green paint on the wall and large brown shelves full of books. Mrs. Johnson sat on the sofa, read the newspaper and chain-smoked. Jeanette was one and half years old, short and thin, and lay on the rug playing with her doll.

"Megan," Jeff started, "I would like to meet Mrs. Shelly Wilson and her daughter, Maria. She also is deaf."

Shelly looked at Megan. The room was bright from the sun and made Shelly's eyes hurt. Jeff put Maria on the floor and pulled her to meet Jeanette. Jeanette felt the vibration on the floor and looked at Maria's feet towards her face, which was big and chubby. It made Jeanette scared, and she ran to her mother and held her.

"Jeanette is scared," Megan said. "She thinks that Maria will hurt her because she's taller and weighs more than Jeanette."

Megan tried to explain to Jeanette that they would not bite he. She wanted Jeanette to meet Maria who was also deaf. Megan brought Jeanette close to Maria and played with the doll. A few minutes later, they got along fine together. Megan stood and went over to the table with a carafe and glasses. She poured wine into two glasses and gave one to Shelly.

"This for you," Megan smiled.

"No thanks," Shelly said.

Megan drank the wine by herself. She put the glass on the table and took another the glass for herself. Shelly wondered why Megan drank too much wine. Shelly did not say anything to Megan. She looked at Maria and Jeanette on the floor. They were playing with toys and ran upstairs to Jeanette's bedroom.

During the middle of the depression years, the two couples parked across the creek at a hill. They were looking for a tree with plenty of shade to avoid the sun and stay cool, since July was so hot and humid outside at noontime. They wanted to eat comfortably under the tree. Megan saw a large maple tree.

"Jeff, I found a tree!" Megan pointed.

"Where?" Jeff looked.

"Right there." Megan pointed again.

Jeff saw the large tree near the hill. He drove under the branches and parked. Jeff got out of the car and walked around the tree.

"Ahh," Jeff said, "it's the perfect place for a picnic here."

Norman and Shelly got out of their car. Norman came over to Jeff and looked at the ground to make sure it was level.

"It's not that bad," Norman chuckled. "Let's get some water right now! I'm so thirsty. This weather makes me crazy!"

Megan got out of the car, but her six-year-old daughter, Jeanette, escaped from the back seat to the front, jumped out of the car and ran to the Wilson's car. Megan laughed at Jeanette in her blue dress, because she was such a wild girl with bright blond hair and a small blue bow on her head. Jeanette loved to play actively and mischievously, that was why she was so thin.

Norman went back to get the basket out of his car. Shelly opened the door and let Maria out with her books and doll. Maria was three months older than Jeanette was; her brown hair tied with a white bow. She was wearing a white blouse and brown suit. She was a little overweight from the sweet candies from the store next door to the beauty shop her mother owned.

Jeanette sneaked to Maria from behind the car. Shelly saw Jeanette, and she tried to scare Maria. Shelly knew Jeanette would like to hide from Maria. Now Jeanette changed her mind and wanted to play tag with Maria. She ran and touched Maria's back. Jeanette ran away from Maria quickly. Maria was looking for Jeanette and was excited to play. She had a plan to run and tag Jeanette, but her mom held Maria's hand. Shelly grabbed the books and doll from Maria, because Shelly did not want Maria to leave her things somewhere over the hill where she couldn't find it. She preferred to keep her things in the car.

"Let's go play with Jeanette." Shelly pointed to Maria's shirt. "Be careful with your new shirt."

Maria nodded and ran with Jeanette over the hill. Shelly threw the books and doll inside the car and watched Maria who ran slowly while Jeanette ran fast. Shelly was laughing at Maria and wanted her to lose weight.

Megan walked past the Wilson's car, started lighting a cigarette and watched the girls run over the hill.

"My poor daughter, Maria," Shelly laughed. "Let's have Jeanette play with Maria more often so she can lose weight."

Shelly was still laughing; she thought that was so funny. Megan didn't say anything to her. Shelly stopped laughing and knew Megan was not interested in her conversation. She walked past Shelly under the branches. It kept Megan away from the sun.

Shelly and Megan were setting blanket, plates, glasses and foods on the ground for lunch. Norman and Jeff set up a fire to cook hamburgers and pork beans. Shelly had planned to look for the girls, but she couldn't see them because they were so high up the hill. Megan was willing to look for the girls.

"I will get the girls back here for lunch," Megan sighed.

Shelly nodded and let Megan go up the hill to look for the girls. Shelly watched carefully while Megan walked up the hill and looked over other hills. Megan saw the girls down the hill; they were picking wild flowers. Megan sat down on the grass and started to smoke a cigarette. She might as well relax and watch them. Jeanette was counting the wild flowers she collected, and at that moment the wind started to blow a little hard. The smoke was flowing to the area where the girls were. Jeanette knew from that cigarette smoke smell that her mother was somewhere around near them. She saw her mother sitting at the top of the hill and waved

11

to her. Megan waved back. Jeanette smiled and ran to Maria to grab her hands. Jeanette put her wild flowers on the ground and put the wild flowers from Maria's hand to the ground. Jeanette started to run one way and Maria ran the opposite way. They were playing "merry-go-round". They were spinning so fast. Megan kept watching them while they continued to spin. She started to tear up and felt her heart break about her daughter.

After War World II, it was over in Germany. Bombs from the air forces damaged other countries. The army went back to America within a few weeks after the end of the war. In America, it was hard for women to leave their jobs while all the men were serving in Europe for almost six years. Now all the men had to go back to their hometowns and find jobs. All the women had to go back to their homes and take care of their children, reverting back to family tradition. But most of the women wanted to stay at their jobs because they liked the taste of work experience more than staying in the house with the children.

Jeanette and Maria grew up together. They communicated by combined method and spoke as well, but they were not used to speaking orally. Jeanette was short and thin, the same as her mother's height, and had long, dark, dirty blonde hair. She always liked to play rough with other kids and flirt with handsome guys from school. Jeanette was a good average student at Culpeper High School. She was involved in clubs and sports.

Maria was pretty tall and bigger boned with a medium brown hair to her shoulder. The boys were afraid of Maria, because she could fight against the boys at school or at the park. If someone started to pick on her for no reason, she would lift him up to the sky then down to the ground. She always liked to read books and wrote in a diary since she was about eight years old. Her father was a professional English teacher in Culpeper High School where Maria attended. He encouraged Maria to read books, because she was unable to hear spoken words. She could increase her vocabulary through the words she read in books. She was the top Honor student at Culpeper High School for four straight years. During school seasons, her father hired a private tutor to teach the two girls any subject, with a note line for their homework, while they attended the classes. They were the only two deaf girls in 150 hearing students in Culpeper High School.

During senior year, Maria and Jeanette were thinking about going to Gallaudet College. They took a test for English and Math to meet the college level. A few months later, the staff from Gallaudet mailed the letters to Maria and Jeanette's house. They were accepted to be freshmen at Gallaudet College in the fall of 1945. They were exited and could not to wait to graduate that spring.

A week after they graduated from Culpeper High School, Maria, Jeanette and her boyfriend, Sean, went to the hill for a nice view of the full blue sky with very few clouds. The land and trees were a very lush green. The weather was very warm and started to become humid in the first weekend of June. Maria lay on the ground with a blanket over her stomach; she brought some magazine, books and a yearbook from high School. She wrote in her diary about her graduation from high school. She looked at the mountain, reminiscing about the past and her freshman year at high school, then her memories appeared as she wrote in her diary.

Sean sat back in the station wagon of the 1938 Ford. He set up the film and checked to make sure it was working. He loved to film for both hobby and pleasure. He looked at his girlfriend, Jeanette; she stood up, looked at the land and could see a house next to the red big barn with sheep and goats. They were spread out around the area, liking the freedom but unable to go out of the fence. Sean started to film Jeanette and walked close to her while the film ran on. He tried to whisper, but forgot that she was deaf and could not hear his whisper. Jeanette did not know that Sean was filming her. She noticed when he tried to get close to her. Then she became an actress like Lauren Bacall and pulled her shirt down her left shoulder like a sexy woman.

"Whoa, come on," Sean laughed. "Go for it!"

Jeanette walked close to Sean while the film ran on; she pointed to Maria's butt. Sean laughed hard.

"Keep the film running for me," she said. "I'm going to scare her to death!"

She jumped on Maria's back like a horse ride. Maria screamed loud, her back turned up, and attacked Jeanette quickly. Maria lifted Jeanette high up into the air; her body was so light that the students from school called Jeanette "feather body." Jeanette tried to escape from Maria raising her body up in the air. Maria ran and caught Jeanette. Sean stopped the film; he knew Maria did not like what Jeanette was doing to her back.

"NO! Please don't touch me," Jeanette begged. "Stop lifting me to the sky!"

"Too bad for you!" Maria laughed like a devil. "How dare you jump me with my big butt in front of the camera. You made me so embarrassed!"

Jeanette was still laughing at Maria for no reason. Maria rolled her eyes up started to pull her hair. It felt like she could pull out the hair from her head to leave a small bald area.

"Give me break! I hope that doesn't happen when we go to Gallaudet College!" She was so upset with Jeannette. "Do you promise me that you will not do to me on campus?"

Jeanette looked up at the sky then down toward the ground with her hands on her hips and her right foot tapping. Maria looked puzzled at what Jeanette was doing to her. Jeanette raised her arms and pretended to play a violin very slowly.

"Poor thing," she said, smiling like a killer. "I don't think that will not happen when we go to Gallaudet College this fall."

Jeanette continued the violin play and walked around the blanket. It made Maria nuts; she felt that she could kill Jeanette, but she knew it was against the law and didn't want to be in jail her whole life. Jeanette looked at Maria and stopped playing the pretend violin.

"Come on, don't be upset," she signed. "Just forget this happened."

Jeanette pulled Maria's hand away from the blanket, ran higher up the hill, stopped and looked at the mountain toward the best view. Jeanette looked at Maria with a smile. The wind started to blow on them, and they looked at the sky, closed their eyes shut, and raised their arms up in the air like they used to do when they were little girls. They always played like airplanes and ran around the hill. They stopped right away because they weren't kids anymore. Now they were women getting ready for a new world of their own without living with their parents.

"Whoa, I don't want to play that again!" Maria's breath was very heavy. "I'm too old for that."

"Wait a minute, I want to play just one more time," Jeanette giggled, "the last one for sure. Please?"

"What?" Maria asked looking puzzled. "The last one? I don't understand what you're talking about it."

"You and me used to play 'merry-go-round' together," she said excitedly. "That was my favorite one. Let's play one more time before we're off to Gallaudet."

"Oh no! I'll vomit on you," said Maria, rolling her eyes up and holding her hands together tight. "OK! OK! This is the last one!"

Jeanette was so excited and grabbed Maria to go to another area that had flatter ground, which was better for playing "merry-go-round". The other side had no slope, and they did not want to fall down and hurt themselves. Jeanette and Maria held each other's hands tightly.

"Are you ready?" Jeanette asked clearly to Maria.

"Umm?" Maria nodded. "Go now!"

They turned like a "merry-go-round" and spun faster into a whirl. They felt like they had come back to old times when they were little girls and had more time to stay on the hill. Sean started filming while they were spinning together.

The sky became dusk. Maria looked at the sun, but it went down. She rushed to pack her things and brought them to the car. Jeanette and Sean folded the blanket and took a bag of food. They came in the car and left for home.

Summer was almost at the end of its season. Jeanette and Maria went shopping with their family. They bought new clothes and personal things for the dorm. Maria wanted to know what the dorm looked like. Jeanette felt that there was no privacy. She knew that they would be sharing the room with other girls. They had to use it for four years. They spent time with their family and friends before going to Gallaudet College. It was hard for them to leave their hometown.

At the end of August 1946, Maria's parent's car was following

Jeanette's parent's car to Washington D.C. early in the morning. They arrived in front of the campus.

"Which girl's dorm should we find?" Jeff wondered.

He saw three students on the sidewalk; they were talking with sign language.

"Can you ask them to find the girls' dorm?" Jeff asked Jeanette.

Jeanette nodded, left the car and came over to the students. They looked at Jeanette.

"Do you know where the girls' dorm is?" Jeanette asked.

"Are you a new student?" the student asked.

"Yes, I am Jeanette Johnson." Jeanette introduced herself.

"I am Julie Ross, nice to meet you." Julie shook Jeanette's hand.

Jeff was in the car; he had no patience waiting so long. He wanted to move right away. The student noticed Jeff's face, which looked like he was about to get mad at Jeanette for wasting his time as he waited in the car.

"Your father has no patience to wait for you," the student pointed.

Jeanette looked at her father in the car. She did not realize that it was too long to wait to ask to find the girls' dorm.

"Where is it?" Jeanette rushed.

"Fowler Hall is right there," Julie pointed.

"There's our dorm!" Jeanette pointed.

"Great! I'm going to park my car there!" Jeff chuckled.

Jeff drove to the parking lots and came out of the car. Norman parked his car. Shelly and Maria came out of the car right away because they did not like to ride long, and the trip took almost three hours.

"Thanks and see you around later," Jeanette said.

"Yes, same to you too," Julie smiled. "We can get together tonight. OK? Bye!"

Jeanette waved at Julie and her friends. She went to her parents and Maria's parents and went in Fowler Hall. That was a dorm for girls only. An older woman was sitting on a chair in the hall waiting for new girls who came to Fowler Hall. She stood up when the people came in the building.

"Those girls are freshmen?" She pointed to the girls.

Jeanette and Maria liked what the woman did to them.

"This is my daughter, Jeanette Johnson," Jeff pointed. "And this is Maria Wilson there with her parents."

"Good, please follow me upstairs," the woman said.

They followed the woman upstairs to the second floor and walked through the hall to the room. Jeanette and Maria looked around each of the rooms and bathroom. They came in the room where they were supposed live for a year. The woman pointed to the bed toward the closet.

"That bed in the corner and the closet there are for you." She pointed to Maria.

"And the other bed near the window is for you." She pointed to Jeanette.

She wondered where her closet was.

"Where is my closet?" Jeanette asked.

"You may share the closet with Maria," she said.

Jeanette was not comfortable with what the woman said. She looked at Maria, who did not like it either.

"Now it's time for you to bring your things in," the woman said.

She left the room to go downstairs. Maria sat on the bed and got homesick already. Jeanette sat next to Maria and hugged her.

"We will get used to it for now," Jeanette signed.

She looked at the other three beds and wondered who the other girls were. They went downstairs to their car, brought their things to their room and unpacked with their mothers. They were in for a bombshell by the deaf culture on campus because there had only been two deaf people in their hometown. However, it was not only them. There were still plenty of deaf people somewhere around the world, either going to deaf schools like Gallaudet College or public schools.

The first day of classes, Maria and Jeanette went to College Hall in the morning. They were in classes with other students. There were only thirty-six freshmen.

During their college years, they gained life experience in their school. They met new faces, learned the Combined Method with other the students from different states, socially explained what they learned from Y.W.C.A. Maria joined the literary society;

she loved to enter poetry contests and submit essays for the school. Jeanette joined G.C.W.A.A. (Gallaudet College Women's Athletic Association). She was interested in playing sports with women, and sometimes with men. She enjoyed activities for a year. Jeanette and Maria joined O.W.L.S. Sorority. A sisterhood from the same group, the four women included Bonnie Lewis from Ohio. She was a very nice person but sometime bossy. Angel Martinez was from New Jersey, but her native country was Cuba. She was very active and stubborn. Vicky Matins, a Penn native, was always passive, and DeeDee Anderson, from North Carolina, was very talkative. They were the closest friends of Jeanette and Maria, since they met during first year.

The school was closed for summer. They went to their hometowns, but it was a short time to stay there. They already missed their friends from Gallaudet. They joined other friends to travel in the United States for three months. They stopped and stayed at their friends' places in other states, then had to go back to Washington, D.C. before classes started in fall 1947.

Jeanette and Maria studied at school through the years. They graduated from Gallaudet College in May of 1949.

Jeanette got Bachelor of Art Degree and became an artist teacher at a deaf school, but it was not the right major for her. Jeanette worked as a secretary at a hospital in Culpeper. A few months after Jeanette got the job, she went out to eat with other hearing single women at a café downtown. At the table, Jeanette was bored with the women because she felt left out. She decided to look at other people around the café. Jeanette noticed a man at a table with his friends. He was a tall with short, dirty blond hair, white shirt and tie. She was puzzled that he kept looking at the women at her table. Jeanette kept watching him. He moved his head toward Jeanette and touched his eyes to her eyes. That scared her to death. She looked down at the table. The women left the café to go back to the car, and Jeanette went into the car with them. The last woman came in and closed the door shut. She scared that a man was trying to catch her before she closed the door.

"Open the window please?" The man gestured.

The woman opened the window.

"What you want?" she asked.

Go to the Hill

"I would like to know her name." He pointed to Jeanette.

"Jeanette. She is deaf," she said.

"She's deaf?" he wondered.

"Jeanette can write on paper or speak as well," she explained.

"Can you tell Jeanette," he asked, "that I'm Paul Dreyfuss."

She nodded and told Jeanette his name. Jeanette was shy.

"She's shy," she laughed. "I'm Susie."

"Nice meet you and Jeanette too," Paul said.

"Donna, Rita and Renee," Susie pointed. "Most of us always go to the café and the bar for a while because we're single."

"Nice to meet you," the women greeted to Paul.

"Good," Paul smiled. "Most of my friends are single too. We will be at the bar this Friday. Will you go there too?"

"Of course we will!" Susie laughed.

"I think I better go for now," Paul said. "See you this Friday. You have a good afternoon. Good bye."

Paul ran to his friend's car on another side street. Susie closed the window. She looked at Jeanette.

"I think he likes you," Susie giggled. "He is cute!"

"Umm, yes," Jeanette said shyly.

On Friday evening, Jeanette and her friends from work went to the bar. Jeanette was not used to hearing people, because she was used to hanging out with deaf people at Gallaudet for four years. She should stay in D.C. and get a job there sometime with deaf people. She already missed the campus. She looked at the people in the bar; they were dancing and drinking beers. Jeanette was still shy about Paul seeing her tonight. She saw her friends at the bar. They were smoking cigarettes. Jeanette wondered why they were smoking. She came over to her friends at the bar, and Susie looked at Jeanette.

"Why are you smoking?" Jeanette pointed.

"The men think it's sexy." Susie explained.

"Are you sure," Jeanette puzzled, "that men like women smoking cigarettes?"

"Yes. You'll look sexy too," Susie nodded.

Jeanette had a hard time deciding if she would smoke.

"I want to smoke a cigarette too," Jeanette said.

The women were surprised that Jeanette wanted to smoke

19

with them. They laughed at Jeanette, because she did not know how to do it. Renee gave a cigarette to Jeanette, who started to smoke. She inhaled the smoke, but coughed. The women were surprised that Jeanette could take it. Paul and his friends arrived at the bar later. He saw Jeanette with her friends.

"I saw the women there," Paul pointed, "that I met at the café last Tuesday afternoon."

They came over to the women. Paul looked at Jeanette while she coughed badly. He gave a puzzling look to Susie.

"What's she doing?" Paul asked.

"Oh well," Susie muttered, "she tried to smoke a cigarette. But she made it."

"Oh poor Jeanette." Paul said.

Jeanette slapped Susie for telling Paul what she was doing with the cigarette. Jeanette pulled Paul's arm to the dance floor. She smashed the cigarette on the floor. Paul wondered why Jeanette brought him to the dance floor.

"Are you dancing with me?" Paul asked.

Jeanette did not realize that the floor was meant for dancing. She changed her mind and did not dance with him. She left the bar with her friends. Paul grabbed Jeanette's arm to dance with him. Jeanette's face turned red. They were dancing for a few minutes. The band on stage changed to a different song. The people started dancing with more fun. Jeanette did not like that and walked back to her friends at the bar. She noticed that her friends liked talking with the men who were Paul's friends. They were enjoying spending the evening together. Jeanette looked at Paul, while he was on the way to the bar with her friends there. Paul asked Jeanette if she would go out with him on a date. Jeanette said, "Yes."

Paul and Jeanette were going out to eat, walking in the park and other places together. They had a good relationship for almost two years. In spring of 1951, they got married in a church at Culpeper. Paul was an engineer for a site and involved in environmental planning in city hall.

He bought a yellow house with fifty acres in the country. They started a new family. Jeanette wanted to keep her job until her daughter was five years old and went to preschool. Jeanette went back to work part-time. One thing that she missed was her best friend, Maria. She was still in D.C. with her job and friends. Maria got a Bachelor of Science degree to be an English teacher. She got a full time job teaching at the Kendall School for the Deaf for a year, but she had lost motivation teaching deaf kids. She decided to go back to school and change majors. Maria got another degree in Math. She wanted to move back to Culpeper and get a full time job in payroll and clerical at the bank. Jeanette invited Maria to her house for a party. Maria met Ray Scott. He worked under his father's business for Heating and Oil for houses and apartments. They already liked each other for a year. They decided to get married right away, because Maria did not like living with her mother since her father passed away from a heart attack while she was in D.C. Her mother gave some money from her father's will for her wedding gifts. They bought a brand new house with two levels. They had four bedrooms with one full bathroom. When Bobby was born, Maria had to leave her job for the new family and to take care of her new son.

Jeanette and Maria were spending time together with their kids. They went shopping and to the theater together. Except, they went to the hill to be alone without the kids.

During the middle of the 1950s, Jeanette and Maria's sisterhood of O.W.L.S. Sorority—Bonnie, Angel, Vicky, and DeeDee—moved to Culpeper with their husbands and family. Most of their husbands were deaf and worked at the print shop for the Culpeper newspaper and to make supplies for papers like memo, bookkeeper and formal letterhead with a company's address and business name. They were together again. They had an active social life with their kids for dinner on Saturday evenings and short trips for a day. They went to the church every Sunday in the morning and Bible studies, with women only, every Wednesday evening.

Chapter 2

On November 22, 1963, early in the morning, President John F. Kennedy and his wife Jacqueline B. Kennedy flew to Dallas, Texas from Washington, D.C. for a downtown tour at one o'clock in the afternoon. Many people were excited to see President John F. Kennedy and the First Lady, who would have to ride with Texas Governor John Connally and his wife.

Jeanette raised her three daughters, Mary Anna, Nikki and Barbara. All were hearing and used sign with their mother. They went to school all day. Jeanette took a full-time job at the hospital again. She started to save some money for a new car. Every night she went to bed, she started to dream about getting a new 1964 Ford Thunderbird Convertible. She wanted to trade her 1953 Buick Road Master Riviera Sedan for the new car.

Jeanette informed her boss that she planned to travel to Charlottesville to get the new car. Her boss let Jeanette take off a day. Jeanette drove to Charlottesville. She arrived at Harry's Ford and parked in front of the store. She came into the lobby. The dealer was waiting for someone to come in. He saw Jeanette and came over her. Jeanette looked at him.

"I'm Andy Wells," he said. "Can I help you?"

She told Andy that she was deaf and showed him to her old car. She wanted to trade her old car for a brand new car.

"What kind of car?" Andy asked.

Jeanette came into the building and pointed to the new 1964 Ford Thunderbird Convertible; it was on model for everyone to look inside the car.

"That the car you want?" Andy asked.

"Yes, I want that car," Jeanette nodded.

"Sure I can do it for you," said Andy certainly. "I will talk to my boss about the Buick Road Master Riviera Sedan. Can you wait for a moment?"

Jeanette nodded and started to smoke a cigarette. Andy went to the boss's office and asked him about trading the car.

She could see through the window in the boss's office. She knew that they were trying to talk about trading the car. Andy and the boss left the office through the lobby to go outside. Andy pointed to the Buick car parked there. The boss nodded and said he wanted the car for himself. She wondered what the boss said about that car and whether he would accept the trade. They came back in the building toward Jeanette.

"She's deaf," Andy said, "but I didn't ask her name."

"Can you read my lips?" The boss asked.

"Sometimes, but not so well," Jeanette muttered.

"What is your name please?" Andy asked.

"J E A N E T T E," she spoke as clearly, "D R E Y F U S S."

The boss and Andy tried to catch her full name. The boss took his pen to write what Jeanette told him. He wrote her full name and showed the note to Jeanette. She checked that it was spelled correctly. She nodded that he got it right.

"All right," the boss smiled, "you can trade it, but you need to fill out some paperwork right away before you can take that car."

The boss told Andy that he could fill out the form and sign her name on it. The boss shook Jeanette's hand and went back to his office.

"Good, we can make it," Andy said. "Please come with me and go to the room for the paperwork."

She was so excited that she was getting a new car. They went to the room. He told Jeanette to sit there.

"I'll get some forms," Andy said, "and I'll be right back."

He rushed to another office. Jeanette nodded and started to smoke again. The car dealership was busy and crowded, because people were buying the same kind of car she bought before JFK was shown on TV at 1 p.m. that afternoon. Andy came back to the room and put the paperwork on the table; they filled out the form and Jeanette signed her name on it. Andy took the paperwork to the office. Jeanette sighed and waited another few minutes. She got tired of waiting and walked to the hall and looked for Andy somewhere in the office. Jeanette saw a tall woman with fur over her shoulder. She noticed that the woman was acting like a bitch. Another dealer came to the woman, but Jeanette could not hear what they were talking about. Jeanette could tell that the woman had a bad attitude toward the dealer. Jeanette saw another woman with a folder who came from the accountant's office. The dealer took the folder from her and gave it to the woman. She left with the folder. The accountant was mad at the dealer and she did not like it that he took it without her knowing. She came to Andy and gave the folder to him. Jeanette knew that Andy would be on the way to the room. She went back to the room and sat on the chair. Andy came in the room and showed Jeanette the key to her new car.

"Here's the key for you," Andy smiled. "Let's go now!"

They went to the new car outside. Andy gave the key to Jeanette. She unlocked the door and climbed into the car. She asked Andy how to open the convertible. He showed Jeanette how to unlock the roof above the windshield. He pushed the convertible over to near the trunk and locked it. She took a pink scarf out of her purse and put it to cover her head, donned her sunglasses, and started chain-smoking. It all made her feel so good! She felt like she was an actress in Hollywood, California. Andy laughed that he thought she looked good in her new car. He almost forgot to give her the folder. He gave it to Jeanette, and she put it in her purse so it wouldn't be lost.

"Thanks! Bye!" Jeanette waved.

Andy waved to Jeanette while she left Harry's Ford. She drove her new car with a high speed on Route 29. It was quiet and there were not many cars on the road, just herself with her brand new car. She speeded up because she wanted to have a fun with her new car! But her scarf began loosen, and a few seconds later, it slipped off her head. She tried to catch the scarf, but it was too late because of she was going over 80 mph. The scarf was gone somewhere on the road. She was upset that her scarf was gone because this was her favorite scarf and a gift from her mother for her 30th birthday. Jeanette had to accept it.

Maria's mother wanted her to come to the Beauty Shop to help with the bookkeeping. The previous woman left her job because her husband found a new job in Colorado. They left town a few weeks ago. Maria brought her daughter, Jobelle, who was three months old. Maria put Jobelle in the crib. She went to the desk and started the bookkeeping. She finished her work around noon. Maria came to see her mother and informed her that her job was done. She took her daughter and drove home. She came in the house and walked toward her bedroom. Maria put Jobelle in the crib and moved the crib closer to her bed. She sat on the bed and took her shoes off. She took a nap for a few minutes.

When Jeanette arrived at Culpeper, she drove to Maria's home and parked at her backyard. She got out of the car and slammed the door hard because she was angry about losing her favorite scarf. Jeanette came into the kitchen from outside. It was a huge room with light oak wood cabinets and dark green tiles on the floor. A long rectangle table with eight chairs was in the middle of the room. There was only a cerulean blue plate with fresh butter on the middle of the table. The kitchen was full of decorations of peaches and strawberries. That's what Maria collected for the kitchen.

Jeanette looked in the mirror and saw her hair was a mess. She tried to fix it, but it still looked awful. She gave up, sat down on the chair, put her purse on the table, took a cigarette and lighter out of her purse and started to smoke. That made her feel satisfied. A few minutes later, the smoke started to flow to other rooms. Maria was in her bedroom and awoke from the smoke, which was bothering her. Maria wondered if someone was there. It was Friday, so it was a workday. She wanted to nap longer because she woke up so early to get her children ready for school and clean up the house. But maybe there was something wrong. Could someone be hurt or have a problem? Alternatively, it could have been one of her husband's friends or cousins stopping by her place for her help or to borrow her husband's tools from the garage. Maria's rule for smokers was that they could smoke in the kitchen, period. She could not stand to smell of cigarettes and therefore didn't allow smoking in any other room. She preferred the other rooms to stay clean and fresh.

She thought she better to check and see who was in the kitchen. She got out of bed, put her shoes on, and looked in the mirror to make sure her hair was a mess. She made sure Jobelle did not wake up yet. Maria came to the door and opened it. She walked to the kitchen and looked at who was there. She found saw it was Jeanette and noticed her face looked sad for some reason.

"What's the matter with you?" Maria asked, concerned. "Did something happen to you?"

Jeanette looked at Maria and her eyebrow raised.

"Well," she exhaled the cigarette, "it's not that important I lost my favorite pink scarf."

Maria wondered why she was spoke about her pink scarf. There were plenty of pink scarves in the drawer at her home. She did not understand why Jeanette was upset over a small problem with her scarf. It bothered her.

"What are you talking about? What favorite pink scarf?" Maria wondered. "I'm confused because you collect scarves. There are still plenty of other pink scarves that you can wear. Which one was your favorite pink scarf?"

Jeanette rolled her eyes up at the ceiling for a few seconds and blew smoke from the cigarette. Maria was standing and staring at her and expecting an answer concerning her problem with the stupid scarf.

"Ok, I will explain it to you," Jeanette admitted. "My favorite pink scarf was a present from my mother, and now it's gone."

"How did you lose it?" Maria asked.

"Well, never mind about it. Just forget about my favorite scarf," Jeanette said. "I want to show you something outside."

Jeanette stood up and walked to the window. Maria was puzzled with Jeanette's quick change of behavior. It was strange because Maria had not seen her act that way before.

"Come here please," Jeanette said excitedly. "Look outside at what I got today."

Maria was still puzzled and walked to the window. Sometimes

she did not trust Jeanette, because she always played a game with her. Maria decided to look outside. She noticed Jeanette's new car.

"You bought a brand new car," Maria said. "WOW! I don't believe it! What kind of car is that?"

"It's a Ford Thunderbird convertible," Jeanette answered.

"What year?" Maria asked curiously. "Is it a 1963 or 1964?"

"Oh that's a 1964," Jeanette answered. "I forgot about it, excuse me!"

Jeanette laughed hard. Maria was shocked that she already bought it. In a few moments, she looked at Jeanette and knew that her scarf flew off her head while she was driving the convertible. That was why Jeanette's hair was a mess.

"Jeanette," Maria asked, "were you upset that your scarf flew off your head while you were driving the new car?"

Jeanette was surprised that Maria could tell she was upset. Jeanette looked down at the floor for few seconds and looked back at Maria again. Maria raised her eyebrow to Jeanette.

"Umm, yes," Jeanette nodded, "that's why I was upset. I lost my favorite scarf somewhere on the road while I was on my way here from Charlottesville."

Maria understood why Jeanette was so upset. She hoped that she could forget about her favorite scarf.

"All right," Maria said, "you'll forget about it. Just forget it. The past is over. Now you have a new car and will have fun riding with the top down."

Jeanette smiled and giggled at her. "Thanks," Jeanette smiled, "you make me feel better."

"You're welcome," Maria smiled. "I'm glad you admitted it to me. It's no big deal. Remember that we are only human, which is the more important than anything is. Isn't that right?"

Jeanette nodded and hugged Maria. That was good advice and it encouraged her to forget about the scarf. Jeanette looked at her new car outside again. Maria lightly patted Jeanette's back.

"I must ask you," Maria asked, "how much did that car cost? I'm just curious, if don't mind telling me."

Jeanette was not surprised that Maria would ask.

"It was very expensive," Jeanette explained. "It cost me

$4,687.54, but it's a good thing I traded my old car. That saved me a lot of money."

"What?" Maria was surprised. "That's lot of money. I can't afford to buy a new car. I prefer to keep my station wagon that's still operating after almost 13 years."

Maria came to the end of the table, pulled a chair out and sat down. She looked at Jeanette. "You're lucky," Maria pointed, "because your husband gets paid well working as an engineer for so long. My husband doesn't get paid as much."

Jeanette rolled her eyes up and slapped her thigh.

"Don't stress yourself," Jeanette signed. "Your husband has a good job, and it's hard to find a good job where he can fit in."

Maria nodded and agreed with Jeanette's good point about their husbands' jobs. Jeanette came over to the table and opened her purse to take out the signed paper from the Ford dealer. She gave it to Maria who unfolded it and read the signed form. She noticed the form that Jeanette signed had a different name on the paper. There was probably something wrong with this signed paper. Maria looked at Jeanette, who was looking at her new car outside. Maria sighed and wished Jeanette would have been more careful and checked that the signed paper was for her and not another person. It looked like either the office or the dealer gave the paperwork to the wrong person by mistake.

Maria started to bang her hand on the table. This caught Jeanette's attention, who couldn't hear but could feel the vibration from the noise. Jeanette looked to Maria.

"What," Jeanette said, "do you have any questions about this signed paper?"

Maria did not say anything, but looked at bottom of paper at the name of the person who signed it. She felt that Jeanette did not read very careful before leaving the auto store.

"Who are you," Maria replied. "Are you Mrs. Ruby Robertson?"

Jeanette wondered why Maria asked such a stupid question about a Mrs. Ruby Robertson. She knew that Maria was trying to give her a hard time, because Jeanette always played with her like a child. She knew that Maria wanted to play back.

"Who are you," Maria repeated. "Hey Mrs. Robertson, it

that you?"

Jeanette rolled her eyes and shook her head. She knew that was joke.

"What are you talking about," Jeanette signed. "I am not Mrs. Ruby Robertson, that lady acted like a bitch! Please don't play with me, ok?"

Jeanette turned her head back to the window and looked at her new car. Maria nodded and looked at the signed paper again. She was concerned about Jeanette if the police happened stop her while she was speeding on the road. The police would ask her for her driver's license and registration. He would find out that the car was not hers. Maybe he would think she stole the vehicle from Mrs. Robertson then he'd take Jeanette to jail. Jeanette felt that she should have checked the signed paper in case someone dealership made a mistake. She wanted to make sure the car belonged to either her or Mrs. Robertson. Jeanette wondered why Maria asked her about Mrs. Robertson, the woman she saw in the lobby at Harry's Ford. The dealer took the wrong folder from the account woman to Mrs. Robertson. Jeanette took the signed form from Maria and read the bottom of the paper. She found out that it was not her signature and realized Maria was not trying to tease her. It was a serious situation.

"I knew that was her," Jeanette said, shocked. "I didn't realize you were serious about me signing the paper. My dealer, Andy, should have checked it before he gave it to me!"

"Yes, it's true." Maria said. "You better back to Harry's Ford and look for that salesman who helped you buy that. Hopefully he'll take care of it and give you the right forms. Better hurry now before it's too late!"

Jeanette felt almost faint, but it couldn't be that bad. She put the cigarette on the butter by mistake because she momentarily lost her mind and did not see the ashtray. Maria was shocked and took the plate of butter to show Jeanette. Maria did not like that Jeanette put her cigarette in the wrong place.

"Hey, why did you do that?" Maria yelled. "That's not an ashtray! You can buy me new butter right away!"

"Ok," Jeanette signed. "Do you want to come with me down to Charlottesville now?"

"Yes," Maria yelled, "I'll go with you to buy butter right now!"

Jeanette took the plate to the table and put the signed form in her purse. Maria took her coat and went to her bedroom to take Jobelle with her. She came back to the kitchen.

"I want you to close the convertible now," Maria said. "I don't want to mess my hair. I will drop off my baby to Dolly's and come back with you, ok?"

Jeanette nodded and ran to her car to close the convertible. Maria locked the door and rushed to Dolly's house. Maria knocked and told Dolly that they were going to Charlottesville right away. She wanted Dolly to watch her daughter Jobelle. Dolly didn't mind taking care of Jobelle while Maria was going with Jeanette to Charlottesville. She climbed into the car and Jeanette started to push her foot on the gas so hard, the rear tires squealed. Dolly heard Jeanette's tires and watched the car all the way to the end of the road. She wondered what was wrong with Jeanette's driver.

Jeanette and Maria traveled an hour south to Charlottesville. Jeanette was very nervous, because something was wrong with Andy that he did not read the folder carefully before giving the wrong one to her. Maria was disappointed with Jeanette for putting her cigarette into the butter. They arrived and parked the car at Harry's Ford; Jeanette ran and looked for Andy. She saw Andy talking to his boss in the office. Jeanette came to the office and called Andy. He heard and knew that Jeanette was there and looked at her. Jeanette showed him the folder and explained that the signature was not hers. Andy nodded and was glad that Jeanette came back, because Mrs. Robertson came back, too, and showed the boss the folder, right after Jeanette left with her new car. Andy told her that he would be more than happy to make another paper for her to sign. It would take about a half-hour. He told them they could go to the showroom and sit on the couch or look around at the car models inside the build. Another dealer came and asked them if he could show them a new car. Jeanette preferred the dealer take Maria, because it kept her from thinking about the butter.

Jeanette pointed to Maria, indicating that she wanted to let the dealer show Maria some cars. The dealer asked Maria to come with him. Maria looked at Jeanette, expecting her to say something to him, but Jeanette nodded and moved her hand like "keep moving" and let him take Maria. Maria was willing to go, and he showed her a model that was the same kind of car Jeanette bought. He opened the door, let Maria go inside the car and look around the dashboard.

Jeanette planned to smoke, she looked for a cigarette in her purse, but they were gone. She decided to ask the dealer if he was a smoker. While Maria was inside the new car, Jeanette acted like a sexy woman from the movies.

"Do you have a cigarette?" Jeanette gestured with a cigarette. "Can I have one please?"

The dealer looked and laughed at her because she was a very smooth actress to him.

"Sure, I have a cigarette," the dealer laughed. He took a cigarette from his suit and held the box to her. "Here, for you."

Jeanette pulled a cigarette out of the box; the dealer lit it. She exhaled and blew smoke out of her mouth. That made her felt better.

"Thank you," Jeanette smiled.

Maria smelled the smoke and knew Jeanette was smoking and had she asked the dealer for a cigarette. Maria knew Jeanette could not live without cigarettes. She became mad and went out of the car very slowly. The dealer and Jeanette looked at Maria who stood up with a serious face indicating that she wasn't stupid. Jeanette wanted her to forget about buying butter before they went to home.

"Butter!" Maria said as a shape.

Jeanette rushed and grabbed Maria out of the show room, because she did not want everyone looking at them while Maria was yelling at her about the stupid butter. The people already saw them while Maria acted like Jeanette was a daughter. The dealer wondered what was wrong with them. They walked out front, and Maria kept arguing with Jeanette on the way to grocery store. People on the sidewalk were looking at Maria because her voice was very high pitched and it hurt their ears. Good thing that Jeanette was deaf because she couldn't hear Maria's voice, but it was embarrassing for her. They got to the store, found the dairy products, looked for the butter, grabbed it, and then went to the cashier with a pack of cigarettes. After Jeanette paid, Maria grabbed the butter and crushed the pack of cigarettes to teach Jeanette not to smoke at her house. Maria walked out of the store to Harry's Ford. Jeanette sighed and felt foolish that Maria damaged the pack in front of the cashier. It was kind of embarrassing to her. Jeanette asked the cashier to replace it with a new one, but the cashier said that she would have to pay for another, regardless of what happened. She was willing to pay for another one and kept crushed one in case she needed it later.

After Jeanette signed the new paper, they went back to Maria's house in the early afternoon. They came in the kitchen, when suddenly, Maria's mother-in-law came and showed her with the plate of butter with a cigarette on it. Maria grabbed the plate from her and threw the butter into the trash. It made her mother-in-law shut up, because she was very tired of her always picking on the things at her house. Jeanette took her coat off, hung it up very slowly, and walked to the living room. Somehow Maria's cousin showed up in the kitchen and called his grandmother.

"Hurry up," Maria's cousin said. "Come on and watch TV while JFK is on the air!"

The mother-in-law rushed to the living room so she wouldn't miss it. Jeanette stood and looked at Maria, who unpacked the butter, put it on the plate, then put it on the table. Maria walked to the living room quickly, but she was starting to point at Jeanette, indicating that she did not want Jeanette to do that again in the future.

Jeanette kept quiet and let her talk about this. The living room was full of people. Dolly, her neighbor, some cousins, two of her husband's friends from his work and her mother-in-law were talking about what was on TV. Maria came in the living room, sat on the couch quietly to watch TV alone. Jeanette came and stood between the living room and the hall. She did not want to be close to Maria because she was mad at her for some reason that morning. It was time to forget it. She preferred to let Maria calm down for a while. Jeanette decided to sit on the couch next to Maria. On TV, President John F. Kennedy was riding with his wife, Jacqueline, and Texas Governor John Connally and his wife in the Lincoln. They rode in downtown Dallas. The people on the side of the streets were excited and waved at them. A few minutes later, the media suddenly moved down to the ground. In the living room, they were puzzled and confused as to what the problem was with the media at Dallas. A reporter showed up on TV and informed the nation that President Kennedy was shot and died at the hospital. They were shocked and started to cry, hugging each other. Jeanette and Maria looked at each other. They did not understand why everyone was crying and hugging over something on TV, and they wanted to know what the reporter was talking about.

"Ask Dolly," Jeanette pointed, "what the reporter is talking about."

Maria nodded and waved, trying to call Dolly's name. Dolly looked at Maria and realized they did not know what was happening on TV.

"Oh, I forgot to tell you," Dolly wailed. "The reporter told us that the President was shot by Oswald."

Maria and Jeanette were shocked and confused; they started glancing at each other slowly, then started crying and hugging each other.

Chapter 3

A few days after the President was shot, Maria and Jeanette went to church on Sunday morning with their husband and children together. At First Baptist Church, there were deaf and hearing people together. The first and second rows of the church were reserved for the hearing-impaired, with an interpreter at the front who was for deaf people only. They could see the interpreter. People were talking, hugging and comforting one another because they were sad about the President's death last Friday afternoon. DeeDee came to Maria with her husband and two sons. Maria was looking at DeeDee's eyes shining and knew that DeeDee was going to cry. DeeDee was holding her hand to Maria's arm for support.

"Ok," Maria nodded, "that happened last Friday afternoon."

"Yeah I know that," DeeDee sounded upset. "Why did Oswald shoot the President for no reason!?"

Maria pulled DeeDee close to her to embrace as her. She started to cry out loud. Jeanette was looking and walking toward them. By the time she stopped, she realized she could not do anything with DeeDee's behavior, because she was so upset after that happened, as if someone hurt her sons or husband. Maria noticed Jeanette from a few distant rows. She was standing and looking at them. Jeanette became uncomfortable with DeeDee's outburst of emotions. Her compulsive crying became so audible that everyone in the church could not help but overhear her display of emotional distress. Her crying was very loud in this building. Everyone knew why she was crying. Some people just stood silently and others began to weep with her. Maria was nodding at Jeanette; she would take care of DeeDee for a while. DeeDee's husband, Chris, came to her and tried to help DeeDee calm down, but she could not stop crying. He didn't want everyone to look at her while she was crying out loud. Maria embraced Chris, and both of them held DeeDee until she stopped crying. Jeanette was holding her hand on her chest breathing in deeply and blinking her eyes shut. This calmed her down; she didn't want to start crying in front of people, because she was a very sensitive person. She preferred hiding from them, so they wouldn't see her while she was crying. She didn't mind crying in front of her husband, but she knew that her children could hear her crying; she sounded like a little girl. Maria sat on the bench with DeeDee and Chris.

The preacher showed up on stage; he knew that people were crying in the audience while he was in his office and could hear their sorrow about the President's death. People saw the preacher on stage and sat down on the bench, trying to calm down. Jeanette sat down with her husband, Paul, and their three daughters. They were next to Bonnie, her husband, Eddie, and their only son. Angel was with her husband, Andy; they didn't have children because she had a problem with her ovaries and couldn't get pregnant. They planned on adopting. Vicky was with her husband, Tim; they had only one son and one daughter. All of them were on the same bench, but it was too full. Vicky's children were moved to the front seat next to Maria. They would hear from his lecture this morning about what happened last Friday afternoon. The interpreter stood up for the preacher's lecture and started to sign for the deaf people what the preacher was speaking to the audience.

"Let us pray for our President, John F. Kennedy," the preacher announced to the audience. "Our Father, we already miss President Kennedy. He was the very power of our country for almost 3 years. Now he has gone to Heaven with God and Jesus. We ask God to take Kennedy to Heaven to live his life forever. Praise the Lord God! Amen in Jesus."

People were in tears from the Preacher's prayer about the President's death. A few hours later, church was over at 10 o'clock in the morning. People walked to the front door of the church where the Preacher stood outside, talking with them about their family and life. He would sometimes go to their homes or out to lunch with a family. Maria and her family went to their car. She noticed DeeDee. Maria knew that she would tell her something about this morning at church. DeeDee came to Maria. She was kind of shy and planned to talk her about helping her calm down her emotions.

"Maria," DeeDee said, "thank you very much for your kind help and for trying to calm me down. You know that I can't control my emotions. Right now, I feel better. So, I will see you this evening. Bye."

Maria was trying to tell DeeDee that she wasn't finished talking to her. But DeeDee she rushed to her husband, who was waiting in the car for her, while she was talking with Maria. DeeDee went inside the car, waved at Maria and left. Maria leaned on her car's side and felt that she could finish talking with her when she saw her that evening. Jeanette came to Maria, leaned next to her, took a cigarette and lighter out of her purse, and started to smoke and relax. Maria looked at the sky for a few seconds then turned to Jeanette.

"I don't believe," Maria signed, "what I did with DeeDee at church this morning. I tried to help her, but I didn't like everyone looking at me while DeeDee was crying out loud. That made me so nervous!"

Maria was holding her arms around her body like she had a shiver. Jeanette nodded; she knew how Maria felt about being frustrated with DeeDee.

"Well," Jeanette said, "you did good job calming DeeDee down, because you made her feel comfortable with you for a while. It was kind of a rough time getting her to control her emotions. I think I better go now and see you later. Bye."

Jeanette kissed Maria's cheek, which made her feel better before Jeanette left her alone.

A few days later, the President was buried in Arlington National Cemetery. Maria's neighbors and relatives were coming to her house for the President's funeral on TV. The living room's window shades were closed so the sun couldn't come through and reflect off the TV. The room became as dark as a black hole. The people were depressed, cried, and were sad while they watched the President's funeral. Maria was tired of sitting all day in the small and dull room. She finally decided to walk to the kitchen. She saw Jeanette sitting alone at the big table, reading the newspaper quietly and smoking a cigarette. Now Jeanette noticed Maria standing at the door between the kitchen and hall; she looked so tired and couldn't stand to see everyone cry all day long. Jeanette understood what Maria felt about their sorrow.

"Get out of here," Maria said, frustrated. " I need to get out of here and go outside for some fresh air."

"Yes, sure," Jeanette nodded, "let's go now and I'll take you to the hill."

"Yes, thanks!" Maria was satisfied.

They put their coats and scarves on and went outside to where Jeanette's car was parked. They walked to the car then got in to leave Maria's house. Jeanette drove to the hill where they used to visit for many years. They arrived at the hill and parked the car near the end where it sloped. Maria got out of the car, walked to the front of the car and sat on the hood. That made her butt warm. She felt so good breathing the fresh air, because her house was too crowded with people watching the President's funeral all day on TV. She needed space for herself. Jeanette started smoking inside the car, got out, walked to the front of the car, and sat on the hood next to Maria. They were thinking and relaxing.

"The air smells so fresh," Jeanette said. "It isn't that cold outside, just a little cooler."

"Yes, that's good," Maria smiled. "I like winter, but not when it's too cold for me!"

Jeanette agreed with Maria; they were very silent at this moment. The mountain trees' leaves were becoming dry and brown and starting to fall away from the branches. The rain pulled the leaves down and the wind pushed the leaves away. All the trees were nude. They could see many shapes and the spread branches. There were no birds sitting on the branches; they had gone south for the winter. Jeanette was looking at the area where the farmer owned land. Maria felt like she was going to fall asleep because she didn't have enough sleep last night. She decided to talk with Jeanette about the President's son, John F. Kennedy Jr.

"Did you see on TV recently," Maria asked, "a little boy trying to escape from his mother arms? John Jr. stood up and saluted like a soldier to honor his own father's coffin. Can you believe it? He's only 3 years old! WOW! That's a brave boy!"

"Really?" Jeanette asked. "I didn't watch TV in the living room. I just stayed in the kitchen and read the newspaper about the President from yesterday. I'll read tomorrow what you saw on TV today. I'm sure someone took a good picture of JFK Jr. saluting his father."

"Yes, of course," Maria agreed with Jeanette. She took off the hood, stood up and straightened her back. "You'll get the paper and see the picture of him."

"Yeah, I will," Jeanette said.

Jeanette and Maria were quiet and watching the mountain again. They stayed there for one and a half hours, till the sun set down the mountain and the sky changed to light orange then became a darker orange. They might have to go home before it was too dark, since Jeanette couldn't see that well through the many complex roads and woods, creek and wild animals. She drove very slowly and watched the road carefully. She finally arrived at a main road from the dirt road, then drove to Maria's home safely.

Chapter 4

On Wednesday evening at the church, gentlemen and ladies were separating for their Bible study groups. The women went to the basement where there was a large room at the right wing. There were six women per each of 10 tables for hearing women and only one table in the corner for the deaf women. They could communicate to each other while they worked on the text and book to find an answer to a question. It was rare to ask a lady from another table, although she was happy to help them find the right answer.

Vicky was trying to find the answer in the book from the text. Angel found and wrote the answer. Maria was reading the question on the text and looking for another book somewhere on the table. DeeDee was playing with her hair and looked like she was daydreaming the whole time. She did not finish her paperwork. Jeanette was still trying to look for the right word in the book, but how could she when DeeDee's kept playing with her hair. Jeanette gave up and looked at DeeDee, wondering what was going on in her mind. Jeanette felt like she should slap DeeDee's hand from her hair. She had a good idea to use her pencil like an arrow and aim it at DeeDee's arm. Bonnie was struggling to find the right answer when she finally gave up from her work. She noticed Jeanette playing with her pencil and aiming it at DeeDee's arm. Bonnie knew Jeanette's personally and knew she always liked to pick on the students at Gallaudet College. She didn't realize that Jeanette still had the same bad habit. Bonnie looked under the table to see if there was an open space. She planned to kick

Jeanette's leg. Bonnie was giggling and looking at the ladies from other tables to make sure they didn't see her kick Jeanette. Just then, Bonnie started to slide her leg back and with great force kicked Jeanette's leg.

"Ouch!" Jeanette yelled. DeeDee was scared to death. Maria, Angel and Vicky saw the intense look on Jeanette's face as she screamed from the pain.

"Hey you! That hurt! I'll kick you back!"

Jeanette was kicking Bonnie's leg back. She was laughing so hard, but trying to stop. Ladies from other tables were looking at them. They were wondering what was going. A woman from next the table told Bonnie to keep quiet. It was embarrassing behavior. Maria rolled her eyes up and her hand became a fist; she felt like hitting two women, but knew she couldn't do that.

"Better stop now," Maria told them seriously. "This isn't drama time and it would be better for all of you if you did your work now."

Bonnie tried to calm her laugh down. Jeanette was mad at her, because her leg had a minor bruise from Bonnie's shoes. They were silent, and searched for the right answer.

A few hours later, the study was almost finished around 9 p.m. They decided to take a break from Bible study for now and discuss their plans for the week and weekend with their families and only ladies' day.

"We better go now," Angel said, putting her Bible and paperwork in her purse. "What are we doing for fun tonight after class?"

They looked at each other and agreed with Angel's suggestion. They decided to go out to eat at Diner's place on Rte. 29. They packed their books and paper work, got ready to leave the church, walked to the parking lot from the room in basement and took their own cars to follow one another to Diner's place. After about 25 minute, they arrived at Diner's. The building was an old train's cart. The restaurant owner bought it few years ago. He was working hard to run the restaurant, and the service was open 24 hours now that the business became successful. Most people liked going to Diner's because it was very cozy and there was lots of silver outside and inside the building. The room was a narrow.

Go to the Hill

The entrance was a muddy room in the middle of the building. There were 10 tables with shiny red benches. One the best foods was an 8 oz. steak and hamburger with French fries, and there was good ice cream in the summertime only.

Bonnie was arrived at Diner's first before Angel.

She looked for an available parking space and found plenty of parking at the end for six cars to park. She rolled her window down, put her hand out, and waved to let them know that she found parking. All of them followed her and parked their cars there. Bonnie parked but left the window open. She signed that she forgot to roll the window up. After she rolled up the window, she locked the door again. DeeDee rushed to the front door of Diner's; she was extremely hungry because she cooked for her family, but did not eat before going to church. Maria put her purse in the trunk of her car and looked for her wallet. She could not see in her purse because it was dark outside. She found her wallet at the bottom of the purse and saw Jeanette, who was furious and walking slowly like an old woman. She passed Maria. She signed and ignored her anyway. Vicky ran to Angel's car while she took the books out of her purse and looked for her wallet. Vicky rolled her eyes up and had no patience with Angel. Vicky knew she always kept them waiting for her to finish something before they left somewhere. Vicky decided to knock on Angel's car window to force Angel to look at her outside. Vicky was going to go inside because it was cold and a little windy outside. Good thing Angel gave up for Vicky's sake. She took her wallet out of her purse and put it in her coat's pocket. She got out of her car and walked with Vicky to Diner's.

They came through the door and waited for the host. The restaurant was busy and full of people. The host saw them and asked them how many people?

"Six of us," Vicky told the host with a gesture. "We needed a circle table please."

"Ok, I will find a circle table for six women," the host stated. She looked and found a table that would be ready in a few minutes. She came back and told them, "The table will be ready in fifteen minutes."

The host would call when the table was ready. Jeanette did

not have the patience to wait 5 minutes. She gave up and walked past her friends and the dinner area to the restroom. They wondered what was wrong with her. People in the dining room were looking at Jeanette while she acted like Marilyn Monroe from the movie, Seven Year Itch. They were in awe at Jeanette's behavior. She was like a sexy woman and movie star actress. But Maria closed her hand over her eyes so she wouldn't see what Jeanette was doing in public. She was already embarrassed from her.

Jeanette went the restroom. She tried to block the door so no one could come in. She gave up trying to block the door, sighed and walked toward the mirror to look at herself and see if her hair was a mess from the wind outside. She checked her leg that Bonnie was kicking at Church. The leg was already bruised, but it was not that bad, just the size of a quarter. Jeanette looked in the mirror again. She sighed and in her mind did not understand why Bonnie kicked her leg. It never happened to her in her life! So she decided to forget the past and go back to the group. She came out of the restroom and walked pass the dining room. This time she didn't walk like Marilyn Monroe, but acted normal, like her personal walk. People in the dinner area were confused as to why she changed to her normal walk. Maria felt better that it was Jeanette's personal walk and not Marilyn Monroe's.

"What's the matter?" Jeanette muttered. "Did you notice my leg was bruised?"

Maria looked at her leg and noticed a bruise the size of a quarter. She thought the bruise would be gone in a few days.

"Don't worry about that," Maria said. "It will be gone in a few days, ok?"

Maria caught Bonnie, who was trying to cover her mouth to stifle a giggle. Bonnie tired to hide it from Jeanette. She did not mean to kick Jeanette's leg that hard. Jeanette saw Bonnie's face making fun of her, but she did not mean it.

"Do you think that was so funny?" Maria signed. "I think you should apologize to Jeanette for what you did to her. It was wrong."

Bonnie stopped her giggle and nodded to Maria that she would tell Jeanette that she was sorry for kicking her leg so hard.

"Jeanette," Bonnie said shyly, "I am sorry. I didn't realize that my shoes were so hard they'd cause you to bruise. So, I won't let that happen again Ok?"

Jeanette was silent and did not answer her apology. Bonnie was shocked that Jeanette would not forgive what happened. Everyone in the group was waiting for Jeanette's answer. Maria pushed her arm against Jeanette's back, indicating that she expected her to tell Bonnie that she accepted Bonnie's apology. Jeanette had to answer with words.

"Yes," Jeanette admitted, "I accept your apology, and I forgive you for what happened."

Jeanette moved and hugged Bonnie. Maria felt good that they were still friends again. All of them started to hug Jeanette and Bonnie together. The host came to the group because the table was ready. She tried to call them, but they could not hear her voice. Vicky saw the host stood and waited for someone to notice her. Vicky told them that the host would take them to the table. They broke their hug and followed the host to a big circle table in the corner of the room. It was next to a window. After they started to walk to the dinner area, Bonnie smiled and grabbed Jeanette's arm. Was she trying to tell her something? Bonnie showed her leg to Jeanette, and she had a bruise too. Jeanette looked at Bonnie's leg for a few seconds then turned to look at her face. Jeanette now started to laugh at her. Bonnie knew she would laugh and Bonnie started to laugh too. Both of them laughed and hugged each other. Angel came to them. They saw her stand and smile at them.

"Are you alright now?" Angel smiled. "Better for both of you to come with me and go to the corner where we can eat."

Bonnie and Jeanette nodded at Angel and walked with her to the table. Maria looked at Jeanette and knew that Jeanette seemed fine now.

They could see each other more clearly than at a rectangle table. The waitress brought a large round tray with six glasses full of the water and menus to the table. She gave the glasses to Vicky and passed them to the last person. The waitress told them she would be back in a few minutes. They looked at the menu and chose what they wanted to eat. The server came back to the table from the kitchen and asked if they were ready to order. They said yes and ordered their food. After a half-hour, servers brought two trays of food to the table and passed it out. They ate their dinner and talked about future plans. They planned on meeting next Thursday evening for a large dinner with their families at Bonnie's Uncle's cabin in Mansion County, which was about 20 miles south of Culpeper. In addition, they planned on a long weekend in the spring to camp outdoors in West Virginia with their families. After they discussed their plans for next week, they noticed that the dining room was full of men, except for the six women. The men were on break came to Diner's from working at the houseplant during the night shift. DeeDee looked at her watch. She told them it was past 1 a.m. in the morning. They were surprised they were there that long discussing plans and enjoying dinner together. But their husbands might be worried they were in an accident or kidnapped. They thought it best for them to go home right away. Maria asked the server for the check. She gave the check to Maria. They paid the server and left the tip on the table. They went to the parking lot and hugged each other before they left for home. The only two women in the parking lot were Maria and Jeanette. They walked to Jeanette's car. She started to smoke a cigarette and lay against her car. Maria looked at the full moon. She thought that April was almost over and May would be coming next week.

"Oh well," Maria said. "Are you alright now?"

Jeanette nodded and exhaled the cigarette.

"Yes, I am doing fine now," Jeanette nodded contentedly. "I think I better go now before I start to fall asleep. It's late, and I need to go bed and get up early tomorrow morning for work."

Maria smiled at Jeanette. "Yes, me too," Maria agreed. "I think it's better for me to go now. Good night."

Maria hugged Jeanette hard like they did when they were best friends, since their mothers made them become friends.

Jeanette told Maria, "Good night and bye." She went to her car, started the engine, and left the parking lot.

Maria walked toward her car and looked at Jeanette's car driving on Route 29 north where she lived. Maria saw Jeanette's hand out the window waved to her. Maria waved back to Jeanette. Maria smiled and opened the door, started her engine and drove home.

Chapter 5

In downtown Culpeper, the main street was the most popular for tourists. There was an old historic building from the Civil War time, but most of the other buildings were added 20 years after that time. The street had a lot of traffic and people walked on the sidewalks. They would look and buy some things from the different stores and eat at good restaurants.

The Beauty Salon had been busy with brides and Maids of Honor the whole month of June. Maria rushed across the street to the store to buy some more nail polish and shampoo for the women. Maria went to a fabric store to buy white and colored fabrics for the bride's and maid of honor's dresses. Maria added a new business in the same store for sewing clothes for special occasions. She came back to the Beauty Shop carrying bags. She arrived at the front door of the Beauty Salon, but could not open the door while holding the bags. A woman was going to the Beauty Salon for her hair appointment. She opened the door for Maria.

Maria walked fast toward the office, put the bags on the desk and took out some nail polish. She brought nail polishes to a private room for the Bride and Maid of Honor. They planned for a wedding at noon at the church. Maria showed the Bride one pink and one white. The Bride told Maria that the pink nail polish was for the Maid of Honor and white for her. Maria gave both of them to the women. They would work quickly with them before they left the store about 15 minutes before noon. Maria came out of the private room to the Beauty Salon. There were six chairs for cuts, four chairs for hot dry curl, three tables for nail polishes and other chairs for the waiting customers.

Maria's mother, Mrs. Wilson, was at the front desk, near the door, talking on the phone about her personal things. She looked at a woman who was mad at the hairdresser because her hair length was not evenly layered. Mrs. Wilson came to the woman and asked her what was wrong with the hairdresser. The woman told Mrs. Wilson that her hair length looked awful. Mrs. Wilson rolled her eyes and turned the chair around back to the mirror where the woman could see it. Mrs. Wilson pulled the woman's hair down and checked if she could change it to a new style. That made her shut up. She walked to the front desk and looked for a magazine on hairstyles. She flipped the magazine pages to find the best picture of a new hairstyle that would look good and fit the woman's round face. Mrs. Wilson showed the hair style picture to the woman. The woman accepted Mrs. Wilson's suggestion. The hairdresser took the magazine from Mrs. Wilson and looked at the picture; she flipped to the last pages and found the directions on how to properly cut that style. Mrs. Wilson watched as the hairdresser cut the woman's hair. After a few minutes, the cut was done. The woman looked in the mirror and was shocked. She loved it. That was the first time she had short hair in her life. It was time for her to change to a new style. Mrs. Wilson smiled and winked at the hairdresser. The woman told the hairdresser that she was doing good job. She gave her $10 for a tip and paid the price. She opened the door, forgetting to tell them "Good-bye and have a nice day."

The hairdresser and Mrs. Wilson were tired and sat on their chairs for a while. Maria was laughing at them because they were doing a good job in convincing the woman to try a new style.

The Beauty Salon closed by 6:30 p.m. Maria was counting the money and checks to deposit it at the bank a few days later. The hairdressers were cleaning up the floor, sink, chairs and tables. The room looked clean and organized for next Monday morning. The hairdressers were planning to leave and one asked Maria if they could go. She said sure and told them to lock the doors after they left the Beauty Salon. She went to the office and worked on the bookkeeping for a few more hours to finish up.

Her friends, Angel and Vicky, arrived at her business but

couldn't come in because the front door was lock. They tired to find a window to Maria's office and made noises to make Maria look. Angel waved her hand to her.

"I'll go to the front door," Maria said, pointing her finger to the front door. She walked toward the front door, unlocked it, and let her friends in. "What were you planning for tonight?"

Angel and Vicky looked at each other and laughed at Maria. She didn't understand why they were laughing at her. Maria was wide-eyed looking at Angel and Vicky, which made them stop laughing.

"You got it," Vicky smiled. "That's why we stopped by to see if you had any plans for tonight."

Vicky looked at Angel while she was staring at Maria. Maria looked at Angel's eyes, then looked at Vicky and wanted to know what was wrong with Angel. Vicky did not know anything about her personally. Now Angel became weak and looked for a chair to sit on. She laughed and thought that it was so funny they were confused at her behavior.

"It's so silly," Angel giggled. "I bet that you're psychic and read our minds before you asked us our plans for tonight."

Vicky nodded and agreed with Angel that Maria already read their minds. Maria never knew they were planning on asking her out.

"That's just what happened," Maria said honestly to them. "I want to get out of here soon. Can you wait a few minutes for me to finish my job?"

Angel and Vicky agreed, and Maria ran to the office to finish her work. Nevertheless, it took her an hour to finish. She worried about Angel and Vicky waiting for her to finish. She looked at them. It was a good thing that they were reading magazines about new styles for women's hair. Maria thought, "Thank God," and was glad they were waiting for her while she finished. She came back to her desk and finished the bookkeeping, put the book in the locker and closed it. She pushed the chair under the desk, took her purse and turned off the light.

She walked to Angel and Vicky and let them know she was ready to go now. However, Vicky asked Maria if she could borrow the magazine for the weekend. Maria told her it was ok, but she wanted it brought back to her at church Sunday morning. She didn't want her mother to find out that she let someone borrow a magazine. Mrs. Wilson would get mad at Maria for lending it without her permission. Vicky agreed to bring the magazine to her at church. She put it in her purse, and no one knew she brought it to the bar.

"What are we going to do tonight?" Maria asked.

"Go to the bar," Angel said. "It's just a few blocks away from here. Our sisterhood is waiting for us to show up tonight. I think it's best for us to get of out here and go to the bar right away."

Maria didn't want to go to the Bar because she was tired from working all day with the Bride and Maid of Honor. She preferred going home, but she changed her mind and decided to join the sisterhood at the bar for a good time.

"I'll go with you tonight," Maria said. "Maybe I'll miss church tomorrow morning because we'll be out late here at the Bar."

They laughed and agreed with Maria. Angel and Vicky left the Beauty Salon; Maria checked each window and the back door to make sure everything was locked up. After everyone left, she went out of the building and locked the front door.

They rushed across the street and walked a few blocks until they saw the 52 year old, two-story, red brick building flashing "Bar" above the entrance. They came in the bar and looked for their friends. It was so crowded because most people came there after the wedding reception. They couldn't find their friends anywhere because the light looked like a dome of heavy smoke above their heads. The paper walls were green with red stripes, and the floor was hardwood. It was too dark to see any faces. Angel saw Bonnie's hands while she tried to wave at them, and Angel told Vicky and Maria. They walked through the crowd of people to the wall where Bonnie, Jeanette and DeeDee sat with their beers. Finally they made it to their friends and hugged each other. Maria looked at Jeanette's shirt collar and hat that had a leopard print.

"Meow," Jeanette acted like a cat. "Do you like my fake leopard collar and hat?"

"It scared me to death," Maria laughed. "It looks so good on you, but it wouldn't on me."

Jeanette laughed and agreed with Maria and told her to get a drink. Maria wanted a glass of red wine so Jeanette called the waiter over. She pointed to Maria and indicated she wanted to order a glass of red wine. The waiter went back to the bar and brought the wine to Maria.

They were having fun talking to other people in the bar. Most of them knew Maria's mother from the Beauty Salon. A customer, Carol, and her husband, Teddy, showed up at the bar to surprise their friends. Carol saw Maria with her friends near the counter and decided to introduce Maria to her husband. She told Teddy that her mother knew Maria's mother, and that she went to their Beauty Salon for haircuts. That's how Carol knew Maria and her mother for such a long time. She started to take Teddy to meet Maria. They came through the crowd and finally got close to Maria. Carol waved at Maria, but she didn't remember her because Carol wore her wedding gown in the shop that morning. Now she was wearing a normal dress since the reception was over. Carol reminded Maria about the pink and white nail polishes and the private room with the Maid of Honor. Maria finally recognized her.

"Good to see you again," Maria smiled with gesture. "Now I remember you at my work. How was your wedding today? Are you planning on going on a honeymoon?"

"The wedding was so wonderful," Carol spoke clearly so Maria could read her lips. "I hated wearing my wedding gown because it was so heavy, and it was hot in the Church since the new air conditioner wouldn't start. We leave for Spain tomorrow morning. I can't wait to get there!"

Carol looked at her new husband, Teddy, and explained to him what they were talking about. She had forgotten to introduce her husband to Maria.

"This is Mrs. Maria Scott," Carol introduced. "This is my new husband Teddy Hall."

Teddy shook Maria's hand and talked about how her services were good and how she did a nice job on his new wife's hair and wedding gown. He made Maria feel good that her business was running well. They had a good wedding experience.

Stevie Platt

DeeDee sat on a barstool and was about to fall asleep at the counter. Her face fell into a bowl full of peanuts. She could not feel anything at all. The people who stood behind DeeDee laughed at her while she slept in the bowl. Angel was wondering why people were making fun of another person. She was curious to see who was there. She came through people to the counter and found DeeDee with the bowl. Angel got embarrassed about DeeDee's behavior in public. She looked at the waiter who told her to take DeeDee out because she was so drunk. Angel slapped her hand against her head thinking, "Why did she drink too much?" She pulled DeeDee's face from the bowl. It was so messy because peanuts were all over the counter. She looked for her friends to leave right away. Vicky looked at her watch and signed that was past 1 a.m. in the morning. She told them to leave because DeeDee had too much wine. They laughed and walked a few blocks to their cars parked in front of Maria's work, and went home.

Chapter 6

The next day, Maria's daughter, Helen, was mad at her mother because she overslept and was supposed take her to the store to buy a present for her friend's birthday party that afternoon. Helen smelled smoke from Maria's hair and her dress lay on the chair next to the bed. She wondered if something was wrong with her mother. Helen knew that her mother did not smoke. She tried to make her mother wake up, but she couldn't. Maria was in a very heavy sleep. Helen tried to push her back hard. Finally, Maria awoke up and slipped out of her bedclothes quickly. Then she stood up, which gave her a headache. She felt she had not gotten enough sleep last night. She had only six hours of sleep, but thought she could take some medicine to make her feel better. Maria told Helen that she would take a hot shower and get dressed so they could get Joy's birthday present. Maria walked to the bathroom and closed the door; she looked at herself in the mirror. Her eyeliner and mascara were a mess from the pillow. Maria looked like she had a black eye, like someone punched her last night. She sighed. She really hated getting up so early, but she had to because of her daughter's birthday party today. She just wanted to get out of the house and hide in a cave with a bear. No one bothered her while she was sleep as well.

She showered, ran to the bedroom to get dressed, then went back to the bathroom again to dry and fix her hair. Helen brought Maria a plate of breakfast, but she didn't want to eat while doing her hair, and told Helen to take it back to the kitchen. After a while, she had finished doing her hair, went to the kitchen and ate her breakfast. But now it was cold. She ate the cold food anyway. Helen had waited for her mother for a long time. Maria finally told Helen to get ready to go to the store. Helen was happy and grabbed a bag with wrapping paper, tape, and scissors to wrap the present on the way to Joy's place. They left the house and drove to the store.

Maria still had a headache and could not wait to cure it. She might have to take a nap after she dropped Helen off at Joy's. They arrived at the store and walked in. Helen asked the cashier about a small music box with a ballerina who spun around by herself. It also had a small rectangular mirror. The cashier told her that it was in the third row at the end of the shelf. Helen and Maria found the music box, and Maria checked to make sure it worked. It worked fine, so she and Helen paid for it.

After they left the store, Helen sat on the front seat, took the music box out of the bag, and opened it. She listened as the music began to play a very familiar ballet. She imagined that she was a ballerina dancing gracefully to the gentle ballet that was playing. She had always wanted to be a ballerina. Maria looked at Helen holding the music box.

"I want one for myself," Helen begged. "Can you buy me one later?"

Maria was still tired, but she agreed to buy the music box for Helen. "Yes," Maria nodded. "I'll buy the music box, hopefully this week. Ok, Helen?"

Helen couldn't wait until her mother bought the music box. Maria was worried the music box might break. She told Helen to close it and wrap it right away. Helen nodded and climbed to the back seat to wrap the music box. Before they were got to the house, they saw many balloons hanging up by a mailbox. They passed it and parked in front of another car. Joy's mother, Mrs. Gina Morris, came to Maria's car and told her to plan on picking up Helen after 6 p.m. Mrs. Morris planned to cook dinner for the children around 5, and after that, would make ice cream with brownies. Maria appreciated it. Helen gave her mother a kiss then get out of the car and ran to Joy, who was standing at the front door waiting for Helen. Helen gave the present to Joy and they ran through the house to the backyard for the party.

Go to the Hill

"What was crazy day," Mrs. Morris said, rolling her eyes up to the sky. "I need to rest for a day!"

Maria agreed with what she said. Gina noticed Maria's eyes looked light black around them, like she didn't get enough sleep. Maria told Gina that she went to bed late last night and might go home and take a nap. Gina told her that she would be happy to bring Helen back call Maria's husband, Ray, to pick her up. Maria said that would be nice and that she owed her one. She offered to take the girls out to the park for a day.

"I'll talk to you later," Maria said. "I'll call to let you know if either me or Ray will be picking up Helen."

"Sure," Gina smiled. "Give me a call soon and please drive safely home, Maria."

Maria waved to Gina as she drove toward home. Gina waved back and watched Maria until she turned left on Main Street.

Maria was still tired and rushed home. She parked in front of the house and ran to the front door. She looked for the key to the front the door, but it wasn't there. She sighed as she walked around to the back door. She unlocked it, came in the kitchen and pulled a chair away from the table to sit down and rest for a while. She put her purse on the table and took her shoes off. She thought about making tea, but decided to wait because it might keep her up. She left the kitchen to go to bed, took off her clothes and put on pajamas. She finally jumped into bed at 12:16, then fell asleep.

Maria's husband, Ray and three kids, Bobby, Jobelle and Jeffery, arrived home from the horse show. Jeffery ran through the kitchen to Maria's bedroom and jumped on the mattress, not knowing she was asleep. He jumped on Maria's back, which made her scared and angry.

"Hey Jeffery," Maria yell, "you're supposed to know that a bed is not for a play, it's for people to sleep on!"

Jeffery was shocked and jumped off the bed. He stood and tried to talk to his mother.

"I'm sorry, mom," Jeffery said. "I didn't know you were on the bed."

Maria was not fully awake and was startled by Jeffery. In a moment, she woke and wanted Jeffery to come into bed and hug her. Ray came in the bedroom and wondered if Maria had been in the bed all the day.

"Are you still in bed?" Ray questioned. "Are you alright?"

"I haven't been in bed all the day," Maria answered. "I took Helen to Joy's birthday party before noon, then I drove back home and went to bed."

Ray heard a car honking outside. He told Maria that someone was in front of the house. Ray walked to the door and opened it. It was Gina's car. She brought Helen home. Helen got out of Gina's car and ran toward her father at the door.

"Mom was home?" Helen asked. "I've been trying to call all day, but no one answered the phone. Joy's mother said she'd bring me home."

"Yes," Ray said, "mom was asleep."

Helen knew that mother was still tired. Helen looked at Joy and waved goodbye to her. Then she came in and walked to her mother's bedroom. Bobby saw Helen on the way to the bedroom and told Maria that it was Helen. Maria was puzzled and looked at the clock; it was already past 6:30 p.m. She was supposed to pick Helen up at Joy's house or call Gina to tell her to bring Helen home. It was too late. Helen came in the bedroom and looked at her mother.

"Are you feeling better now?" Helen asked. "Did you get a good nap this afternoon? It's all right that you forgot to pick me up at Joy's house. Everyone is fine now."

Helen walked around the other side of the bed where Maria lay and hugged her hard.

"Thanks, darling," Maria smiled. "I fell asleep this afternoon but didn't realize I slept so long."

Helen nodded and hugged Maria again. Rob came in the bedroom and looked at them on the bed. Rob smiled and told Bobby and Jobelle to join them. All of them climbed into the bed and hugged Maria together.

Chapter 7

Bobby came in Maria's bedroom, woke his mother up and told her it was past 8 a.m. Maria looked at the clock and thought, "Oh no! I'm late!" She overslept, got out of bed, and ran to the bathroom for a hot shower. She rushed back to her bedroom and got dressed while Helen brought her a small breakfast Maria to take with her. She ran to her car, left home, and drove to work. She was worried her mother would get mad because she supposed to show up for work at 7:30 to set up and be ready to open by 8. She knew that customers would be waiting outside.

Maria parked behind the Beauty Salon. She tired to avoid the front door and used another door at the back. She knew her mother would be sitting at the desk by the front door, and didn't want her to see she was late. Maria tried to sneak in another room and turn the light on, but her mother was behind the door. It scared Maria to death; her mother knew that Maria was late. She came close to Maria's face, which looked like a devil who would try to kill her for not getting to the Salon until 8:30 a.m.

"Why are you late?" Mother asked, disappointed. "I planned on picking up my nieces at the train station today. You better be here all the day with the other workers, ok?!"

"Yes Mom," Maria nodded. "I will stay here late this evening, ok?"

Mother stared at Maria's eyes to see if she was telling the truth. Mother was satisfied with Maria's words, walked away from Maria and turned back to her desk near the front door. Maria felt guilty and her legs began to shake. She looked for a chair and found one in the corner. She walked to the corner and moved the chair move to the middle of the room, where she could sit comfortably and not feel so trapped. She sat down on the chair and her breathing calmed down. In her mind, she did not understand why her mother got mad at her just for arriving late. She would not let that happen again.

Maria's mothers looked at the clock on the wall and saw it was five minutes before 1:30. She decided to leave her office early before picking up her nieces at train station. She started to clean up her desk and put things away in a drawer. As she was reaching for her purse, she told Maria that she was going to pick up her nieces. Mother wanted Maria to recheck the bookkeeping from last week, because Maria had rushed to finish and go to the bar with her friends. It was a bad weekend. She hoped that would never happen again.

"Ok," Maria signed. "I'll recheck the books tonight."

Mother smiled and kissed Maria's head. She waved and rushed out the back door.

Maria was looking around her desk for something that she knew her mother would come for, but it looked like her mother didn't forget anything. That obviously meant her mother would not come back this time.

Vicky was showed up at Maria's work and brought the magazine she borrowed on Friday evening. Vicky promised to bring the magazine to church on Sunday, but they had overslept. Vicky took the magazine out of her purse and gave it to Maria, who put it under the schedule book.

"Thank God," Maria said. "That was perfect timing. My mother left here a few hours ago. I'm glad she didn't catch me lending this magazine to any one."

"That's wonderful!" Vicky giggled. "I'm glad your mother wasn't here."

Vicky left to go back to her work. Maria asked Vicky if she could come back there again after the business closed, around 5:30 in the afternoon. Vicky agreed then left the Beauty Salon.

After the Salon closed at 5:30, Maria and coworkers cleaned up each room and tucked everything away in drawers. After they were done, the coworkers told Maria that they were going to leave.

Go to the Hill

She let them out and locked both doors. Now Maria was alone in the building and was able to work on the bookkeeping. When the sun set, the light was coming in through a window and was reflecting off a mirror. It became brighter and started to bother Maria. She decided to pull down the shade to block the sun. Maria felt better now and could concentrate on her work. An hour later, some people were standing in front of the window. Maria could see their shadows and saw their bodies and arms moving around the air. She knew it was her friends who were supposed to come by after work. She thought she better open the door. There stood Angel, Bonnie, and DeeDee waiting for Maria to open the door. Maria called them all inside. Maria saw Vicky across the street come slowly running in her high heels. Finally, Vicky arrived at Maria's work. Maria closed the door and locked it.

"Guess what," Maria said. "My mother wasn't here today. She went to the train station to pick up my cousins, who are coming from Ohio to stay for the week."

"That's good," Angel said. "Let's sit and read some magazines while you finish your work tonight, ok?"

Bonnie and DeeDee agreed with Angel. However,

Vicky did not pay any attention to Angel. She was massaging her foot. After running in high heels, her feet were killing her. Vicky asked someone to explain what everyone was talking about. Angel repeated herself so Vicky understood. They were thrilled that Maria's mother would not be there until the next morning. They lounged on the sofa and looked at some magazines, talking about personal things.

"Let me finish my work today, ok?" Maria asked.

Maria went to the office and finished up the bookkeeping. It took her a long time to recheck and correct the totals. DeeDee wasn't in the mood for reading magazines, so she decided to go to another room. The middle room was painted pink and had long lace covering the window. There was a phonograph and some records on the tall dresser. She looked for a record and found the new Beatlemania. She thought why not play it? It would help her feel relaxed and peaceful. DeeDee closed her eyes and danced by herself in the room. However, she couldn't feel anything from the sound, so she decided to turn the volume high.

At that moment, Maria's mother and nieces were pulling up in the parking lot behind the Beauty Salon. They got out of the car and walked to the door. They could hear the music from the building. It was too loud. Her nieces knew it was "Beatlemania." Mrs. Wilson looked puzzled and unlocked the door. When she came in the hall, she heard the music next door. Mrs. Wilson and her nieces walked in the room and saw DeeDee dancing alone. Mrs. Wilson's nieces, Liz and Ruby, were older than Maria and knew DeeDee was deaf and was probably feeling the music on the floor. Mrs. Wilson turned the volume off because the music could was so loud, it hurt her ears. DeeDee stopped dancing, opened her eyes, and wondered why someone turned the music off. She looked back to the phonograph and saw Maria's mother there. That scared DeeDee to death. She ran from the room to the front where her friends were sitting and reading magazines. Angel noticed DeeDee run through the hall with her arms up in the air like she was scared. Angel took off after DeeDee.

"What's wrong with you?" Angel asked.

Bonnie and Vicky looked at each other person then looked at DeeDee.

"What are you doing, DeeDee?" Bonnie asked, concerned.

DeeDee was breathing heavily, sat down on the sofa, and pointed at Mrs. Wilson. Bonnie, Angel and Vicky followed DeeDee's finger to Mrs. Wilson, who stood in the middle of the room with her nieces behind her. They stared at them. That made Bonnie, Angel, and Vicky scared to death.

"Where is Maria?" Mrs. Wilson asked.

"Maria is in the office finishing her work," said Angel. "We're just sitting and reading some magazines until Maria is finished and we can all go out."

Mrs. Wilson was silent now and walked to the office where Maria worked. Mrs. Wilson came in the office with her nieces and see Maria. Maria could smell her mother's perfume and knew she was there right then. Maria saw her mother standing by the front desk with Maria's cousins behind her.

"I didn't expect to see you here with my cousins," Maria said, shocked. "I thought that you were on your way home."

Mrs. Wilson was not at mad at her; she just wanted to make

sure Maria was still in the office. It was fine since she knew Maria's friends well.

"That's ok," Mrs. Wilson said. "I would like you to see your cousins, Liz and Ruby, before you're too busy making plans with your friends. Why not to give them hug, Maria?"

Maria nodded and walked to Liz and Ruby; she hugged and talked to each of them for a while. She saw her friends in the other room who watched Maria to see if everything was all right. They knew she was concerned about her mother. Maria winked and let them know that she everything was fine with her mother and cousins. Bonnie, Vicky, Angel, and DeeDee felt better now and sat back on the sofa.

After Maria left her friends at a small café near the Beauty Salon, she planned to go home. But she decided to visit Jeanette at her home. Maria wanted to see how she was doing since they hadn't seen each other for a few days. At Jeanette's house, her older daughter, Mary Anna, sat on a bench that had chains holding it to the ceiling. She saw Maria's car coming down the dirt road and ran into the house. Mary Anna looked in the kitchen, but Jeanette wasn't there. Mary Anna knew that Jeanette must be upstairs, so she ran to the hall and switched the hall light upstairs for Jeanette to see the flashing.

"Yes, Mary Anna?" Jeanette asked.

"Mommy," Mary Anna told her mother, "your friend, Maria, is coming here now."

Jeanette came down the stairs and walked to the screen door and looked at Maria's car was parked next to hers. Maria got out of her car, walked up the porch and hugged Jeanette.

"How was your day?" Jeanette asked. "It's been a long time since I've heard from you."

Jeanette took a cigarette out of her thin jacket and started to smoke.

"I'm fine, just busy at work," Maria smiled. "Do you know my cousins, Liz and Ruby? They stopped by my office for a while and are staying at my mother's house."

"Umm," Jeanette sounded interested. "How long will they stay here? I mean in Culpeper?"

"They'll be here a week." Maria said.

Jeanette was pretty quiet. At that moment she saw Canadian geese flying to the lake. Maria and Jeanette watched the geese swimming around the lake. Maria looked at Jeanette then turned to the sun; it was almost sunset.

Chapter 8

Winter was ending and spring was starting to arrive. The temperature warmed, and leaves were beginning to show up on branches. The birds flew and sat on the branches, singing for spring. Jeanette opened the front door and smelled the outside. It made her feel so bold. She saw the mail carrier stop by her mailbox and drop off some letters before leaving for the next mailbox. She put on her jacket, pushed the screen door to get out of the house and walked through the porch. Jeanette started to smoke a cigarette as she walked to the mailbox. She looked through the mail and noticed a letter for Paul from the Pentagon. She looked for Paul in the house and wondered why they sent him such an important letter. She hoped nothing was wrong. Jeanette went in the house and looked for Paul. He was in the bathroom shaving, and she thought she'd wait until Paul was finished.

Jeanette went to sit on the bed. Her hands held the letter, and for some reason she didn't want to give it to him. She stared as Paul splashed his face with lukewarm water to wash the shaving cream from his cheek. He wrapped his face in a towel to dry. Paul noticed that Jeanette looked sad and wondered what was wrong with her. Paul hung up the towel and walked to Jeanette. He noticed Jeanette tried to hide a letter from him.

"Who's that letter for?" Paul asked. "Is it for me or what?"

Jeanette nodded and gave the letter to Paul. He saw it was from the Pentagon. He started to get mad and crushed the letter in his hand. He did not want Jeanette to know, but she already knew the Pentagon must have wanted him for something. Jeanette stood

61

up close to Paul.

"Tell me," Jeanette stared. "What do they want you for?"

Paul did not answer Jeanette. He opened the letter and read it carefully. Jeanette wanted to read the letter, let Paul read it completely first. After he read the letter, he looked at Jeanette like he wanted to tell her something.

"Paul," Jeanette said, "let me read the letter please."

Paul nodded and gave the letter to Jeanette. The Pentagon wanted Paul and his family to report to Fort Belvoir, near Washington, D.C. They had a house for them to live in and a school for their children to attend. Paul would have to join the army and prepare for the draft before flying to Vietnam. Paul and Jeanette were to leave Culpeper in two months. She became angry and took the letter away from Paul's hand. She destroyed it and threw it at Paul. He grabbed hold of Jeanette's arms while she lost control. Paul tried to calm her, but couldn't. She pushed Paul away from her, ran down the stairs toward the kitchen and grabbed her jacket and car keys. She ran to the car and left the house. Paul tried to stop her, but she got away. He knew Jeanette wouldn't like him going to war in Vietnam.

Jeanette drove to the hill, parked her car, and vented her anger about Paul having to join the army and serve in Vietnam. She slapped the steering wheel and hit anywhere in the car she could. She started to cry aloud. She felt like she would vomit, so got out of the car and ran. She fell down on her knees and started to vomit. She didn't want Paul to leave her and her daughters alone while he served in Vietnam. She stood up with her arms hugging her stomach and walked to the front of the car. A few seconds later, she started to cry and bend her knees down to the ground again. Her body became weak and she started falling toward the ground. She rolled her body and looked skyward as she continued to cry.

The sun went down and it became dark. Paul stood on the porch and worried about Jeanette. He started to give up hope and was about to call the police. He pulled the screen door opened and heard a car coming on his property. It was Jeanette. She got out of the car and walked slowly to the porch. Paul was glad that she was home safe. Her three daughters ran out of the house to hug their mother. Paul hugged Jeanette with the three girls together. They went into the house.

A few days later, Jeanette was very quiet at work in the hospital. She tried to figure out what she would tell her sisterhood about leaving Culpeper to move to northern Virginia so her husband could serve the Army in Vietnam. A woman came and gave Jeanette a note. The note was from Maria who wanted to inform Jeanette that she was in a car accident. Maria wrote that she was in the emergency room, but not to worry. She was all right, but had broken her left arm. She had to wear a cast for six weeks. Jeanette almost fainted. She left the office and ran down the hall to go downstairs. She walked toward the emergency room and looked for Maria, but she was not there. Jeanette decided to go back to her office to see if Maria was waiting for her. She planned to go upstairs when she noticed someone was sitting on a chair next to the vending machine. Jeanette looked at her face to see if it was Maria, but the patient's hair was a mess and covered her face. Jeanette knew it must be Maria and came to her. Maria saw Jeanette make her way over.

"Jeanette," Maria said, "I'm all right now. I just need to get some sleep. The nurse gave me some medicine for the pain."

Jeanette came close to Maria and said, "I'm glad you're all right now. Let me take you home and let Ray know you were in a car accident."

Maria nodded and showed Jeanette her left arm in the cast. It was uncomfortable. She wanted Jeanette to take her home so she could get some rest. Jeanette called the nurse to wheel Maria to the front of the building. Jeanette ran up the stairs, grabbed her purse, then ran to her car. She drove to the front of the hospital; the nurse opened the door and helped Maria in. Jeanette wanted to smoke, but she didn't because she knew it would bother Maria.

Jeanette drove to Marie's house and parked close so Maria would only have a short walk. She opened the door and walked Maria slowly toward the back door. Maria gave Jeanette her purse to find the door key. Jeanette unlocked the door and they walked into the kitchen. Jeanette took Maria's coat off and hung it up on the wall. They walked to Maria's bedroom from the kitchen. Maria sat on the bed and lay down. Jeanette took Maria's shoes off and dressed her in pajamas. Jeanette brought an extra blanket to keep Maria warm, kissed her on the cheek and started to leave when Maria threw a pillow at her. Jeanette looked puzzled and brought the pillow back to Maria.

"What?" Jeanette asked. "Do you want me to do something for you before I go to Ray's office to inform him you're home?"

"No, it's ok. Thanks anyway," Maria yawned. "After I was in the accident, the police suspected that my vision was poor. He suggested I see an eye doctor. If they're bad, I'll need to get glasses before driving again."

Maria was drifting asleep. Jeanette covered Maria with the blanket then drove to Ray's work.

The next morning, Jeanette picked Maria up at her house and drove her to the optical store. When they arrived, Jeanette told the woman that Maria needed an eye test. The woman told them that Dr. Zone would be glad to test Maria. He was with a customer but would see them in a few minutes. They watched TV and read some magazines while they waited. A half-hour later, Dr. Zone came over to them.

"Which one of you is Mrs. Scott?" Dr. Zone questioned. They did not hear him. He thought they were trying to ignore him. The woman at the front desk forgot to tell Dr. Zone that they were deaf.

"Dr. Zone," the woman called, "I forgot to tell you that they're deaf."

Dr. Zone sighed and waved his hands to Jeanette and Maria. Finally they looked at Dr. Zone's.

"Mrs. Scott?" Dr. Zone replied. "Which one of you is here for the eye test?"

Jeanette pointed to Maria. Dr. Zone wanted Maria to come with him to another room for the eye test. After the test was done, Dr. Zone told her vision was blurred. Maria knew that must have caused her car crash, because she couldn't see far. The doctor told her that she would need new glasses. Maria was pretty shocked that her eyes were not good anymore and that she'd have to wear glasses for the rest of her life.

Go to the Hill

She went to another room to find some frames to match her face. It was hard to find good frames. Jeanette was smoking while Maria and the doctor looked for frames that fit Maria's face. Jeanette had no patience in waiting for Maria to find the right ones, so she picked up some black frames, which looked like Siamese cat eyes, and put them on Maria's face. Jeanette took the mirror to Maria. She liked the glasses immediately. Dr. Zone thanked Jeanette for finding good frames and told Maria that her new glasses would be ready in about two weeks. Maria couldn't wait to get her new glasses.

Chapter 9

About two weeks later, Maria's new glasses arrived at the optician's office. Dr. Zone called Mrs. Wilson at the Beauty Salon and informed her that Maria's glasses had arrived and that she could pick them up any time. Mrs. Wilson told Maria that her new glasses ready. Maria left the Beauty Salon right away, and her mother told the doctor that Maria was on her way to his office. Maria walked quickly, but she had to be careful because it was hard to see far in front of her.

When she got to the building, she told the woman at the front desk that she wanted to see Dr. Zone. Dr. Zone told Miss White to send Maria into his office. When Maria arrived in Dr. Zone's office, he pointed to a chair for her to sit. He took out the new glasses and put them on Maria's face. She finally had good vision. She looked around the room and could see everything more clearly, and she could look out the window and see far away. It felt so good to see again. Dr. Zone fixed the glasses around Maria's ears and asked if it was comfortable or too tight. He checked the glasses to make sure they were level. He held a small mirror so Maria could see herself. She smiled and looked at Dr. Zone.

"Thank you," Maria smiled. "They're comfortable, and I'm so glad I can see everything far away."

When Maria exited Dr. Zone's, she stood on the sidewalk and looked around Main Street. She could clearly see the stores' signs and people's faces. That made her feel good. She decided to go back to her work.

"You got new glasses now," Mrs. Wilson said, surprised.

"Now can you see everything when you wear them?"

A little past noon, Maria began to feel hungry. She thought she would stop by and see if Jeanette wanted to join her for lunch. Maria took her purse and went to look for her mother, but she wasn't there. Maria went to her mother's desk and wrote a note telling her she'd be back in about an hour. She put it on the phone knowing her mother always picked up the phone when she returned to her desk.

Maria rushed to Jeanette's office in the hospital, which was about a mile away. She walked up the stairs to Jeanette's office, however, Jeanette wasn't there. Maria hoped Jeanette hadn't eaten in the cafeteria; she wanted to eat out. Maria thought she'd try and catch her at the cafeteria. She was about to run down the stairs when she ran into Jeanette leaving the women's restroom. Jeanette got hurt from the frames pushing into her back and got mad at the person for not paying attention to what she was doing. However, she didn't realize it was Maria who ran into her.

"I didn't notice you, Maria," Jeanette said, shocked. "You look different because of your new glasses."

Maria laughed at Jeanette's shock. "I'm sorry that I ran into you so hard." Maria said. "I was trying to catch you to see if you'd like to go out for lunch."

"Umm, yes, I'd like to go with you for lunch today," Jeanette nodded.

Jeanette went to the office and took her purse from the desk. She told her manger that she would be out to lunch with her friend. Her manger said it was okay and to take her time.

They went to Jeanette's car and drove to a restaurant near their old high school. They spent an hour together before Jeanette dropped Maria off at work. When Maria left Jeanette's car, she said, "Thanks for taking me to the restaurant and dropping me off here. Talk with you later. Good bye."

She left Jeanette alone. Jeanette felt she needed to talk to Maria right away. She got out of her car and walked to the Beauty Salon. Maria was in the office. Jeanette walked to the office, and Maria looked at her quizzically.

"What's wrong with you?" Maria asked. "Do you want me to

help you with something?"

Jeanette didn't know what to say. "Would you like to join me," Jeanette asked, "at the hill after work? I'll pick you up around 5:30, ok?"

Maria was still puzzled with Jeanette's face. It looked a bit sad. Maria had no idea Jeanette was trying to tell her something at lunch. Maria suspected Jeanette might be having problems that were hard to share and felt she should meet her after work.

"Ok, I'll go with you," Maria nodded. "Please meet me at the backdoor, ok?"

Jeanette smiled and hugged Maria and went back to the hospital. Jeanette was pretty upset and nervous about telling Maria she was leaving. What if Maria got so upset that she wouldn't see her she moved to Northern Virginia?

Jeanette was busy with paperwork for patients and putting folders into files. She looked at the clock; it was past 5:30 already. She left her office and drove to the ally behind the Beauty Salon. Maria came outside and locked the door the same time Jeanette arrived.

"Perfect timing!" Maria laughed.

Jeanette stopped and let Maria in the car. They left and drove to the hill.

In less than an hour, they were at the hill. Jeanette parked her car near the slope and opened the convertible. Maria looked to the mountain with her new glasses. It was the first time she could see so well. Jeanette started smoking and looked at Maria while she looked at the mountain. Jeanette moved her hand to Maria's shoulder and tried to talk to her, but couldn't say anything. Jeanette opened the door and got out of the car. Maria watched Jeanette walk to the front of the car holding her head in her hands. She wondered what was wrong with Jeanette.

Maria slapped the side of the door to make Jeanette look at her, but Jeanette raised her hand up in the air with a fist, like "hold." Maria decided to get out of the car, but Jeanette came to Maria. Jeanette didn't say any thing for a second. She took the car key out of her jacket pocket and showed it to Maria. Maria was surprised and confused. Jeanette tried to put the key in Maria's hand, but Maria wouldn't lift her hand up. Jeanette decided to take Maria's hand, put the key in it, and squeeze it tight.

"This is your present," Jeanette said. "Now you can have it since your old car was a dump."

"Oh, this is for me?" Maria was shocked. She looked around the dashboard inside the car. "Thank you for your support for me."

She came out of the car and hugged Jeanette hard. Jeanette went to the front of the car and started cried. Maria didn't understand why Jeanette was crying. She sighed and walked to Jeanette, who took her hands from her face and looked at the sky. Maria stood and stared in Jeanette's eyes, which started to tear. Jeanette looked at Maria, thinking she should explain what was wrong.

"Ok, let me explain to you what's wrong with me," Jeanette finally said and walked with Maria. "The Pentagon wants Paul to go to Vietnam because he's an engineer. He's being drafted into the army to lead somewhere at Vietnam."

Now Maria understood why Jeanette was so upset for weeks after the accident.

"No wonder," Maria said, "you've been trying to tell me this for a while time."

Maria thought Jeanette's husband would have to leave her alone.

"I'd like to help you while Paul's at the Pentagon or Vietnam or whatever," Maria said.

Jeanette shook her head and said, "No." She walked away from her, disappointed that Maria didn't understand Jeanette's point that she and her family would have to move up there with Paul.

Maria still did not understand what Jeanette was trying to tell her. Jeanette looked back to Maria.

"Maria," Jeanette signed, "we'll have to move to Northern Virginia and live on base while Paul is in Vietnam."

Maria was shocked and looked from the car keys to Jeanette. "Are you sure?" Maria asked, confused.

"Yes," Jeanette nodded.

Maria looked at Jeanette's face and could tell she wasn't making up a story. She wanted to give Maria the car while she was on base. Maria felt like she was in a hole.

"Why?" asked Maria.

Jeanette came and hugged Maria for a long time while they cried and laughed.

"Why don't you drive your car now?" Jeanette smiled. "Let's have fun tonight."

Maria kept quiet and raised her finger with the key ring hanging from it. She looked at her left arm with the cast and didn't think she could drive without both hands. She showed her broken arm to Jeanette.

"You can manage to drive," Jeanette said. "I'll help you while you drive, ok?"

Jeanette pulled Maria's arm and walked to the car, but Maria wouldn't move.

"What's the matter with you?" Jeanette signed.

Maria was quiet and stared at Jeanette. She showed her the cast again. Jeanette rolled her eyes skyward. Just then, Maria realized she forgot to ask Jeanette when she would be leaving town.

"Jeanette," Maria asked, "when do you have to leave?"

"We plan to move," Jeanette said, "after our daughters finish the school year. Not until the end of May."

"I see," Maria nodded. "We'll have at least two months to spend time together."

They were silent and stood looking at each other, not saying anything. Jeanette was still waiting for Maria to drive her "new" car. Maria had a hard time deciding how she wanted to spend her time with Jeanette before she moved.

"Maria," Jeanette asked, "are you planning on driving your car? I'll help you, ok?"

Maria looked to the car and slowly walked toward it. She opened the door and sat down. Maria turned the ignition on and held the steering wheel with her right hand. She looked at Jeanette standing right in front of the car. Jeanette felt sick that she already gave Maria her favorite car.

"I'm ready to drive," Maria said anxiously. "I'll try my best to drive with my right hand only. Are you coming?"

Jeanette was staring at Maria. She started to smile, then laugh.

Maria was confused with Jeanette's odd behavior.

"You look good in the car," Jeanette laughed. "Yeah, let me join you for a long ride."

Maria started to laugh and watched as Jeanette got into the car. She looked at Maria with tears in her eyes.

"Yes, we're ready to ride now," Jeanette spoke softly.

Maria put her foot on the gas too hard and the rear tires spun too fast. She wasn't used to this car. Jeanette laughed hard as Maria drove her car. After she got used to it, they traveled south on Route 29 to eat out and have some fun before going back home late that night.

Chapter 10

The Junior High School had red bricks, four columns and large steps from the sidewalk to the front entrance. The halls were quiet and empty because students were in their classes. The bell rang, and children ran out of the classrooms. They were excited and threw away their papers and pencils. It was the last day of school. The children ran to their buses and parents' cars to go home.

A bus stopped at Jeanette's house, and Mary Anna, Nikki and Barbara got off, waved to their bus driver then walked the dirt road home. Jeanette was in living room packing books in a box. She saw the three girls walking home and knew they weren't happy about leaving Culpeper and losing their friends from school. Jeanette knew that she'd be parting from her friends too. She thought she should tell her daughters that she understood how they felt about leaving their friends.

The girls came through the door. Jeanette ran to the foyer and called the girls who wondered why she wanted to talk to them.

"Can I talk with all of you?" Jeanette asked. "Please come in the living room so I can explain things to you, ok?"

The girls refused to talk with her and walked to the kitchen. Jeanette sighed and came back to the living room, sat on a chair and started smoking. She knew the girls were still mad at their father. She was quietly smoking and looking around the room. She decided to get back to work and pack more books.

A few hours later, Paul arrived home from work. He got out

of the car and looked longingly at the house. He already missed this home. When he came in, he looked for his girls. He found them in the kitchen eating their snacks. Then he left and found Jeanette in the living room. He leaned against the doorframe and watched Jeanette while she sat on the floor reading a book next to the fireplace. Paul came in the room and walked to Jeanette. She noticed Paul's shoes and slowly looked at Paul's face.

"How was your day?" Paul said. "Was it kind of rough for you?"

Jeanette did not say any thing to Paul. She looked back to her book. Paul said nothing and left her alone. He went to the kitchen and looked at the girls, then walked upstairs to his bedroom. Paul looked at the bedroom, which was already packed by Jeanette. Paul walked around and sat on the mattress; he was tired and lay down. He looked at the ceiling and wondered how his four girls felt about him going to Vietnam.

On Saturday morning, Jeanette sat alone on the bench on the porch thought about it being her last weekend before they moved out the house the next day. Mary Anna went out of the house and looked at Jeanette with a sad face.

"Are you all right now?" Mary Anna asked. "We're ready to go to your friend Bonnie's for a farewell party."

Jeanette blinked her eyes closed and nodded at her. The other two girls came outside and Paul pulled the door shut and locked it. He came to Jeanette and put his hand on her shoulder. Jeanette looked at Paul's hand on her shoulder, then turned to look at him.

"Time for us to go now," Paul said. "We're supposed to be at Bonnie's house before noon."

Jeanette stood up and walked with Paul and the girls to the car. They drove to Bonnie's place in about a half-hour. Bonnie's house was a hundred years and had a green roof. They parked next to DeeDee's car, got out and walked together around the house to the backyard. The backyard had a large grill for cooking BBQ chicken, ribs, hamburgers and baked potatoes. The sisterhood and their husbands were helping to set up the tables and chairs for lunch. The children played croquet near the woods. Jeanette saw a long brown paper printed with "Farewell to the Dreyfuss's. We'll

Stevie Platt

miss you lots. Love, your sisterhood and families." She smiled
with tears in her eyes. Angel put paper plates on the table and saw
Jeanette, who was on her way to the back yard with her family.
Angel dropped them, came to Jeanette, and hugged her.

"I'm glad you're here," Angel smiled. "We'll miss you so
much."

Angel waved to Bonnie at the grill. Vicky noticed Angel's
hand trying to get Bonnie's attention. Vicky walked and patted
Bonnie's back; she turned and pointed to Angel. At last Bonnie
saw Angel and Jeanette.

"Oh," Bonnie said. She ran and hugged Jeanette, Paul and
the girls. "I'm glad you and your family are here."

Vicky and DeeDee came to Jeanette and hugged her. Jeanette
saw Jeffery. He ran to the grill, and she looked around the backyard
to see Maria was there, but no one was there.

"Where's Maria?" Jeanette asked Angel.

"She was here," Angel said. "Maria went to the kitchen and
will be right back. She brought some food to the table."

Jeanette was glad that Maria was still around here. She saw
the screen door open, and Maria was carrying a large bowl full of
tomatoes. She put the bowl on the table.

"I need someone to help me," Maria said, and she noticed
Jeanette behind Angel. Maria came and hugged Jeanette. "I'm
glad you're here with your family."

Maria wanted Jeanette to join the sisterhood at the table to
cut tomatoes so they could have time to catch up on the news.
Paul went to join the men, and the three girls joined the other kids
to play a game. The food was ready. Everyone lined up to get
food and find a place to eat. Jeanette had a good time spending the
day with her sisterhood. They gave some presents for Jeanette
and her family. She opened the presents and showed them to her
family. DeeDee and Vicky ran into the house and brought out a
large cake with "Best Wishes and Good Luck" written on top of
the cake. They brought it to the table to show Jeanette. Maria
gave a knife to Jeanette and Paul so they could cut the cake.

The sun went down. Everyone looked at the sky and looked at
their watches. It was time for them to say "Good Bye" and hug
Jeanette and her family before they left.

74

Jeanette and Maria stayed at Bonnie's place and were talking about their plans to keep in touch and write letters. Maria and Jeanette were standing on the porch. Maria held Jeanette's hand.

"I'll come to your place tomorrow," Maria said. "We'll help you move your furniture into the moving van."

Jeanette nodded and sat quietly, looking at her husband and the girls, who were already in the car waiting for her.

"Yes," Jeanette said. Bonnie came on the porch from the screen door. "I appreciate your offer to help us move tomorrow morning. Bonnie, thank you very much for a warm farewell party with the sisterhood and their families. It was so nice to see my good friends from Gallaudet College."

Jeanette hugged both Bonnie and Maria and told them she better leave. Jeanette ran to the car, opened the window, and waved to Maria and Bonnie as they drove off. They drove and stopped by the store. Paul went in to get something for breakfast in the morning. They were home in a few minutes.

They arrived home and parked near the porch. Jeanette walked to the porch, then stopped and looked at the sky. It was a clear night with no clouds in the sky, and the stars were so bright, especially the Northern star. It was the biggest and brightest of them all. She wanted to fly up to the sky and catch that star. She imagined the star was like a rock or crystal that she could grab before coming down to earth.

Paul unlocked the door let the girls in the house. He was about to come in when he noticed Jeanette wasn't there. Paul looked for Jeanette and found her gazing at the sky. He came to Jeanette and looked at the sky with her. Jeanette looked at and put her head on Paul's chest. Paul hugged Jeanette warmly. Jeanette wanted to keep holding his body like that. She did not want to let him go to another country. Both of them watched the stars.

Mary Anna went to her bedroom, and it was very hot. She thought she'd open the window to cool down her room. Mary Anna lifted the window up and saw her parents standing outside. She called Nikki and Barbara to come in her bedroom. They came in, and Mary Anna's told them to keep quiet. She pointed to their parents outside. The girls went to the window, saw their parents standing outside, and smiled at them. Mary Anna watched them, but she suspected that Jeanette and Paul were looking at the sky. Mary Anna decided to look at the sky, too, and didn't realize there were so many stars out. She told the girls to look at the stars. The girls looked up and were in awe of the beautiful night sky.

Chapter 11

The sunrise lit the blue sky early in the morning. The flowers at the front porch, called "Holland", were starting to open and let the sun come to them. The birds flew from their nests to the sky or the trees. The light came through Jeanette's bedroom window to hit the blank, country white wall. The bedroom became brighter and woke Jeanette, who looked up at the ceiling. She wondered if this was her last day in this room. She looked around the room with its boxes and bags. She looked out the window to the maple trees. She wanted to keep these memories fresh in her mind so she could remember everything when they lived in a different house on base. She took off her bedclothes, walked to the window, and looked at the road. Paul turned his body to the other side of the bed and moved his arm over to Jeanette's shoulder, but Jeanette wasn't in bed. He looked around the room until he saw her. She was standing by the window, looking somewhere outside. Paul sighed and knew that she already missed this house and her friends. He got out of the bed, walked to Jeanette and hugged her. Jeanette looked at Paul and moved her head to Paul's chest to feel his heartbeat. Paul was holding his breath, wishing he didn't have to go to war in Vietnam. But he had to go. The Pentagon drafted him. Paul kissed Jeanette's head and went to the bathroom for quick shower. Jeanette went to wake the girls up and clean their bedrooms for the move. After Paul finished his shower, he let Jeanette in the bathroom. She looked at the mirror, which was steamed up from the hot shower. She wiped the steam off the mirror and looked at herself. She brushed her teeth and took a

77

shower.

Paul and Jeanette went downstairs to the kitchen. They would have to clear the table for their last breakfast in this house. Paul cooked bacons, eggs, pancakes, and ham on the stove. Jeanette set the table and made toast. The girls could smell breakfast from their bedrooms. The smell made them hungry, so they came to the kitchen. Paul put a large plate of food on the table. Jeanette made homemade orange juice and poured it in each of the glasses. Paul and Jeanette liked showing off their cooking skills. The girls were surprised with their parents, because they never cooked such a large breakfast before. The girls sat down and ate with Paul and Jeanette.

After they had finished eating, the girls went back to their bedrooms and started to pack their clothes. Jeanette and Paul washed the dishes and glasses, then wrapped and packed them in a box. Paul heard a knock at the front door; he told Jeanette that someone was there. Paul opened the door, and there were Angel and her husband, Andy. They brought some food for lunch. A few minutes later, Paul saw another car coming down the dirt road. It was DeeDee and her husband, Chris. DeeDee opened their trunk and pulled out a basket. She walked to Paul on the porch, opened the basket lid and showed Paul that she had made some homemade meatloaf.

DeeDee said, "This was my first time making meatloaf. I hope it tastes good."

"It smells so good! I can't wait to eat that for lunch," Paul smiled.

He pulled the screen door open and let the warm air come into the house. They walked through the foyer to the kitchen and looked for Jeanette. She and Angel were packing dishes in a box. Jeanette saw DeeDee standing with a basket and her husband, Chris. Jeanette came to DeeDee and hugged her and Chris. She took the basket to the counter and opened the lid.

"Is that meatloaf?" Jeanette asked.

"Yes," DeeDee smiled. "I tried my best to cook meatloaf. Do you think everyone will like it?"

"Come on," Jeanette giggled. "Everyone will love it. I'm sure they'll tell you the meatloaf was delicious. You should be proud of yourself."

A moving van with a green and yellow strip and the world "Mayflower" came to the house from Northern Virginia. The men came to the porch and knocked on the screen door. Paul saw them and told Jeanette that the moving van was there now. Jeanette told her friends to wait for her while she showed the men around the house. The men chose to take the mattress from the master bedroom first; they carried it downstairs to the moving van.

Maria and Bonnie arrived at Jeanette's house next. Maria and her husband brought three large watermelons. Bonnie brought bags with rolls for hotdogs and hamburgers leftover from last night. Her husband had five boxes of Budweiser beer. A half-hour later, Vicky arrived. She was late because her car had a flat on the road. Her husband, Tim, changed the tire and drove to the store. They bought boxes of canned pork bean and corn on the cob.

The men carried boxes and heavy furniture out of each room to load in the moving van. When a room became empty, the women would clean it up. The children played outside on the swing under the tree and talked about the plan to write letters to keep in touch with each other while they lived on the base.

The house was almost empty around noon. The men needed to rest a few minutes and grabbed some beer from the icebox. DeeDee washed the bathroom's tiles floor with some chemical that gave her head a headache. And because she was bending her knees to clean the floor, her back was killing her. Her arms were sore too, so she decided to take a break and open the window in the bathroom. DeeDee tried to open the window, but it was stuck. Someone nailed the frame closed so it couldn't be opened. She sighed and left the bathroom to the hall. She stood and looked out the open window. The fresh air made her feel better. She stuck her out the window and saw the men outside in the backyard; they were talking and drinking beer. DeeDee felt like joining them for a beer and thought all the women should take a break from working get some beers with their husbands. DeeDee saw the women in another room; she used the light switch to flash the women so they would look at her.

"Why don't we take a break?" DeeDee asked. "I saw the men

outside drinking beer. Let's go outside with them, grab a beer and rest."

The women agreed with DeeDee's idea and walked outside to the men. The women started to walk around the house to the backyard when Bonnie told them to "stop" because she had an idea.

"Can you act sexy for the men?" Bonnie asked. "Why don't we act like we're in West Side Story?"

The women looked at each other for a moment and laughed. They thought it was so funny. They opened their blouse buttons to let the men see their breasts, and they practiced acting sexy. They walked slowly to the icebox, and opened it to take a beer out, turn the cap, and drink it. The men stood, talked, and looked at the women, wondering why they were acting sexy in front of them. The women walked and sat on their husband's laps and drank the beer. The moving men and the children were laughing at the women's behavior. When they saw their children watching, they got embarrassed.

Jeanette had a good time drinking beer with her husband and friends around her. She looked at her watch and saw it was past noon. She called Maria and Angel to help her get something ready for lunch. Jeanette told Paul to collect some wood for the grill and light a fire to cook the hamburgers and hot dogs. Jeanette and two women brought paper plates and cups outside. Jeanette turned on the oven to warm up the meatloaf. Vicky showed up to help Jeanette and cooked the pork beans in a big pan.

In the backyard, the moving men had a good idea of using plywood and boxes to make a long table. Maria and Angel walked outside to the backyard and were surprised at the long table that was already ready for their last lunch. They set up the plates and forks on the table. Chris and Andy started to cook the hamburgers and hot dogs on the grill. The children came to the table and sat on a long piece of wood supported by concrete, and waited for some hamburgers and hot dogs. All of the people came and sat at the long table like an Amish family from Pennsylvania. Andy brought a large plate full of hamburgers, and Chris brought a large bowl of hot dogs to the table. A half-hour later, they were all enjoying a good lunch. When Maria was finished, she decided to look for Jeanette. She found Jeanette on the porch. She was sitting on the bench and smoking a cigarette. Maria knew that Jeanette wasn't happy to leave. She came onto the porch and sat next to Jeanette.

"I'll miss you," Maria said. "We'll write to each other every week."

Jeanette was silent and did not respond to Maria's words. Maria nodded and sat back quietly on the bench.

After lunch was over, everyone was full and started to clean up the table. The men took all of the boxes and plywood back to the truck, then closed and locked the door. Paul told them that they would meet at the base around 6:00 that afternoon. The men got in the truck and left to go to Northern Virginia.

Maria watched the truck leave and looked for Jeanette; she knew that Jeanette was somewhere in the house. Maria went into the house and checked each floor until she found Jeanette in the master bedroom standing near the window. Maria came in the bedroom and flicked the light switch. Jeanette would not turn around to look at Maria. Maria knew that Jeanette was not happy to leave the house. She tried to talk to Jeanette, who wouldn't say anything. Maria decided to back off and leave her alone. After Maria left the bedroom, Jeanette turned to make sure Maria was not there. She preferred to be alone. Jeanette looked out the window again and started to tear for a moment.

Jeanette's friends were waiting for her to show up so they could say goodbye. Jeanette came out of the house and stood on the porch; she was just being quiet and looking at the view to always remember it. Paul came to Jeanette and told her he was going to make sure they had everything before they left. Jeanette nodded as Paul went in the house. He walked around each room. In the master bedroom, he stood against the wall and looked at the ceiling. He did not want to leave this house either, but he had to go for the Pentagon's sake. Paul went downstairs, looked at the living room and fireplace, then opened the door to go outside. He locked the door, walked to the end of the porch and looked at Jeanette standing outside. Jeanette came to the porch.

"The house is empty," Paul said.

Jeanette looked at the ground. Paul didn't say anything because

Jeanette refused to look at him.

"Well, let's go hug our friends before we leave." Paul said.

Jeanette went into the porch alone. Paul knew that she did not want to leave this house. He came to Jeanette and tried to pull her out of the porch toward her friends for one last hug. Jeanette walked to the car, looked at Maria, and realized she forgot to hug and talk to Maria.

Jeanette came to Maria and muttered, "I forgot to say goodbye. I'll write every week. I do remember what you told me before I went into the house."

Jeanette hugged Maria as hard as she could and started to cry. Maria knew it was hard for them to be apart and was glad Jeanette heard Maria wanted to keep in touch through letters. Jeanette got into to the car and looked at Maria and her friends. She started to weep.

"I miss you already," Jeanette cried. "I'll keep in touch with you and I love you, sisterhood."

Her daughters then hugged and talked to Jeanette's friends and children before getting in the car. Paul started the engine and drove around to the road. They waved and followed the car to the end of the dirt road. Jeanette was starting to cry again. She didn't turn back to look at her friends behind the car. The car turned left on the road and kept going. Maria walked and waved until the car gone. The sisterhood came to Maria and comforted her since she would be apart from her best friend, Jeanette, for first time since lived in D.C. for a year.

Chapter 12

Paul kept driving north on Route 29, away from Culpeper, for three hours. Jeanette was quiet and looking outside. The girls in the back seat slept for a while during the trip. Paul and Jeanette noticed the one lane road become two lanes in Fairfax County. More houses, stores and cars appeared, and they realized this area was much more commercialized than their hometown.

They arrived at the front gate of Fort Belvoir, which was about thirty minutes away from Washington, D.C. Paul gave his Pentagon letter to the security guard. He read the letter and told Paul that he was required to call headquarters at Fort Belvoir to make sure they had his name on the list to join the army for the Vietnam War. The security guard wanted Paul to drive through and park near the gate and wait for headquarters to call back in a few minutes. After twenty minutes, the guard received a call indicating Paul was on the list. The security guard gave Paul an envelope and explained that it was for his new home on base.

Paul opened the envelope and found directions to his new house from the gate. He left the gate and kept driving straight down the same road. They saw army recruits running with a leader. They followed the road till the end and looked for house #86, which they finally found in the circle. They parked in front of the house. Jeanette saw a middle-sized brown envelope stuck between the door and the frame. Paul told Jeanette that he would get it and told the girls that they had arrived.

The girls woke up, got out of the car, and looked around the houses on the base. They weren't used to this area. Most of the houses were of standard design, with the two stories and plain red brick. They weren't used to red brick houses so close to other houses. Paul opened the envelope and read a small yellow paper that informed him he should stay there and wait for a person who would show up at the house after Paul arrived. Paul told Jeanette that a person would be there any time. He saw a car park next to his car and get out. The man wore an army uniform and brought a briefcase; he came to Paul and asked him to show his ID. Paul took out his wallet and showed his ID to the man. He looked at Paul's ID and asked him for the first letter from the Pentagon. Paul showed the letter to the man, who read Paul's draft notice for Vietnam. He gave the ID and the letter back to Paul and introduced himself as Mark Collin.

Mark had the keys for the house. He went to the front door, unlocked it and let Paul's family in the house. Jeanette came in the house first, followed by the girls and Paul. They all spread out. Jeanette walked through the dining room to the kitchen. The first thing she saw was a dishwasher, which she did not have at her old house. She looked around the cabinets and walked to the breakfast room with a bay window. It was larger than her old house. The building was about five years old with new appliances. The washer and dryer were on the same floor as the kitchen. Mary Anna walked around a bedroom, stopped by the window, and saw the moving van coming to her new home. She ran downstairs to the kitchen and looked for Jeanette who was standing by a window looking outside at the backyard. Mary Anna looked for a switch to flick, but couldn't find one. Instead, she stomped her foot on the floor to make Jeanette notice her.

"I saw the moving van," Mary Anna said. "They're here now."

Mary Anna ran to the front door. Jeanette didn't have to worry about the men losing their things on such a long trip. She was glad that the driver found their new house. She walked to the front door and saw the moving van drive over the grass to get close to the door. The men wanted to work quickly before it was dark. They opened the van doors and pulled the ramp under the bumper down to the ground. They carried furniture and boxes into the house. Each time they brought something in, they asked Jeanette which room to put it in. All of their belongings were unloaded by 10 p.m. The men gave Paul a form to sign.

"Thank you for giving us lunch today at your old house," the man said. "You have a good evening."

The men left the house and Paul closed and locked the door. Jeanette walked to the living room. It was so full of boxes that she couldn't walk through it. She saw Nikki on the love seat sleeping with her pink blanket. Jeanette gave up trying to move Nikki to her new bedroom, because the love seat was in the middle of the boxes and she couldn't get through. Paul laughed at Jeanette. It was so funny. She decided to leave Nikki there for the night. Jeanette came to Paul and hugged him. Paul was so tired, and he looked at Jeanette.

"Are you all right now?" Paul asked. "Can you tell me what you think about this house? I was surprised there was a dishwasher. We don't have to worry about dishpan hands for a long time. Did you see that?"

"Yeah," Jeanette smiled and laughed. "I'm we have dishwasher. We might need to break the habit of hand washing. I suppose this house will be fine. I need to go to bed as soon as we find the bed sheets. Tomorrow we'll start unpacking boxes, ok?"

Paul nodded and hugged Jeanette again. They decided to go upstairs to the master bedroom and look for the sheets. Jeanette found the sheets, and she and Paul made the bed to sleep together for the first night in their new house.

For a week, Jeanette and Paul unpacked and moved the furniture around the room. They argued over where to hang pictures in the living room and hallway walls. Mary Anna, Nikki and Barbara helped each other unpack their bedrooms. The phone was ringing in the foyer near the stairs. Mary Anna ran downstairs and answered the phone.

"Hello," Mary Anna said. "Ok, I'll get my Daddy right away."

Mary Anna called for her Daddy. Paul was outside and heard Mary Anna's voice calling him to get the phone.

"It's some guy from the Pentagon," Mary Anna whispered to his hear. "It scared me to death because I'm not used to his military voice."

Mary Anna ran upstairs again. Paul watched her go to her room.

"Yes, sir?" Paul asked.

"Are you Dreyfuss?" the Chief asked.

"Yes, I am." Paul said.

"Ok. First thing you need to do is meet me in my office tomorrow morning, 8 o'clock sharp," the chief ordered.

"Yes, sir, I'll be there tomorrow morning," Paul said.

"Good, see you tomorrow," said the chief.

Paul hung up the phone slowly. He sat on the chair and looked at his hands, which looked nervous. He held his hands to his chest and closed his eyes shut. He heard someone come, opened his eyes and saw Barbara. She stood in the foyer and staring at Paul. She wondered why the Pentagon made Paul so nervous.

Early in the morning, Paul rushed to the Pentagon in Arlington, VA. He did not realize the building was so huge. He would have to ask someone for help in finding the chief's office. Paul was lost in the parking lot. Good thing he was able to park close to the building. He ran into the lobby and showed security his letter. The security guard called the chief and informed him that Paul Dreyfuss was in the lobby. The guard then told Paul that the chief wanted to see him right away. He gave Paul directions to go to the third floor towards a set of brown wooden doors that said "Headquarters" on them. Paul's heart beat so fast when he found the doors and pulled them open. He saw a woman at the front desk. Paul walked to the front desk and gave the letter to the woman. She opened and read his letter.

"Mr. Dreyfuss," the woman said, "I will tell Captain White that you are here. Please have a seat there."

The woman gave the letter back to Paul. He went and sat on a chair. He saw the woman dialed Captain White. In ten minutes, Paul heard her phone ring. Paul knew it was the Captain. She spoke on the phone and looked at Paul.

She pointed to a door. "Captain White will see you now."

Paul went into the office. Captain White stood up from his chair and came over to Paul.

"Mr. Dreyfuss," Captain White shook Paul's hand. "Thank you for stopping by. Please have a seat."

Paul sat on a leather chair. Captain White went back to his

chair, opened a long, cream folder and read Paul's background as an Engineer.

"You know a lot about bridges and roads," he stated. "You have a lot of knowledge in that area."

"Thanks, sir," Paul said softly.

Captain White closed the folder and came to Paul. "Welcome to the army," Captain White said.

Paul was surprised at what he said. He stood up and shook hands.

"Thanks again, sir," Paul said.

"First thing you need to do is go back to your base," Captain White explained. "Go to the hospital for a physical, then go to the main area for your new uniform. A soldier there will give you a schedule for your military practice. Within six months, you'll leave for Vietnam."

"Yes sir," Paul said. "I'm on my way to base to follow your orders. Sir."

Captain White and Paul stood straight like soldiers. Paul left the office and drove back to the base. He parked at his house, which was close to the hospital, then went straight to the hospital. He asked a nurse to find a doctor to give him his physical so he could join the army. The nurse pointed to a door that was for health checks only. He went into the room and told the doctor that he wanted health checked. After Paul passed his physical, he went to get his new uniform. He was not used to a uniform of all green. The soldier gave him a practice schedule for his military group.

Once he was done, he went home. He walked in the foyer and put his bags on the stairs. Paul looked for Jeanette somewhere in the house. He knew that she would be in the kitchen. He came to the kitchen and saw Jeanette at the sink. He knew Jeanette would be upset at seeing him in an army uniform. Paul came over and kissed Jeanette on her cheek. Jeanette looked at Paul.

"Oh you're wearing a uniform," Jeanette said, surprised. "I'm not used to seeing you wear that! But I'll get used to it."

Jeanette hugged Paul hard. He was surprised that Jeanette did not get upset. He looked into Jeanette's eyes to see if she looked sad.

"Are you all right, darling?" Paul asked. His face looked

concerned.

Jeanette did not answer; she went to the table and put a cigarette to her lip. She lit the cigarette and exhaled. Paul didn't know if Jeanette was all right or not. Jeanette sat on a chair and looked at Paul. He stood near the sink.

"Jeanette," Paul asked, "please would you say something?"

"Hey, Paul," Jeanette answered. "I'm fine. You don't have to worry about me, ok?"

Jeanette walked out of the kitchen to her bedroom upstairs. Paul thought he'd better leave Jeanette alone for now. He took the paper out of his shirt pocket and read his schedule for his first military group meeting. It was tonight.

During six months, Paul practiced with the military at 4:00 a.m. every morning. He became used to it and knew the practices would help protect his life in Vietnam. He spent time with his family when he was at home.

On Thanksgiving Day, Paul ate his last good dinner with Jeanette and his daughters at home. He was leaving for Vietnam early the next morning. He noticed Jeanette's behavior seemed fine and she ate normally. After the dinner was over, Paul and Jeanette cleaned up the kitchen. The girls cried and hugged their father. They went to bed early so they could get up with their father. Paul kissed each of his daughters, then went to his bedroom. He closed the door and looked at Jeanette who was sitting in a chair next to the window, smoking a cigarette. She did not change her clothes yet. He knew that Jeanette did not want him to leave her alone for a few years. He came over to her and bent his knees on the floor. He took the cigarette and put it out in the ashtray. His hands rubbed Jeanette's thighs, which turned her on. They started to kiss and he took Jeanette to their bed. They removed their clothes and made love all the night.

The alarm clock was loud. Paul turned it off, got out of bed and took a shower. Jeanette awoke from the light of the bathroom. She thought that she'd join Paul in the shower. She rushed into the bathroom and jumped in the shower. Paul laughed as they bathed each other and was happy they were still in love.

It was getting late, so Paul went to wake up their daughters.

Go to the Hill

They changed clothes and brushed their teeth. The girls had a hard time getting up so early, but they managed anyway. Jeanette got dressed and went downstairs to the kitchen. She had planned to cook a nice breakfast, but there was no time. She decided to eat cereal with Paul and the girls. After they finished, they left the house for the base airport. More than a hundred soldiers were there with their wives and children. Jeanette noticed one soldier's wife crying that she did not want to see her husband killed in Vietnam. Jeanette held her breath and hoped she wouldn't cry like that in public. Paul hugged his girls, then Jeanette last. She hugged and kissed him before he got on the airplane. Paul put a five pound, long, dark green bag over his shoulder and waved at them. He followed the other soldiers into the plane. The girls waved and cried as their father walked toward the airplane and went upstairs to the door. He looked at Jeanette and the girls and blew them a kiss. Jeanette found it hard to control her emotions. She gave up and started to cry for Paul. The girls looked at Jeanette while she cried; they hugged their mother. Paul started to tear up and went in the airplane. Jeanette refused to leave until the airplane flew into the sky. Then they all left for home.

Jeanette and Maria wrote letters every week since Paul left his family to go to Vietnam. Jeanette had been alone with her three daughters for a month without Paul. She decided to stop writing Maria because she couldn't stop thinking about Paul while risking is life in the jungle with the other men.

After three weeks, Jeanette was still so upset that her stomach felt sick. She went to her bed to rest a while. A woman from the next door knocked on Jeanette's door. Nikki opened the door.

"Hi, Mrs. Wright, can I help you?" Nikki said.

"Hello, Nikki," Mrs. Wright smiled. "I'd like you and your family to have this turkey for dinner tonight."

She gave it to Nikki. It was very heavy to hold.

"Thanks for give us a half turkey." Nikki said shyly.

She brought the turkey to the kitchen and left it on the counter. Barbara and Mary Anna came into the kitchen from the family room. They smelled the turkey.

"That turkey smells so good, Mary Anna said, "I think you

should tell mother that Mrs. Wright gave us a turkey for dinner. I'm hungry now!"

"I plan on telling mom now," said Nikki, rolling her eyes up. Nikki went upstairs and came in her mother's bedroom. She woke Jeanette, who started to wake up slowly, and looked at Nikki standing there.

"Yes, darling?" Jeanette sounded tired.

"Mrs. Wright gave us a turkey for dinner tonight," Nikki said. Jeanette's looked at Nikki's face and saw she wasn't joking. Jeanette came out the bed, grabbed a cigarette and started to smoke. Nikki waited for Jeanette to respond. Jeanette came over Nikki.

"Are you sure?" Jeanette asked seriously.

"Yes, I swear it." Nikki crossed her heart and raised up her right hand.

Jeanette looked puzzled and wanted to check the kitchen. She followed Nikki downstairs.

"Look at the turkey on the table," Nikki pointed. Jeanette was surprised Nikki wasn't teasing her. Barbara and Mary Anna set the table with plates, forks and knives. Jeanette put her cigarette out into the ashtray and sat on a chair. She looked at the turkey. Barbara put glasses of water on the table. The girls sat down and waited for Jeanette to cut the turkey. Mary Anna gave a sharp knife to Jeanette. She planned on carving the turkey, but at that moment, she started feel sick, like she could vomit at any time. She dropped the knife on the floor and ran to the powder room to vomit into the toilet. The girls suspected something was wrong with Jeanette. Mary Anna came to the powder room.

"Are you all right?" Mary Anna asked.

"I'm fine," Jeanette nodded her head. "You can cut the turkey yourself, but be careful with the sharp knife, ok?"

"Yeah, I'll do it," Mary Anna promised.

She went back to the kitchen. She picked the sharp knife off floor, washed it, then came back to the table to carve the turkey.

The next morning, Jeanette was still bothered by her stomach and decided to go see a doctor. Jeanette went to the hospital and told the doctor something was wrong with her stomach. The doctor told Jeanette to change into a hospital gown in another room. When she came back, she sat on a chair. The doctor came and checked her health first, then checked at her stomach and vagina. He told Jeanette to put her clothes back on and meet him in his office. Jeanette wondered what was wrong with her. She changed her clothes and entered the doctor's office. The doctor and a nurse looked at Jeanette with smiles on their faces. She wondered what they were smiling about. The nurse came to Jeanette and brought her close to the doctor.

"It's not your stomach," he explained. "Mrs. Dreyfuss, you're three weeks pregnant."

Jeanette was shocked at what the doctor told her. She looked at the nurse.

"Your baby due will be due in the middle of July," the nurse said.

Jeanette started to faint. The doctor and nurse held Jeanette and brought her on a bed. A few minutes later, Jeanette woke up, looked at the ceiling, and looked around the room. Nobody was there. She got out of bed, took her coat and purse with her and left the room. The doctor and nurse were in the hall; they saw Jeanette leaving the room. They came and asked Jeanette if she was all right. She nodded her head that she was fine and left the hospital. Jeanette walked on the sidewalk to her house. She started to smoke a cigarette but thought it was a bad idea since she was three weeks pregnant. She threw the cigarette into the street. She scared and worried about having a fourth baby without Paul. She thought she'd write Paul a letter to inform him that she was pregnant. She wondered if he would be upset or happy.

Chapter 13

Norma Gina Dreyfuss was born on July 12, 1969 at 8:24 a.m. She was nine pounds and had blond hair and hazel eyes. Jeanette went home with her baby. The girls were happy to play with their little sister. It was hard for Barbara to be jealous of Norma because Norma was twelve years younger than Barbara was. When Norma was a year old, she loved to play outside with her older sisters. Jeanette got tired of cleaning the house by herself, so she deiced to move to a three bedroom apartment on the base. At first the girls weren't happy living in an apartment because it was too small, but they got used to it an about a month.

Three weeks before the Vietnam War was over, Paul had been gone for a little over seven years. Jeanette and her four daughters had lived in the apartment for almost five years. Mary Anna was 18 years old and a senior in high school in Alexandria. Nikki and Barbara were in junior high. And the last girl, Norma, was six years old. She had never seen her father since he left before she was born. They were watching Little House on the Prairie on the TV in the living room. Mary Anna asked the girls if wanted some popcorn, which they did. She started to make the popcorn when a military vehicle drove up their street and stopped in front of their place.

An officer got out of the car and looked for Jeanette's apartment number. He found her apartment, walked upstairs and knocked on the door. Mary Anna heard knock the knock and moved the popcorn pan to the other side of the stove. She opened the door and looked puzzled at seeing a military man standing outside. Mary Anna figured he was there for Jeanette.

"Can I help you?" Mary Anna asked. "Are you looking for my mother?"

"Yes, I'm here for your mother," the officer said softly. "Is she here? Can I speak with Mrs. Dreyfuss please?"

Mary Anna took the man to the living room. Jeanette was sitting on the sofa and smoking a cigarette next to Norma. Jeanette looked at Mary Anna.

"This man is here for you," Mary Anna said.

"What?" Jeanette asked, puzzled.

"He wants to talk to you," Mary Anna said. "He needs to see you right away."

"Why does he want to talk to me?" Jeanette asked.

"I don't know," Mary Anna sighed. "He said he needed to tell you something."

Jeanette thought she better check the door and see if an officer was waiting for her. Jeanette pushed her cigarette into the ashtray and followed Mary Anna to the kitchen. Jeanette came in the kitchen and saw the military man. Mary Anna left the kitchen to go in the living room with the girls. Now Jeanette was alone with the man. He walked into the kitchen and closed the door to talk to her. Jeanette could not understand what he said. She pointed to her ear and shook her head "No," trying to convey that she could not hear him. The officer didn't understand; he did not realize she was deaf. Jeanette motioned towards the officer to stop speaking by putting her hand up. She could not hear what he was saying and his lips were moving too fast for her to read. Jeanette called Mary Anna to help interpret. Mary Anna came back to the kitchen again.

"Can you tell me what the officer is saying?" Jeanette asked. "What does he want to tell me?"

Mary Anna explained to the officer that Jeanette was deaf. The officer pulled a letter from his coat pocket and gave it to Jeanette. He slowly looked at Mary Anna.

"This letter is for Mrs. Dreyfuss," said the officer as he gave it to Jeanette. "I'll stay here until she reads it."

Mary Anna spoke to Jeanette in American Sign Language

and explained what the officer said. Jeanette suspected something happened to Paul in Vietnam. She looked at the letter then looked at the officer. She opened the envelope and read the letter:

Dear Mrs. Dreyfuss,

We, the Pentagon, would like to inform you about the death of your husband, Paul Dreyfuss. The base at Vietnam will send Dreyfuss' coffin to Fort Belvoir, Virginia, tomorrow at 0730. Please come with your children to the airport at Fort Belvoir.

Paul Dreyfuss was killed in the line of duty by an enemy land mine in the jungle. We are honored to give you a Medal of Honor for Paul's bravery. We will communicate more about supporting your children and yourself after his burial. Again, we offer you our deepest sympathy and condolences on the loss of your husband.

Sincerely,
The Pentagon

Jeanette was shocked, then started to cry aloud and crumble to the floor. Mary Anna knew that her father was killed in Vietnam. She hugged Jeanette.

"Why did the Pentagon ask Paul to go to Vietnam?" Jeanette screamed.

Nikki and Barbara heard Jeanette's voice. They ran to the kitchen and saw the officer standing at the door and Mary Anna hugging Jeanette on the floor. The girls were confused.

"What's wrong?" Barbara asked.

"Daddy was killed in Vietnam," Mary Anna cried.

Nikki and Barbara were shocked and saddened. Mary Anna told them to come to their mother. The girls came and hugged Mary Anna and Jeanette. Mary Anna looked at the officer who was looking at Norma. Norma stood near the kitchen and stared at them. She didn't understand what they were doing. Mary Anna knew that Norma never knew their father. Mary Anna looked at the officer. He opened the door and left. Then she looked at Norma and motioned for her to join them in grieving their father's death. Norma finally came over to them.

The next morning, Jeanette and her four daughters got up early, rushed to shower, got dressed and grabbed something to eat for breakfast. They were sad, but not as depressed as the night before. A black limousine was waiting outside to take them to the memorial service. They got in and were driven to the airport at Fort Belvoir. They got out of the car and walked into the building to join other people waiting for the Air Force to arrive from Vietnam.

They saw a plane arrive and land near the building. A line of military personnel waited for the plane to stop and open its back door. Soldiers went in and carried coffins out of the airplane. They brought the coffin of Paul Dreyfuss to Jeanette. They put the coffin in the funeral car, and Jeanette and her daughters went in the limousine. They procession went to Arlington National Cemetery, about half-hour from Fort Belvoir.

The funeral car arrived at Arlington National Cemetery and drove to the place where Paul Dreyfuss was to be buried. Soldiers carried the coffin with the United States flag draped over it. There five chairs in front of the grave for Jeanette and her four daughters. They came to the chairs and sat down. The soldiers walked back to the other side and stood straight. A preacher arrived at the gravesite and met Jeanette and her daughters. He stood next to the coffin and prayed for Paul Dreyfuss. Jeanette stared at the coffin toward another burial less than 800 feet away. There, a soldier's wife and two sons, about Mary Anna's age, were crying at the loss of their father. The wife cried and hugged her husband's coffin; she did not want him to leave her alone. Jeanette started to tear up at seeing this scene. An officer came over to Paul's coffin and started to fold the flag; he then gave it to Jeanette. The started to shoot their guns in the air. The loud shots frightened Jeanette and her daughters.

After Paul's burial, they went home. Jeanette walked toward her bedroom. She put her purse on the dresser, sat on the mattress, and stared at the mirror for a while. She took her black hat off and cleaned it up to use another time. She walked to a tall dresser, put the hat in its box and closed it. At that moment, she got so angry that she swept everything off the dresser with her arms. Things were falling to the floor, and some were breaking. She started to cry, then pulled a drawer out of the dresser and threw it against the wall. She pulled another drawer out and threw it across the room. Then she pushed the dresser down from against the wall and started to scream over her husband's death. Jeanette became weak and fell down on the floor near the wall. She never stopped screaming and hitting her hand against the wall. Norma ran to the kitchen and hid under the table. She held her hands over her ears because she didn't' like hearing Jeanette's voice so loud. Mary Anna held her other two sisters together on the sofa. The girls were scared and cried.

The apartment became silent. Norma awoke and crawled out from under the table. She walked through the living room to her mother's bedroom. She looked at the girls on the sofa who were sleeping together. Norma came in her mother's bedroom and looked for her mother. She found Jeanette on the floor between the dresser and bed. She was holding the flag. Jeanette woke up, but her vision was blurred and she should not see clearly. She rubbed her eyes again. Jeanette then saw Norma standing and staring at her while she lay on the floor holding the flag. Jeanette looked at Norma's face and saw she looked confused about Jeanette's behavior and outburst that morning.

Jeanette got up from the floor. She didn't realize she had slept with Paul's flag. She decided to put the flag away in the closet near the bathroom. Then she turned on the bathroom light and filled the sink with water. She cupped her hands together and splashed water on her face. When she dried her face, she noticed Norma by the mirror. Norma stood by the door and stared at Jeanette washing her face. Jeanette tried to talk to Norma, but couldn't say anything. Jeanette putted the towel back and looked at her bedroom. It had clothes strewn all over the room and looked such a mess. Jeanette sighed. Norma pulled Jeanette's hand to have Jeanette look at her.

"Mommy," Norma said. "You slept on the all night."

Jeanette was surprised that she slept on the floor by herself.

She sat on the mattress and pulled Norma to hug her.

Mary Anna awoke with stiff arms from the way she was sleeping. She pushed her sisters away from her body, and Barbara and Nikki moved to another side of the couch. Mary Anna got up, stretched her back and yawned. She went to the kitchen to pour a glass of cherry Kool Aid. She drank the whole thing then put her glass in the sink. She looked under the table as saw Norma wasn't there. She figured Norma was in their mother's room and, indeed, found Norma there. Mary Anna was glad that Norma didn't run away from home. Mary Anna came close to the bathroom and waved at the mirror. Jeanette looked at Mary Anna's reflection.

"Are you all right now?" Mary Anna asked. "I know it's so hard to lose a good man from our family."

She started to cry and sat next to Jeanette. She moved her arm over Jeanette. Mary Anna heard the phone ringing. She told Jeanette that the phone was ringing and ran to the kitchen to answer it.

"Hello?" Mary Anna asked.

"May I speak with Mrs. Dreyfuss, please?" an officer asked.

"She can't speak on the phone, because she's deaf," Mary Anna explained.

"Ok. Would you please inform her that she can come to the office and pick up her husband's box any time," he said.

"Ok, I'll let her know right away. Thanks," Mary Anna said.

She hung up the phone and walked toward the bedroom. Jeanette was on the bed with Norma. She looked at Mary Anna.

"Who was on the phone?" Jeanette asked.

"A military officer called," Mary Anna said. "He'd like you to come over to the office and pick up a box of Daddy's personal things."

"They bought Paul's things here?" Jeanette asked.

"Yes, that's what he said," Mary Anna believed.

Jeanette stood up from the bed and walked to the dresser to get her purse, but it wasn't there.

"Oh no! My purse is gone! It must be somewhere in the room," Jeanette said, sounding upset.

"Don't worry, mom, I'll help you find it," Mary Anna said.

Mary Anna and Jeanette looked for the purse in the disheveled room. Norma stood and watched at them; she noticed something brown under the bed that was probably her mother's purse.

"Mary Anna, I see the purse under the bed," Norma pointed.

"Where is it?" Mary Anna asked.

"Under the bed," Norma pointed again.

Mary Anna followed Norma's point and grabbed the purse from under the bed.

"Thank you Norma," Mary Anna smiled.

She showed the purse to Jeanette.

"Where did you find my purse?" Jeanette asked.

"Norma found it under your bed," Mary Anna said, pointing to Norma.

"Oh thanks, Norma!" Jeanette smiled.

Jeanette got her purse and ran to the kitchen to grab her coat.

"Which building should I go to?" Jeanette asked.

"Good question," Mary Anna answered. "I'm sure it's in Human Services."

"Yeah, I probably should go there first," Jeanette said. 'I'm sure they can tell me the right building to get your father's box."

"Yes, I'm sure they can," Jeanette nodded her head.

She put her coat on and kissed each of girls' cheek.

"Mary Anna," Jeanette called, "would you please take care of Norma for me? I'll be back in a minutes. Thanks!"

"Ok. Goodbye." Mary Anna waved.

Jeanette went downstairs and walked on the sidewalk. She looked up at the window where Mary Anna and Norma stood watching her. She waved at them, and the girls waved back. She kept walking straight to the building.

Jeanette came in the building, walked through the lobby to the front desk and asked the receptionist for paper and pen. Jeanette wrote the woman, asking her if she knew where one went to collect a soldier's personal belongings. The woman wrote something on the paper and gave it back to Jeanette. Jeanette read the note that said to go upstairs, turn left, and keep walking until the eighth door on the right, which would have a sign that said "Personal" on it. Jeanette nodded and left to find the right office.

When she came to the room, saw a man behind a front desk.

He needed to see Jeanette's ID. He looked at the ID and looked at another book to find the matching name. Then he gave the ID back to her. The man called another person on the phone. In few minutes, the man brought out a box and put it on the table. He nodded to Jeanette and left her alone. Jeanette watched him leave and moved to the table where the box sat. She opened the box and looked inside to make sure it really had Paul's things. It did. Jeanette closed the box and brought it home.

When she arrived home, Jeanette put the box on the kitchen table. She hung up her coat and opened the box quickly. Mary Anna watched Jeanette as she looked inside the box and slowly took a bag out. Mary Anna continued to peek at her mother. Jeanette put the bag on the table and started to open it slowly to see what Paul had from Vietnam. She put her hand in the bag and felt something funny. Jeanette took it out and saw it was a small silver lighter. She wondered why Paul had a lighter and figured he was probably smoking in Vietnam. Jeanette closed her hand tightly around the lighter and held it to her chest.

Chapter 14

The newspaper boy threw a paper against Nancy's door. Nancy, Maria's neighbor, picked up the newspaper, walked into the kitchen, and dropped it on the table. She poured herself a cup of coffee and started to read the paper. First she read the obituary list of soldiers who were killed in Vietnam. She read each the soldiers' name to see if she knew any from Virginia. She saw Paul Dreyfuss's name on the list. She was shocked and knew that he was the husband of Maria's friend, Jeanette's. Nancy decided to bring the newspaper to Maria' house. She came through the door to the kitchen and looked at Maria, who was cleaning the stove. Maria noticed the shadow of a person on the floor. She looked and saw it was Nancy. Nancy's face was so sad and shocked that it scared Maria. She thought Bobby must have fallen off the roof again. He had already broken his arms several times.

"Did Bobby break his arm again?" Maria asked nervously.

"No," Nancy said, "read the paper."

"What are you talking about, read what newspaper?" Maria asked, looking confused.

Nancy put the newspaper on the table and opened it. She pointed her finger at the paper. Maria suspected something was wrong.

"What is it?" Maria asked.

She walked slowly toward the table and sat down. She looked at Nancy's finger on a list.

"What?" Maria asked, puzzled.

Nancy pointed her finger to the list of soldier's killed. She saw Paul Dreyfuss' name on the list. It hit Maria hard. She was shocked and wondered how Jeanette was feeling.

"Are you all right?" Nancy asked.

"I haven't kept in touch with Jeanette," Maria muttered. "We haven't written for seven years."

Maria was concerned about Jeanette. Nancy hugged and comforted Maria. At that moment, Nancy heard the phone ring. Maria watched Nancy go toward the hall. She knew the phone must have been ringing.

Nancy ran and grabbed the phone. "Hello?" she answered.

She heard something that sounded very quiet on the line and thought it was probably from TTY.

"Hurry up," Nancy said, "it's for you."

Maria went to the hall, put the phone into the TTY and turned a machine on. She started to type.

"Hello, who is this calling?" Maria asked.

"Hello, this is Jeanette. Is that you, Maria?" Jeanette asked.

Maria was shocked that Jeanette called her for the first time in seven years. She looked at Nancy.

"It's Jeanette on the phone now!" Maria said, surprised.

She typed back to Jeanette on the TTY. "I am glad that you are all right now," Maria said. "I heard what happened."

Jeanette knew that Maria found out about her husband's death. She typed back to Maria on the TTY.

"Yes, that is correct," Jeanette said. "It was hard for me to be accept the fact he has gone away. Right now I am planning to move back south again."

Maria was surprised that Jeanette wanted to move back to her hometown again. Maria thought Jeanette might need a place to live and offered her house to Jeanette until she found her own place.

"You can live with us until you find your own place to live, ok?" Maria asked.

Jeanette smiled and was grateful to live with Maria for a short time.

"That will make it so much easier for me to move home," Jeanette said. "I appreciate your help."

"Sure, it's no problem at all," Maria said. "I'll prepare a

room or two before you and your daughters arrive."

"We'll leave base next Saturday," Jeanette said. "I'll probably clean up the apartment before we lave. We can talk about it next Saturday, ok? Thanks again for your help. I love you. Goodbye."

"Sure, same to you too," Maria said. "I'm glad that you're all right now and can't wait to see you again. Talk to you later. Be careful when you drive here next Saturday. I love you, sisterhood. Goodbye for now."

Jeanette hung up the phone and turned the TTY off. She pulled the paper from the TTY and walked to the window. She read their conversation again.

When Maria hung up the phone, she was glad Jeanette was all right and planned on moving back to her hometown.

"Jeanette's moving back here next Saturday," Maria smiled.

"I'm glad she's all right," Nancy said, "but I am sorry to hear about the loss of her husband. I hope she can be brave now."

"Yes, I'm sure Jeanette will be brave," Maria said surely.

Maria stood up and hugged Nancy; she went back to the kitchen and grabbed the newspaper.

"Thank you for showing me the paper." Maria gave the newspaper back to Nancy.

"You're welcome," Nancy said. "You can keep it if you want."

Maria thought about it and said softly, "Ok, I'll keep it. Thank you."

Nancy smiled and hugged Maria, then went home. Maria watched through the window as Nancy walked home. Maria had to call the sisterhood and tell them about Jeanette moving back. She called Bonnie, Angel, Vicky, and DeeDee to informed about Jeanette's husband death and that Jeanette would be moving in with her. They went to Maria's house to plan a "Welcome Home" party for Jeanette and her daughters next Saturday.

A week later, Maria and the sisterhood were at Maria's house. They were making a simple poster that said, "Welcome back home Jeanette," and hung it on the back the house. They set up plates and food on the table in the kitchen. They sat and watched through the window for Jeanette to show up. She was supposed to be there any time after 1:00. After a while, they gave up and went to the living room to watch TV with the kids.

About fifteen minutes later, Angel was thirsty and got up to get a drink of water. While she was in the kitchen, she noticed a yellow and brown Ford station wagon, full of personal things, parking on the street. Angel wondered who the woman was with short blond hair. The woman came out of the car, and Angel finally recognized her to be Jeanette, who just arrived with her daughters. Angel put the cup on the table, ran to the living room, and told them Jeanette was there. They were so excited and ran through the hall to the kitchen. They opened the door and saw Jeanette smoking and standing next to her car with her four daughters. The sisterhood ran to Jeanette and hugged her. They were thrilled to see Jeanette after seven years. Maria arrived last. She knew that Jeanette was very depressed about her husband's death. She hugged Jeanette, who started to smoke again. She went ahead hugged Jeanette anyway. They hugged for a while then broke apart to look at each other.

"Well," Maria said, "I'm so glad to see you again. Welcome back home Jeanette."

Jeanette nodded and cried at what Maria said. Jeanette looked at Norma, who was holding Jeanette's pants. Norma was not used to being with other deaf women because she did not see any deaf people around the base. Maria looked at Norma hiding behind her mother.

"Who is she?" Maria asked Jeanette quickly. "Is she your daughter?"

"Yes, this is my last daughter, Norma," Jeanette said. "I got pregnant right before Paul left. She never even met him and doesn't fully understand her father was killed in Vietnam."

Maria understood and bent down to Norma, but Norma moved behind Jeanette's leg to hide. Maria knew that Norma must be shy.

"Hello, my name is Maria," Maria introduced herself. "I've known your mother since we were little girls like you."

Norma started to smile, then laughed and hugged Maria. Maria picked Norma up and held her. Jeanette was surprised that Norma felt so comfortable already.

"My name is Norma" Norma said, with sign language.

Maria smiled and tickled Norma's stomach, which made her laugh out loud out. Maria introduced Norma to her children and knew they would have fun playing together. The kids wanted to play with Norma, but she was hungry and needed something to eat. Maria brought Norma in the house; there was plenty of food. Bonnie and Angel came to Jeanette and brought her to the house. Jeanette was kind of tired from not sleeping much the past week.

The kids ate lunch then ran outside to play with the other kids. The men went outside to drink the beer and chat. Sometimes the men watched the kids while the women were in the house chat with Jeanette. The six women in the kitchen were together again for the first time in seven years. Jeanette told them the story about moving to base and how it difficult for Jeanette keep control when she was away from Paul and Maria for so long.

Jeanette went to the refrigerator, opened the door, and looked for a beer. She grabbed one and closed the door. Jeanette opened the beer and sat back down. Angel, DeeDee, and Bonnie stared at Jeanette while she drank the beer. They suspected she had become an alcoholic after Paul died. Jeanette put her beer on the table and looked at Maria. Jeanette noticed that Maria didn't like Jeanette drinking beer in front of her daughters and the sisterhood. Maria left the table to go to the bathroom. Jeanette looked at Maria and wondered what was wrong with her and the sisterhood women.

When Maria went to the bathroom, she closed the door and locked it. She looked in the mirror, thinking to herself that she was stuck with Jeanette, who was now an alcoholic. Maria decided to talk to Jeanette about the situation. She got out of the bathroom and went back to the kitchen. She looked for Jeanette who was no longer there. Bonnie came to Maria with a sad face.

"Do you know what happened to Jeanette?" Bonnie asked. "She became an alcoholic."

Maria nodded and knew that Bonnie could tell Jeanette had a drinking problem. Vicky came to Maria slowly.

"Jeanette fell asleep on the couch in the living room," Vicky pointed to the living room. "She was tired from driving all day. Or maybe she's tired from drinking so much beer this afternoon."

Maria moved her hands to hold Vicky and Bonnie's hands warmly. Maria told them she was going to ask Mary Anna if she knew what happened to her this past year. Maria decided to check on Jeanette first before going to Mary Anna. Maria came into the living room and looked at Jeanette asleep on the couch. Angel put a blanket over Jeanette to keep her warm and comfortable. Maria looked at DeeDee who was staring at Jeanette while she slept. Maria knew that DeeDee had never seen Jeanette's behave this way in her life.

"Poor Jeanette," Angel said with a sad face. "It's so hard for me to believe what Jeanette was doing in front of us."

"Yeah, I know," Maria said. " I plan on talking to Mary Anna right away."

Angel nodded. Maria went downstairs to look for Mary Anna. She found her in Helen's bedroom. Mary Anna and Helen were on the bed talking to each other. They were close in age. Maria stood near the door and asked to speak to Mary Anna for a moment. Maria knew Mary Anna would be uncomfortable telling her about her mother's condition. Mary Anna looked at Maria.

"Yes, Maria?" Mary Anna asked with a sour voice. "Do you expect me to explain my mother's strange behavior this afternoon?"

Maria was stuck with Mary Anna and her three sisters and felt responsible for the girls while her mother was suffering.

"Yes," Maria said, "I want to know when you mother started drinking so much."

"After my father's burial," Mary Anna explained.

Maria was glad to hear Mary Anna's information about Jeanette. She looked at Helen, who looked so sad, and wondered if Jeanette's drinking would cause a problem with her family.

"Mary Anna," Maria said, "don't worry about your mother's problem. I'll be glad to help her straighten up if I can, ok?"

"I hope you can help her. Thanks, Maria." Mary Anna smiled.

"No problem," Maria said. "If you ever have a problem, you can find a safe place here with Helen, ok?"

"That sounds good to me." Mary Anna nodded her head. "Thanks for the advice."

"Good," Maria said. "I'll talk with you and your sisters later, ok?"

Maria left and walked down the hall. She was nervous about whether she could control Jeanette if she got drunk. Maria stood near the stairs, but wouldn't go up. She was still thinking about the problem of Jeanette and trying to resolve the situation. She finally went up the stairs to the living room. The sisterhood looked at Maria who stood quietly at the moment. She explained to them what Mary Anna had told her, that Jeanette became an alcoholic after Paul's death.

The sunset went down. The women cleaned up the kitchen and wrapped the leftovers to bring home with them. Maria checked on Jeanette's girls. They were in bed and asleep. Maria went back upstairs, walked through the hall to her bedroom. She looked at the living from her bedroom. She decided to check on Jeanette before going to bed. Maria walked to the living room and looked at Jeanette on the couch; she was still sleep. Maria sighed and sat next to Jeanette. She touched her hair, which felt dry from being dyed blond so much. Maria dropped Jeanette's hair on her face by accident. Jeanette shook her head like someone was bothering her, and turned her head to the other side. Maria decided to leave Jeanette alone and turned off the light. She hoped Jeanette would be all right for one night.

She walked toward her bedroom and slowly closed the door. Maria was tired. She noticed her husband Ray was in bed and still awake. She felt like she should tell him about Jeanette. Maria came to the other side of the bed where Ray lay and put her hand on his leg.

"Ray," Maria said as she tried to comfort Ray, "are you all right today?"

Ray shrugged his shoulder and said nothing. He just watched the news on the TV. Maria nodded and left Ray alone. She decided to put on her pajamas and get ready for bed. She lay down next to Ray. Maria told Ray goodnight and kissed his cheek before falling asleep.

An hour later, Jeanette awoke on the sofa. She couldn't see anything because the room was dark. She could see through a window at a light in the street. She stood up and walked slowly, trying to not make any noise. She went in the kitchen and looked for her pack of cigarettes and lighter. She unlocked the door and walked outside. Jeanette smelled the fresh night air. She preferred living in the country, because there was less traffic and people around than in the city. She would not go back to Northern Virginia again. Jeanette lit a cigarette, sat on the porch and looked at the sky with a quarter moon. Jeanette was glad she decided to move back to her hometown again.

When Maria woke up in the morning, she started walking to the bathroom when she noticed Jeanette in the kitchen making coffee. After Maria went to the bathroom, she saw Jeanette looking in the cabinets for a coffee mug. She came in the kitchen. Jeanette looked at Maria quickly.

"The cup is there," Maria pointed, "near the refrigerator."

Jeanette opened the cabinet and saw plenty of cups inside. She took a white cup.

"Thanks, Maria," Jeanette yawned.

"You're welcome," Maria said.

Jeanette poured the coffee into the cup and drank it. She went to the table with her coffee and sat on a chair looking at Maria.

"Can we visit my old yellow house now?" Jeanette begged.

Maria nodded her head sat down with her arms on the table. "Yeah, we can see your yellow house today," Maria agreed.

"Right after we drank coffee," Jeanette asked, "can we go there?"

"Ok," Maria nodded her head. "I'll get dressed and we'll have breakfast before we leave."

Maria pushed the chair back from the table, stood up and left the kitchen. Jeanette watched Maria walk to her bedroom, and then she lit a cigarette. Maria changed her clothes, brushed her teeth and fixed her hair. She joined Jeanette in the kitchen.

"I'm ready to go now," Maria said. "We'll drive to the yellow house now, ok?"

"Yes, good." Jeanette blinked.

Jeanette took a can of beer and put it in her purse. Maria took her wallet. They got in Maria's car. Jeanette forgot how to get her former home from Maria's and hope Maria knew the way. Maria drove through downtown, and Jeanette noticed some of the stores had changed. Maria kept driving. Jeanette remembered the place; there was still plenty of woods. She saw a barn on the left side and knew they would be arriving at the yellow house any minute.

"We'll be there soon," Jeanette said anxiously. "Slow down. There's the mail box on the fence."

Maria slowed down and stopped her car before turning down the driveway. Jeanette lit a cigarette and got out of the car. Maria watched Jeanette going toward the driveway. She stopped walking near the driveway and looked at the house, which was about a quarter of a mile away from the road. She looked at the trees on each the side, which were now nearly nine feet tall. She remembered when Paul and the girls planted the year-old trees on each side of the driveway. Jeanette saw some young boys at the house; they were playing on the porch. One of the boys saw Jeanette standing on the driveway and went to find his parents. They came with the boy.

"What's the matter?" asked the Mother.

"I saw a woman there," he pointed.

"David, would you please help the woman," Betty said.

Jeanette saw David on his way to see her. She threw down the cigarette on the dirt road and walked fast. Maria thought something was wrong with Jeanette's behavior. She thought she should take Jeanette away from the house because she didn't want Jeanette to get in trouble for being on their property. Maria got out the car and ran to catch Jeanette in the middle of the driveway. David stopped and watched the two women. Maria held Jeanette's stomach and wouldn't let her go over to that man. Jeanette tried to escape.

"Let me go now!" Jeanette yelled.

Maria refused to let her go there. She brought Jeanette to the end of the driveway. Jeanette got mad and wrenched away from Maria.

"Please calm down," Maria said. "They might call the police for being on their property."

Maria looked at the man. Betty came to David and held his hand.

"What are they doing here?" Betty asked.

"I have no idea," David said.

Jeanette got mad at Maria and went to the car. Maria looked at Jeanette then toward the man standing in front of the house. She waved and left him alone.

Go to the Hill

"I think she must be nice," Betty stated. "She was trying to help her friend."

"Yeah, that's good." David nodded.

They went in the house with the boys. Maria climbed into her car and looked at Jeanette.

"What do you want?" Jeanette asked.

"Please don't do that again, ok?" Maria asked seriously.

Jeanette turned her head to the door and tried to ignore Maria.

Maria was mad at Jeanette and started to drive back home.

Chapter 15

Jeanette worked in the office at the hospital again. She was not happy with her job because her new boss hadn't given her a raise, even though she'd been there for one year now. Jeanette wished that her former boss were still there. He retired three years ago. Jeanette had been fighting her new boss for a few weeks now. She kept asking for a raise, but without any success. She felt it wasn't working out and decided to leave the office. She grabbed a cigarette and went to the hall to smoke. Jeanette needed to cool off for now. At 4:30 p.m., she turned the typewriter off and put the papers into a file. She took her coat from the closet when she saw her boss making his way over to see her. Jeanette didn't want to talk to him and left the office. She rushed downstairs and left the hospital. Jeanette would not turn back to look at her boss. She knew he would follow her to her car. She got in her car and closed the door. She looked for her boss somewhere in the parking lots and felt good that he didn't follow her. She was so mad, she felt like she could kill her boss, but she wouldn't do that because she didn't want to go to jail.

She drove home. Jeanette and her daughters still lived with Maria this past year. She parked her car, got out and started to smoke again. When she came in the kitchen, she grabbed some beers and went downstairs to her bedroom. She closed the door and changed into a uniform, which she wore for her second job at a restaurant. She worked as a cook and cleaned up the kitchen as a part-time job in the evening. Jeanette wanted to nap for fifteen minutes. However, she fell into a heavy sleep, and when she awoke, she realized she slept for over thirty minutes. She got out of bed, ran to the kitchen and grabbed some more beers to take to work. She put the beers in her large purse on the way to her car. As she was running to her car, she saw the school bus stop on the corner. The students came out and walked to their homes. Nikki and Barbara came to their mother.

"Mom," Barbara asked, "are you coming back tonight? I need your help for my homework, ok?"

Jeanette nodded and felt like she didn't want to help her with her homework. Barbara knew that Jeanette had problem with alcohol, but it wouldn't do anything to argue with Jeanette.

"Maria can help you with your homework," Jeanette said.

She jumped in the car and rolled down the window. "Don't wait up for me. I'll be home late. I love both of you."

She started to drive away and waved to Nikki and Barbara. They waved back until their mother's car was gone. Barbara was disappointed with her mother.

"I know it's not easy for her," Nikki tried.

"What are you talking about?" Barbara asked moodily.

She walked toward the house. Nikki was not happy with her mother, because she was stilling drank beers for a year now. She kicked rock on the ground and went in the house. Barbara went to the kitchen, took off her coat and hung it up on the coat rack. Nikki came in and closed the door.

"Barbara," Nikki called, "I know how you feel about mom."

Barbara ignored Nikki's voice and kept walking downstairs.

"Barbara, Barbara!" Nikki yelled.

Barbara did not stop and kept walking to her bedroom.

Nikki knew that Barbara suffered and had been mad at their mother for a long time. She thought it might be best to leave Barbara alone, but decided to go see her. She dropped her coat and bag and went to the hall. Maria's ran into Nikki and accidentally hit her shoulder.

"Oh, I'm sorry. I didn't see you!" Maria gasped.

"That's all right. I'm going downstairs," Nikki said.

Maria wondered why Nikki was going downstairs. She stopped thinking about it and went to the kitchen. She saw Nikki's bag and coat on the chair. Maria was pissed off at that; she didn't like the kids putting their things on the chair. She put Nikki's bag on the floor and hung her coat on the rack.

Nikki went down the hall and heard Barbara crying. She opened the bedroom door slowly and went in. It was dark, and she couldn't see anything. She turned the light on and looked at the bed, but Barbara wasn't there. Nikki sighed and tried to hear where Barbara was hiding. Nikki listened carefully and found Barbara in the closet. Nikki opened the door and pushed the clothes out of the way. She saw Barbara sitting in the corner with her head bent down in her arms, like she was trying to hold herself.

"Barbara," Nikki sighed, "please listen me."

Barbara did not want to talk to her. Nikki bent her legs and tried to help Barbara, but she pushed Nikki on the floor.

"You better leave me alone!" Barbara yelled. She ran to the hall. Nikki knew that Barbara was frustrated with their mother. She stood up and walked to the hall, looking in each room for Barbara.

"Barbara, please don't be so serious," Nikki said.

She had given up on helping Barbara and went to her bedroom. Nikki sat on her bed and was quiet.

At five o' clock in the afternoon, Maria planned to go shopping for dinner and clean up in the kitchen. She took her bookkeeping back to her bedroom. She did not want it to get messed up and figured she'd finish the job later that night. She took her coat and purse and went outside, but realized she forgot the shopping list. She went back to the kitchen and found the list. Barbara heard Maria's feet in the kitchen from the basement. She wanted to see Maria, so she walked upstairs to the kitchen. Barbara stood and started at Maria reading the note. Maria noticed Barbara's shoes and looked at Barbara's face. She was not happy. Maria knew something was wrong with Jeanette, because she did not take care of Barbara. Most of the time, Maria took care of all of them since they moved in. Maria came close to Barbara.

"Are you all right?" Maria asked. "I know it's not always easy to talk about things."

Barbara did not answer Maria, but ran and hugged her. Maria could feel Barbara to start cry. Maria thought she'd see if Barbara wanted to go shopping with her. It might make her feel better than staying at home.

"Do you want to go shopping with today?" Maria asked.

"Yes, I'd like to go with you now," Barbara said.

Barbara took her coat and ran outside to Maria's car. They arrived at the store and bought some food. Then they went back home again. Maria and Barbara unpacked the food and started to cook a T-bone steak and mashed potatoes before Ray got home around six. However, he was 30 minutes late. Maria told Barbara to call Norma and Jeffery to come home for diner. Barbara went outside and looked for Norma and Jeffery. They were playing with their friends cross the street.

"Norma and Jeffery," Barbara called, "time for dinner now!"

Norma and Jeffery heard Barbara's voice and left their friends. They ran to the house and came in the kitchen. They dropped their coats on the floor and sit down, waiting for Maria to finish cooking. Barbara came in the kitchen and saw Norma and Jeffery sitting there.

"Hey Norma and Jeffery," Barbara said, "pick up your coats and put them on the rack. Then go wash your hands before dinner."

Norma and Jeffery did as Barbara told. Then they came back to their chairs and waited for dinner. Maria laughed at Barbara because she acted like a mother with the kids. After dinner, Jobelle and Nikki washed the plates and pots in the sink. After they dried and put the dishes away, Maria cleaned the whole kitchen. She put the broom in the closet and looked out the window. She wondered what Jeanette was doing after work. Maria knew that Jeanette always went to the bar before she came home. Jeanette was supposed to come home early and take care of her girls. Maria had given up arguing with Jeanette. She turned off the light in the kitchen and walked to her bedroom.

An hour later, Jeanette came home from the bar. She dropped her a long yellow coat with blue fur and her purse on the chair. She took a pack of cigarettes and her lighter out. She didn't want to wake Ray and the kids since it was after midnight. She went to the living room and turned on the TV. She forgot to turn the volume off. Jeanette took the ashtray from a side table and put it on the coffee table. She picked a cigarette out of the box and lit it. She watched TV until her eyes became tired. She started to fall asleep on the sofa.

Norma had a hard time sleeping; she could hear the TV blaring in the living room. She needed a drink of water, so she got out of bed and went upstairs. She saw a light in the hall and knew her mother was in the living room alone. She walked to the living room slowly, looked at the TV and turned the volume off. She looked at her mother asleep on the sofa, holding a cigarette with her fingers together. Norma came over to Jeanette and got the cigarette out of Jeanette's fingers. Norma snuffed the cigarette into the ashtray. She saw the silver lighter on the pack of cigarettes. She was curious to see the silver lighter that looked so shiny. Norma took the lighter and looked at it, then she took a cigarette out of Jeanette's pack. She walked through the hall to the kitchen door and went outside. She looked for a place to hide because she didn't want anyone to see her. She was only seven years old. She found a large old tree near the detached garage that she thought would make a good hiding place. She ran behind the tree and started to smoke like it was a game. Norma did not know how to smoke a cigarette.

Chapter 16

Microwaves were becoming popular all over the country in 1981. Maria was in the living room reading the newspaper when she saw a commercial about microwaves on TV. You could cook food without using a stove. She thought it would be easier for her to not use the stove. It would also save her some time when she came home late from work. Since microwaves were so expensive, she decided to save her money to buy one.

The next year, Maria had enough money to buy her children's Christmas presents and new microwave. A week before Christmas, Maria bought a brand new microwave from a Sears in Charlottesville. When she arrived home, she took the box out of the trunk and carried it into the house. Maria couldn't turn the knob while holding the box, so it was a good thing Jobelle was in the kitchen reading a book. She saw Maria standing outside and opened the door to let her in. Jobelle wondered what Maria bought. She put the box on the table, took her coat off, and hung it up on the coat rack. Maria was excited about her microwave. She opened the box, took the microwave out, and put it on the counter. Jobelle was curious. She walked over and looked at the microwave.

"What is that?" Jobelle asked. "It looks strange to me."

"That's a microwave," Maria explained. "This is used to cook food without a stove. I'll show you how to use it, ok?"

Jobelle wanted to learn how to use the microwave.

Jeanette continued to look for her silver lighter in her bedroom and other rooms for a long time, ever since it was missing. She had never lost her husband's silver lighter, which he got when he was in Vietnam. She decided to take a break and went outside to sit on the porch. She started to smoke a cigarette. Jeanette looked at a tree toward the detached garage. She noticed smoke coming from somewhere near it. She watched the smoke carefully and saw it was coming from behind the tree. She suspected someone was smoking cigarette or pot. She checked to see who was hiding behind the tree and slowly walked around it. She found Norma there. Norma was only 14 years old and seemed used to smoke cigarettes. Jeanette was mad at Norma, because she was too young to smoke.

"Norma, please put the cigarette out now," Jeanette said. Norma smashed the cigarette on the ground. She walked away from Jeanette.

"Hey, Norma," Jeanette yelled, "please give me the pack of cigarettes and matches right away."

Norma stopped and took out the pack of cigarettes and lighter from her coat pocket. She handed them to Jeanette's. Norma went to the house while Jeanette just watched her. Jeanette opened her hand and saw a pack of cigarettes and the silver lighter. She was shocked to see the silver lighter on her hand. She had looked for that lighter for a long time. Jeanette got so mad and yelled at Norma, "Norma!"

Norma heard Jeanette's angry voice. She was afraid and ran into the house before Jeanette could hurt her. In the kitchen, Maria set the timer on the microwave with Jobelle and Jeffery watching. Norma came in the kitchen and slammed the door hard. It scared Maria to death. Norma ran downstairs to her bedroom and hid under the bed. She did not want Jeanette to find her. Jeanette came into the kitchen and slammed the door as hard as Norma did.

"Please don't slam the door!" Maria yelled.

Jeanette nodded and walked downstairs. Maria felt that Jeanette might hurt Norma. Jeanette came in Norma's bedroom. She looked around and found Norma hiding under the bed.

"Norma, get out from under the bed now!" Jeanette yelled. "Don't you dare take my husband's silver lighter! You bitch!"

She pulled the covers off the bed and pulled the mattress out. Norma was shocked. Jeanette dragged Norma out from under the bed and threw her against the wall.

"Why are you still thinking about your fucking silver lighter?!" Norma yelled.

Jeanette came close to Norma's face and showed her the silver lighter.

"So what?" Norma asked harshly.

Jeanette pushed Norma against the wall then threw her on the floor. Jeanette was jumped on top of Norma, with her legs around Norma's stomach, and beat Norma's face with her fist. Norma put her arms in front of her face for protection.

Jobelle and Jeffery heard noises from downstairs. "I hear something downstairs." Jobelle said.

"What?" Maria asked, surprised.

"Sounds like they're in a fight." Jobelle said.

Maria thought she better call Ray to help with Jeanette. Maria ran to the hall.

"Ray, I need your help now!" Maria yelled.

Ray heard Maria's voice and dropped the newspaper on the living room floor. He ran to Maria before she started going downstairs.

"I heard a door slam twice," Ray said. "Who did that?"

"Jeanette and Norma did that," Maria said anxiously. "I hope Jeanette won't hurt Norma."

"Oh shit! Where are they?" Ray yelled.

"Downstairs!" Maria hurried.

Ray ran downstairs. Maria followed him, but she forgot to tell Jobelle and Jeffery.

"Please don't touch the new microwave," Maria said. "Stay here while I go help Jeanette and Norma."

"Ok, we'll stay here." Jobelle promised.

Maria ran downstairs to Norma's bedroom. When they came in, they were shocked to find Jeanette and Norma fighting. Maria told Ray pull them apart. Ray tried to take Jeanette, while Maria held Norma and tried to calm her down. Ray held Jeanette for a second before she pushed Ray's arms away and left the bedroom. Jeanette kicked the wall with her foot. Maria went to the hall and checked to see if Jeanette was all right, then went back to the bedroom. She was overwhelmed at seeing the room in such a mess.

Jeanette had taken the whole mattress off the bed frame. Norma sat on a chair and her head went down. Maria looked at Norma's face and saw a bruise starting to form on her left cheek, near her eye.

"Does your cheek hurt?" Maria asked.

"Yes," Norma said.

"Better go to the kitchen," Maria suggested. "We'll get a bag of ice and hold it on your cheek for a few minutes."

Norma nodded and walked through the hall where Jeanette was standing in the corner with Ray. Jobelle and Jeffery close to the stairs and heard that the basement was now silent. They heard someone coming up, so they headed back to the kitchen. Jeffery sat on a chair and read the newspaper, and Jobelle looked at the microwave before anybody would show up in the kitchen. It was Norma; she stopped and looked at Jobelle then looked at Jeffery. Norma came over and showed Jobelle her bruised cheek.

"Norma," Jobelle asked, "are you all right? Can I help you get a bag of ice for your cheek? It'll get better, ok?"

Norma nodded but said nothing. Jobelle wanted Norma to sit. She told Jeffery to get off his chair and let Norma sit there.

"Jeffery," Jobelle said, "please go to the bathroom and find a bag for ice."

"Ok, I'll get it for you," Jeffery nodded.

He ran to the bathroom and looked in a small closet full of sheets and towels. He could not find any bag until he looked under the towels. Jeffery took it, ran back to the kitchen and gave it to Jobelle. She took ice from the freezer and put them in the bag until it was full, then she gave it to Norma. Norma put the bag on her cheek. It helped the bruise go down in a few minutes. Maria and Ray stared at Jeanette in the corner. Jeanette went upstairs by herself. Maria and Ray followed her. Jeffery and Jobelle heard Jeanette's feet and knew she was on the way up.

"I think you better move to another room," Jeffery said, "right away. I don't want your mom to hurt you again."

Jeffery and Jobelle quickly took Norma to the living room before Jeanette could hurt her. Maria followed Jeanette to the kitchen. Maria was worried that the kids were still there and didn't want Jeanette to hurt Norma again. Jeanette came in the kitchen.

Go to the Hill

Maria rushed in to look for the kids, but they weren't there. She felt relieved. Jeanette took her coat off the coat rack and grabbed some beers. Maria followed Jeanette to her station wagon. Maria wanted to go with Jeanette to the hill. She grabbed her coat and ran to Jeanette's car. Maria got in and felt nervous with Jeanette driving. Jeanette started the engine and pushed the gas hard. This made the rear tires spin up some rocks that hit another car and the garage. Maria wanted to tell Jeanette to be careful, but was too afraid. Jeanette was too out of control of her emotions.

Jeanette drove through the woods to the hill, which was covered with snow. Nobody was there. This was Jeanette and Maria's first time there since winter began. Jeanette drove carefully on the snow and parked her car near the hill. She couldn't drive up the hill with her station wagon because it was too big and heavy. She stopped there and got out. Jeanette opened another door, got her beer, and walked up the snowy hill. Maria opened the door watched Jeanette. Jeanette made it to the top. She opened a beer and threw the cap away. She drank the whole beer in one gulp. She looked inside the empty bottle, threw it away and got another beer. Maria was glad Jeanette made it up the hill safely and started to follow Jeanette's footprints. Maria was relieved that she didn't slip down the hill. She looked at the mountain full of snow and thought it looked so beautiful. She wanted to talk about the mountain and hoped Jeanette would forget about the silver lighter and her fight with Norma.

"Jeanette," Maria pointed. "Isn't the view so nice? The mountain looks so beautiful full of snow."

Jeanette didn't say anything about the view. Maria felt hurt. She no longer liked Jeanette's personality and thought she was not a nice person anymore. Maria wished that Jeanette should change back to her old self. But Jeanette couldn't change back. Jeanette drank another beer and stopped to show it to Maria. Jeanette took out a cigarette and the silver lighter and started to smoke. She looked at the silver lighter. It made her feel better to hold it and was glad she no longer needed to look for it. She kissed the silver lighter and put it in her pocket.

Jeanette looked at her beer. "This is important to me," Jeanette

119

smiled. "Thank God!"

Jeanette drank the beer again. Maria was shocked at what Jeanette said. She got mad and slapped the beer from Jeanette's hand and pushed Jeanette's shoulder. Jeanette was confused and started to push Maria back.

"What's the matter with you?" Jeanette shouted.

Maria hit Jeanette's lip, knocking Jeanette to the ground. Jeanette was shocked that Maria hit her; it was the first time in her life. Maria hurt her hand hitting Jeanette's lip so hard. Jeanette crawled through the snow and tried to escape. Maria still followed Jeanette and pulled her ankle. Jeanette started to scream and kicked Maria's breast to get free. She kept crawling as fast as she could and stood up quickly. Maria followed Jeanette again. Jeanette got angry and pushed Maria away from her. Maria stopped and stared at Jeanette. Jeanette grunted heavily and couldn't believe Maria was fighting her.

"What's your fucking problem?" Jeanette breathed. "How dare you hit my face for no reason!"

Maria became so angry hearing Jeanette's words.

"What are you talking about it?" Maria cried. "Do you think beer or a lighter are more important than your own daughter?"

Jeanette didn't care about Maria's concern for Norma, and that made Maria lose her temper. She hit Jeanette's lip again. Jeanette was knocked out and fell down to the ground. She almost blacked out. She tasted blood and touched her lip; there was blood on her fingers. She started to crawl again, but Maria caught Jeanette and pulled her legs so she couldn't escape. Jeanette grabbed some snow tried to throw it against Maria's face, but she didn't make it. Maria caught Jeanette's hands and put them between her knees so Jeanette couldn't move at all. Maria hit at Jeanette's eye. Her knees weakened and lost their hold on Jeanette's hands. Jeanette slapped Maria's glasses off so she couldn't see at all.

Jeanette threw snow at Maria's face, pushed Maria off her stomach, and started to run down the hill toward her car. Jeanette got to her car and looked for her keys. She couldn't find them. She finally found her keys in her coat pocket. Maria started to stand up and look for Jeanette. She looked down the hill and saw Jeanette standing next to the car. Maria started to walk down.

Jeanette was very nervous. She watched Maria as she unlocked and opened the door to get in. She locked the car and would not let Maria get in. Jeanette tried to put the key into the ignition, but her hands were shaking so badly that she dropped the key on the floor. She looked for the key. Maria walked toward the car and started to bang on the hood. Jeanette was scared to death and kept looking for the key. Maria tried to open a door, but it was already locked. Maria lost her temper even more and started kicking the door. Jeanette was screaming for her help. Maria gave up struggling to open the door and tried to damage the windshield. Maria beat on the windshield until it cracked, but it didn't break. Jeanette covered her arms, turned her body over the seat, and started to cry. Maria gave up trying to break in the car and walked away. She bent down on the ground and tried to cool off. Jeanette was still screaming for help. The crows started to fly away from the trees, because they could hear Jeanette's screams.

An hour later, Maria's body became colder and it made her wake up. She got up and looked in the car. Jeanette was still inside. Maria wanted to stop fighting. She stood up slowly, but her back was wet and cold lying in the snow for an hour. It was hard for Maria to see without her glasses. She stood up, walked to the car and looked at Jeanette asleep on the front seat. Maria hit the window to try and wake Jeanette. She shook the car like an earthquake. Jeanette woke up, saw Maria and started to scream.

"You better leave me alone," Jeanette screamed. "Don't ever touch me again, period!"

Maria was shocked at seeing Jeanette's face. It was swollen with blood all over it. Maria did not say anything. Maria pointed to the rear seat, indicating she wanted to sit there and would leave Jeanette alone. Jeanette nodded and unlocked the rear door. Jeanette watched the rearview mirror as Maria sat in the back seat. She did not want Maria to touch her again. Maria closed the door and looked in the mirror at Jeanette's eyes. Jeanette moved her eyes to the steering wheel and started to leave the hill. She drove through the woods full of snow. Jeanette drove to Maria's house.

Chapter 17

Jeanette arrived at Maria's house. Maria got out of the car and was about to close the door, but Jeanette braked too early and made the door closed by itself. Maria moved back so a tire wouldn't roll over her feet. She tried to calm Jeanette down, but Jeanette kept driving and looked at Maria in the rearview mirror.

Jeanette rushed to hospital where she worked. She parked her car near the emergency room and walked through the doors to the front desk. In the sitting room, people stared at Jeanette's face. They thought her husband beat her. The nurse at the front desk saw Jeanette's face. It was sallow looking and there were bruises around her eye and mouth. The nurse called a doctor and told Jeanette to go to the emergency room right away. Jeanette went into emergency room; another nurse pointed to a chair for Jeanette to sit in and wait. The nurse came to Dr. Porter and told him that Jeanette had bad bruises on her eye and lip. He followed the nurse to Jeanette. Dr. Porter checked Jeanette's face and told her that she might need a shot to prevent infection. Dr. Porter went to a lab room, got the shot, then came back to Jeanette. He told Jeanette to take her coat off and pull her shirt down so he could administer the shot on Jeanette's shoulder. After he gave her the shot, she buttoned up her shirt. In a moment, she became dizzy and almost fell on the floor. Dr. Porter and the nurse held Jeanette, put her on a bed and let her rest for a few minutes. He could smell alcohol radiating from Jeanette's body. He knew that she had a drinking problem. The nurse stared at Jeanette's face, and it looked scary to her.

"Should I call the police?" the nurse asked. "It looks like her husband nearly beat her to death."

"No, I don't think so," Dr. Porter said.

"Why not?" the nurse wondered.

Dr. Porter put Jeanette's arm close to her body while she slept. He pointed his finger to his nose to smell the alcohol coming from Jeanette's body. The nurse moved her head close to Jeanette's face and could smell the alcohol too.

"Oh, she reeks of alcohol," the nurse said, shocked. "What are we going to do with Jeanette after she wakes up?"

"Don't worry about it. I'll take care of it myself." Dr. Porter said.

They left Jeanette alone. The nurse took care of her and waited for her to wake up. Dr. Porter went to his office. He was thinking that Jeanette needed help. He sat at his desk, took out a pad, and wrote a note to Jeanette telling her he had something to discuss with her. Dr. Porter went to the emergency room to find the nurse; he gave her the note to give to Jeanette. He went back to his office.

Jeanette woke up and looked at the nurse who was sitting on a stool doing paperwork. The nurse noticed Jeanette's body start to move. She looked at Jeanette.

"Are you all right now?" the nurse asked.

"Yes, I'm fine," Jeanette nodded.

The nurse gave Jeanette the letter from Dr. Porter. She was puzzled that he would write her a note. She opened the letter and read that Dr. Porter made an appointment for her to see him the next day. Jeanette nodded and put the letter in her purse. Then she left the emergency room. She started to walk towards her car, but changed her mind and went to the bathroom to look at herself in the mirror. She looked at her left eyebrow and saw she had nine stitches and a black eye. Her lip was badly swollen, too. She didn't realize that she looked so awful. She put on her sunglasses to hide her eyes from people. She left and drove home.

Before she arrived at Maria's house, she slowed down because she didn't want to see Maria's face. Jeanette stopped worrying, parked her car and walked into the house. She went in the kitchen and looked for Maria, but she wasn't there. She looked around carefully then went downstairs to her bedroom and closed the door. She looked around the bedroom and noticed the chair in the corner; she thought she'd use it to block the door. She put it under the knob so Maria couldn't come in. Jeanette lay on her bed and looked at the door. She was scared to death.

In the morning, Jeanette got out of bed and went to the bathroom for a quick shower. She did not eat breakfast. Instead, she stopped by the store and bought some doughnuts and a cup of black coffee, then she went back to her car. She drove to the hospital to see Dr. Porter. She came in the lobby and went upstairs to Dr. Porter's office. A nurse was working at her desk; she looked up and saw Jeanette standing there.

"May I help you?" the nurse asked.

"Yes," Jeanette pointed at Dr. Porter's door.

"You can wait in his office," the nurse nodded. "Dr. Porter will be back in a few minutes."

Jeanette nodded, walked into the office and looked for a chair to sit in. Dr. Porter returned to his office. Jeanette looked at him while he dropped a long white folder on his desk. He sat in his leather chair. He got some papers and a pen to communicate with Jeanette.

"How are you doing today?" Dr. Porter asked.

"I'm fine," Jeanette nodded.

"Good to hear that," Dr. Porter smiled.

He opened the folder, picked a brochure and showed it to Jeanette. She looked at the brochure but did not understand. She just looked at him.

"What is that?" Jeanette asked, pointing to the brochure.

"I suggest you go to the Betty Ford Center," Dr. Porter said. "It's in Rancho Mirage, California. You might think about moving there and starting a new life for yourself."

Jeanette still did not understand what his point was.

"What are you talking about it?" Jeanette questioned.

Dr. Porter was silent and thought about how he should answer Jeanette's question.

"Jeanette," he stated, "you have a problem with alcohol. Read this brochure. The Betty Ford Center has many programs and information about alcohol and drug abuse. I want you to think about going, if you can do it for yourself."

Dr. Porter gave the brochure to Jeanette. She looked at it and opened the folder to read information about the programs and how they offered treatment services for alcoholism and drug addiction. It hit Jeanette hard that Dr. Porter thought she was an alcoholic. She didn't want to discuss it anymore and left Dr. Porter's office.

Jeanette walked quickly down the hall. She was trying to understand why she started drinking when her husband was killed in the Vietnam War so long ago. She kicked the wall and ran downstairs through the lobby area to the parking lot. Jeanette kept running and stopped to catch her breath. She went to the parking lot, but forgot where she parked her car. Jeanette was out of control. She kept looking around for her car, but couldn't find it. She started to scream, "WHY ME!" Weeping, she fell down to the black top and held her hands on her head.

Chapter 18

Christmas had passed a week ago. Jeanette's bedroom was dark and messy with clothes strewn all over the room. She sat and smoked cigarettes in the corner alone. She had missed work for two weeks. Jeanette was afraid to see Maria around the house. She never used the kitchen, because Maria was there all the time and her bedroom was close to the kitchen.

A few days later, Jeanette made the decision to move to California and check into the Betty Ford Center. She wanted a new life in California with her three girls. Her oldest daughter, Mary Anna, wanted to live with her boyfriend from in Northern Virginia.

Jeanette went to see Dr. Porter's. He wondered what Jeanette was doing there and told her to come into his office. Jeanette sat down, and Dr. Porter next to Jeanette.

"Do you want to say something?" he asked.

Jeanette took the brochure out of her purse and showed it to him.

"I want to go to California," Jeanette said.

"What?" Dr. Porter was surprised.

"I want to go there no matter what," Jeanette said.

"I'm glad you want to go there," he nodded. "I'll be more than happy to help you out. I'll call the Center and set it up for you."

Jeanette called her relatives in Boston, and they informed her that a cousin lived in Venice, California. She was willing let Jeanette and the girls come to her place. Jeanette was happy and started to pack her things in boxes. The girls helped to put everything in the station wagon.

Angel, DeeDee, Bonnie and Vicky came over to Maria's house and were talking to Jeanette outside while she packed and checked that everything was packed in her car and rental storage. Nikki sat in the front seat; Barbara and Norma sat in back with the boxes and some books for Norma to read while traveling. Norma still did not want to talk to her mother since their fight. Jeanette kept looking at the back door; she did not want Maria to come out of the house and see her. Maria was alone in her bedroom and did not want to see or talk to Jeanette before she left. They were not the best of friends any more. Jeanette's hands were shaking, and she was still afraid Maria would yell at her. She wanted to leave right away, but the sisterhood wanted to hug her goodbye before she left. Jeanette hugged and talked to each woman, then rushed in her car and drove away. They waved at Jeanette until the station wagon went down the hill. They stopped waving and turned around to go back in Maria's house.

"I don't believe it," Angel signed. "What's happened between Maria and Jeanette?"

Bonnie and Vicky also found it hard to believe that Jeanette and Maria were now enemies.

"Why did Jeanette move out of state?" DeeDee wondered. "What she will do in California?"

Angel rolled her eyes up; she knew DeeDee must not have been paying attention when Jeanette told them she was going to the Betty Ford Center to stop drinking.

"Jeanette told us," Angel explained. "She wants to go to the Betty Ford Center to help her be strong and keep away from alcohol. I hope Jeanette will be successful."

Angel looked at DeeDee, who walked away and started to cry. Angel followed DeeDee into the kitchen. DeeDee sat down and bent her head on her arms, which were on the table. Angel tried to help her, but DeeDee would not listen. Bonnie came in the kitchen, walked past DeeDee and sat next to her. Vicky was the last person to come in. She walked to the table and sat next to DeeDee. Angel looked at them and gave up. She then went to sit next to Bonnie. Vicky tried to call Angel and waved at her.

"What?" Angel asked softly.

"I think it would be better for you," Vicky pointed at Angel toward Maria's door through the hall, "if we discussed this with Maria."

Angel nodded and walked to Maria's bedroom. She opened the door and saw Maria in the mirror. She sat on her bed looking out the window. Angel tried to wave to Maria, but she didn't notice Angel's hand.

Angel decided to flick the lamp to get Maria's attention. Maria looked at the mirror where Angel stood by the door.

"What?" Maria asked moodily.

"I need you to come with us right away," Angel said seriously. "It's important that we talk. Please, Maria."

Maria nodded and looked out the window again. Angel closed the door, came back to the kitchen and sat down. DeeDee turned her head up and looked around the table. Bonnie and Vicky were staring at her with wide eyes.

"I told Maria to come here," Angel said.

After a few minutes, Maria did not come. Bonnie and Vicky asked Angel to get Maria again. They did not like to play games. Angel went back to Maria's bedroom, opened the door and went over to Maria while she watched the birds outside. Maria looked at Angel quickly.

"Please come with us right now," Angel said with anger. "It's very important that we talk to you about what happened to Jeanette's face."

Angel left the bedroom to sit down again in the kitchen. Finally, Maria was moving. She walked toward the kitchen from her bedroom. She sat on the chair and put her arms on the table. Maria looked at the sisterhood around the table. She knew they were shocked that she beat Jeanette up.

"Why did you beat up Jeanette?" Bonnie asked.

Maria did not say anything at all. Vicky looked at Angel because Angel had a hard time understanding what happened between Jeanette and Maria on the hill a few weeks ago. Angel looked at Maria with tears in her eyes.

"Do you want to know," Maria muttered, "why I hit Jeanette?"

Angel looked at Bonnie, Vicky and DeeDee. Angel sighed

and looked back to Maria again.

"Yes," Angel nodded, "we'd like to know what happened between Jeanette and you. So could you explain it to us, and please be honest with, ok?"

Maria nodded with a little smile.

"I'll ask you one question," Maria asked. "What is more important, a silver lighter or Norma?"

They looked puzzled and didn't understand what was Maria's point.

"Please tell us," Angel inquired, "what caused the problems between Jeanette and you?"

Maria sighed and tried to get to the point. "I got mad at Jeanette," Maria explained, "because she told me that the silver lighter was more important to her than Norma. I felt sorry for Norma and sickened with Jeanette. I lost my temper and hit her. Do you understand why now?"

The women were shocked and silent now. Maria looked at them carefully. The sisterhood looked at each other without saying anything. They were disappointed with Jeanette.

Jeanette drove on Route 29 south through Charlottesville to I-64 west. She drove carefully on the icy roads. The weather became cloudy and it started to lightly snow. Nikki and Barbara already missed their friends at school and didn't want to move to California. Norma sat quietly in the rear; she had not been happy with her mother for a long time.

Chapter 19

Jeanette drove on I-81 and I-40 through bad weather since she left Virginia, and was now in west Tennessee early in the morning. Jeanette arrived in Memphis just a few miles from the Arkansas border. She almost fell asleep, because she drove so long by herself. Barbara sat on the front seat and saw a motel on the right. Jeanette thought that she should to take a break and decided to check into the motel for a night. Jeanette parked her car in front of the office and put on her sunglasses on; she didn't want anyone staring at her face. Jeanette told the girls to come with her in the building to warm up inside. They came in the small lobby with two chairs and an old vending machine. A tall man with curly black noticed at Jeanette's lip. Nikki came to the front desk by herself. She saw the man's badge and his name was Nile.

"Nile, can we have a room with two double beds for one night please?" Nikki asked.

Nile looked at Nikki. "Sure, I'll see what we have."

He found a room and took the key from a key cabinet. "Yes, I have a room for you tonight," Nile said.

Nikki told Jeanette that the room was ready for them to stay one night. Jeanette felt relieved and needed to get to bed immediately.

"The price, plus taxes, is $18.43," Nile said. "Either cash or credit card will be acceptable."

Nikki signed to Jeanette the price of the room. Jeanette took her wallet out of her purse and paid with her Visa card. Nile gave them a key and told them their room was number 134 on the first floor. They went back to the car and got their suitcases. They came back in the building, walked through the lobby and found room 134. Jeanette opened the door and let the girls in the room. Jeanette put her purse and the key on the dresser next to the TV and walked to the sink. She looked in the mirror and took her sunglasses off. She noticed her eye was almost healed, but that it still would take a few more weeks. Norma came out of the bathroom. Jeanette looked at Norma, but they did not say anything. Jeanette looked back in the mirror while Norma sat on the bed and watched TV. Barbara ran to the bathroom and closed the door. Jeanette closed her left eye, which still had stitches on it.

The next morning, Jeanette woke and looked at the clock; it was five o' clock in the morning. She got out of bed and took a shower. After she finished, she woke the girls up, who showered and got dressed. They walked across the street from the motel to a "Big Boy" restaurant. They were the first customers.

An hour later, they left the motel and got back on the highway. The weather was sunny and cold. Jeanette had a good time driving all day. She spent time talking to Barbara and Nikki in the front seat. Norma sat in the back seat again. Jeanette still smoked, but hadn't had a beer in five days.

The sun went down in the west, and Jeanette had a hard time seeing the road from the sun's glare. She tried looking at the white line in the road to help her drive until the sun set and she felt comfortable again. She looked at the girls in the front seat; Barbara was napping and Nikki looked outside. Jeanette looked at Norma in the rear view mirror; she was reading a book. Jeanette hoped that Norma would be all right.

A little later, Nikki saw a sign that said, "Welcome to New Mexico". She woke Barbara up and told her to look outside. Jeanette couldn't see the highway very well at night, because there were no lights. She had given trying to drive all the way to Albuquerque, and got off the highway in a small town called Clines Corners. The town had four stores on Main Street and an old motel with six units of cottages. It was built in the early 1910's by the family/owners. Jeanette arrived at the motel and looked for the office, but she could not find it. Jeanette came back to the car and started to leave. From the back seat, Norma saw a man running

131

out of his small cottage. Norma patted Jeanette's shoulder, who had already started driving away. Jeanette braked as hard and looked at Norma.

"That man is trying to get your attention," Norma pointed. "I heard him call you to stop." The man came over to Jeanette. She rolled the window down so Nikki could hear him.

"Did you want to stay here for the night?" he asked.

"Yes," Jeanette nodded.

"Go ahead back and park by the office," the man said, pointing to the office. "I'm Mark Irwin, and I'll meet you there right now."

Mr. Irwin went in the office and turned the light on. Jeanette drove back to the office and parked her car there. She went to the office with her girls. They came in the living room and looked at the many pictures of Indians on the wall. Mr. Irwin came over the desk, pulled out a drawer and looked for a cottage's key. But he couldn't find it, so he checked another drawer and still couldn't find it. Finally, he found the key in a cup in the drawer. He came to the living room with the key. Norma looked at Mr. Irwin. He was tall and had a long ponytail. He looked to be in his mid-40s.

"Here's the key." Mr. Irwin hung the key ring on his finger. "The cottage is nice. You'll all have a good night's sleep tonight."

He gave the key to Jeanette.

"You can pay me in the morning," Mr. Irwin said. "My wife, Roseanne, will be cooking a large breakfast for you and your daughters for when you wake up, ok?"

Jeanette and the girls were happy to hear about breakfast. Jeanette looked at the key, which had no number. She told Nikki there was no number.

"What the cottage's number?" Nikki asked.

"I'll show you," Mr. Irwin said. "Are you ready to find the cottage now?"

They followed Mr. Irwin to a cottage next to his. Mr. Irwin asked Jeanette to give the key to him, and he unlocked the door. He turned the light on. The girls came in the living room and looked up at the loft above the kitchen. Nikki and Norma ran upstairs to the loft and jumped on the bed together. Barbara sat on the couch and looked up at the ceiling made of pinewood. Jeanette walked through the living room to the bedroom. She looked around the bedroom and bathroom. There were double beds with log frames and a nightstand between the beds. She sat on the bed and rested for a while. Mr. Irwin came in the bedroom and saw Jeanette's eye from the mirror. Jeanette saw him and put her sunglasses on. She stood up and came over Mr. Irwin.

"Thank you very much for letting us stay here," Jeanette said. Mr. Irwin nodded and told her good night. He wondered what was wrong with Jeanette's eye.

Jeanette went to the car and brought a suitcase back with her.

In the morning, Nikki came to Jeanette's bedroom and woke her up. She started to wake up slowly and see Nikki. "Yes, what?" Jeanette asked, tired.

"Breakfast is ready for us," Nikki said. "It's in the kitchen. Mr. Irwin's wife made it and brought it here. The food looks so delicious!"

Nikki pulled Jeanette's hand to lift her body up, but Jeanette wouldn't budge. Nikki gave up and left Jeanette alone. Jeanette tried to fall back asleep. She smelled the breakfast, though, and it made her hungry. She gave up trying to sleep and walked to the kitchen. Jeanette was in awe of what Mrs. Irwin made. The table was filled with pancakes, eggs, bacons, ham, French toast and a pitcher of orange juice. Barbara took plates out of the cabinets and put them on the table. After the delicious breakfast, they rushed to start heading west again. Jeanette dropped off the key and paid for the room; she decided to pay a little extra for the breakfast. Then she went back to her car and headed for the highway.

It was quiet on I-40; the weather was pretty nice and cold outside. Snow was on the summit and at some places around the highway. Jeanette drove through the Grand Canyon area and didn't see any trees in this area because there were lots of light pink and white rocks around. They had a good time traveling through the different environments of each state. Barbara was in the back seat and felt she was about to vomit. Barbara told Nikki to move the car to the shoulder right away.

"You better stop, mom," Nikki pointed. "Barbara thinks she might vomit any time."

"Ok, I'll pull over now," Jeanette nodded.

Jeanette drove her car to the shoulder and stopped. Barbara

went outside and started to vomit. Nikki came over and held Barbara's hair back. Jeanette came out of the car and walked over to the fence. She started to light a cigarette. Norma got out and walked over to the fence and looked at Barbara after she was done. It made Norma sick, so she turned to look at the canyon. Jeanette looked at Nikki and Barbara as they went back to the car, then looked toward Norma. Jeanette stared at Norma, and Norma started to look at Jeanette. Their eyes met for a few seconds, then Norma blinked and walked to the car. Jeanette looked toward the canyon. She held the silver lighter to her chest and thought about throwing it away so she wouldn't be reminded of her fight with Norma. Jeanette decided to throw it away and start a new life in California. Jeanette kissed the silver lighter and threw it hard. The silver lighter flew over the fence to the canyon and hit the ground about three times before it stopped.

Jeanette came over the fence and looked for the silver lighter, but couldn't find it. She felt sad, and it broke her heart that Paul's silver lighter was gone. Jeanette stood and waved to the canyon, turned and went to the car. She came in the car. Nikki and Norma sat up front and looked at Barbara in the back seat sleeping.

"Is she all right now?" Jeanette asked Nikki.

"Yeah, she's fine." Nikki said.

Nikki looked at Norma with a smile; she knew that Jeanette wanted to forget about the silver lighter. The car moved to the highway. A few hours later, Norma noticed a sign that said, "Welcome to California."

"Look at the sign," Norma said excitedly. "We're finally here!"

Jeanette drove through the California border and kept driving until I-40 changed to I-15 south of Los Angeles. She decided to stop at a motel in Barstow, because she was tired from driving all day. They stayed in the motel overnight and left early the next morning. It took two hours to drive to Los Angeles from Barstow. Finally, they arrived in Los Angeles. They looked around the town; there was a huge highway and lots of buildings. Jeanette looked for her letter from her cousin, Julie. She found it and read the directions on how to get to her house in Venice. She kept driving until the end of I-10 west, then turned left on Pacific Ave. She looked for Julie's address. Nikki looked for a house with #23 on the door. She couldn't find it. Jeanette and Nikki kept looking when Barbara noticed the number 23.

"Are you looking for 23?" Barbara asked Nikki. "I think it's right there in front of us."

"Where is it?" Nikki asked.

Barbara pointed to a white house with green and blue mixed on each window.

"I see it," Nikki told Jeanette. "Better park here so we can walk to Julie's house over there."

Jeanette looked at the house where Julie lived. She parked her car on the street, got out, and walked across the street to Julie's house. Barbara ran to the door and rang the bell. The door was already opened for them to come in. Jeanette looked through the screen to the hall when Julie came to the door.

"Come in," Julie said while she walked to the front door. "I'm glad you made it safely from the East Coast."

Barbara opened the screen and went inside the house. Julie hugged Barbara. Jeanette, Nikki and Norma came in the house. Julie then hugged Jeanette, Nikki and Norma.

"How was your trip across country in four days?" Julie asked, speaking clearly to Jeanette. "Was it fun with your girls?"

"Yes, thanks," Jeanette said, nodding her head.

Julie guided them to the living room. Two boys close to Mary Anne's age were sitting on the couch watching football on the TV.

"Boys," Julie called to her sons, "please come over here and meet your cousins."

The boys stood up and came over.

"This is Don and Lee," Julie introduced them to Jeanette and her girls. "Boys, this is Jeanette and her three daughters, Nikki, Barbara and Norma."

They shook each other's hands and sat on the coach to talk to each other. Julie wanted Jeanette to come with her. They went outside and walked to another house. Julie showed a key to Jeanette.

"What's this for?" Jeanette asked.

"It's the key to your house," Julie said, putting the key in Jeanette's hand. "You can have it for now. There's plenty of furniture inside, so you don't have to worry about that, ok?"

Julie pushed Jeanette to the house. She walked toward the

front door and looked back at Julie.

"Go inside," Julie said.

Jeanette put the key in and opened the door. She came in the hall and looked at the furnished living room with a fireplace. She was surprised that Julie was so nice to her, especially since it was the first time they'd seen each other since they were little girls. Julie was two and a half years older than Jeanette.

The next day, Jeanette sent her girls to Julie's house. She drove to the Betty Ford Center, but got lost somewhere on the highway. Jeanette arrived there late. She ran through the door to the front desk and asked a woman to give Jeanette a paper and pen to communicate with her. The woman was short long, dirty blonde hair. She used American Sign Language.

"Are you Jeanette Dreyfuss?" Terri asked.

Jeanette nodded her head.

"Ok, I am Terri Bowman," Terri introduced herself. "I've been working for the Betty Ford Center for about two months. I'd like you to come with me to a room. The interpreter will be right back. He just went to get some soda from the vending machine, ok?"

Terri came out of the office and met Jeanette in the hall. They walked through the hall to a room. Terri opened the door and let Jeanette come in the room. She saw a group of people in the room. They were there for alcohol or drug treatment. Terri pointed Jeanette to a chair where she was supposed to sit with the group. Jeanette was uncomfortable for a moment.

"This is Jeanette Dreyfuss," Terri told Mike. He was the group counselor. "The interpreter will be here soon."

Terri was about to leave when she noticed Mike's hand go up.

"Can you tell Mrs. Dreyfuss to take her sunglasses off, please?" Mike muttered.

Terri closed the door and came to Jeanette. "Can you please take your sunglasses off? Terri asked.

"Why?" Jeanette wondered.

"That's our policy," Terri explained. "It's not fair for other people to not be able to see you. They would like to know who you are."

Jeanette nodded and took her sunglasses off. Jeanette looked at Terri's eyes. Terri was pretty shocked to see that Jeanette had a black eye and stitches on her eyebrow.

"Ok. Would you like to put your sunglasses into your purse?" Terri asked. "You look fine to me."

Jeanette did as she was asked.

"Thank you, and you have a good day. Goodbye," Terri said.

Mike winked at Terri, and she could tell he was glad she asked Jeanette to take off her sunglasses. She nodded and went to the hall and pulled the door closed.

Chapter 20

Jeanette and her daughter lived in the rental house of her cousin. After three months, they adjusted to California living. The girls were homesick for a while, but they seemed happy to live in California.

Jeanette kept attending Alcoholics Anonymous meetings at the Betty Ford Center. She learned a lot from the lectures and various programs. She cleaned up her body from alcohol and quit chain-smoking. Jeanette was changing her way of life. She was a new person now that she had stopped drinking and smoking. She began to exercise and take better care of herself and her children. She helped her girls with homework, played games and went to the mall with them. She got a full-time job at a data processing company. Jeanette shared with the group her bad experience with alcohol since her husband was killed in Vietnam. Jeanette sat next to Sean Collins. He was tall and good-looking, with dirty blond hair, and was about three years older than Jeanette's. Sean had been a heavy alcoholic for a long time. After his divorce was final, he was very depressed and drank too many beers. Sean was traveling on I-10 east, when he lost control of his new, 1983 Porsche. It went off the road and crashed into a large rock. Sean was in the hospital in Palm Springs. His car was a total loss, and the court in Palm Springs ordered Sean to check into the Betty Ford Center. He'd been there three months before Jeanette came.

Sean and Jeanette were working together as partners. He wanted to learn sign language in order to communicate better. They had a common background with their family and education.

Go to the Hill

One night, they left the meeting and drove to Venice. They went out to dinner and took a walk on the beach. Sean saw a man carrying a basket with three different colored roses. The man showed the basket to another couple, but they did not want to buy one. Sean wanted to buy a red rose for Jeanette. He gave one dollar to the man and picked a red rose. Sean held the rose close to Jeanette's face; she could smell the fragrance. She looked at the rose and then at Sean. It was the first rose she had ever been given. She smiled and knew that Sean had fallen in love with her, but she was too shy to move their relationship further. Jeanette took the rose and told Sean how much she really liked him. Sean reached his hand over to Jeanette's face and touched her very gently. They came closer together, and he embraced and kissed her.

Sean and Jeanette had a good time traveling to different places in the area. Sean was raised in southern California, so he was very familiar with the area. He had custody of his two children, Rob and Amy. His ex-wife didn't want the children, because she remarried and moved to France. Rob had dark, dirty blond hair and was as tall as his father. He was a year older than Nikki. Amy was shy, with long blond hair, and she was close in age to Norma. They did not get along with Nikki, Barbara and Norma because of their different lifestyles. Jeanette's children were middle class, and she had to work hard to support them. Sean's children were upper class and stubborn. But after a few weeks, they got used to each other and learned things from each other's lifestyle. They became friends, almost like a family.

Two years later, Jeanette and Sean were still alcohol-free and no longer attended group meetings. They had a good relationship for a long time. Jeanette moved into Sean's house near the Hollywood area. After they married, they bought a beach house in Malibu. Jeanette quit her job and went back to college as a full-time student. She was an art major. She learned and practiced with oil and water painting and made clay. Jeanette was very talented and became a successful painter. She received an award for her oil and water paintings. Sean bought Jeanette a cozy store in Venice to sell her paintings and crafts.

Mary Anna moved to the West Coast. She lived with her mother after she broke up her boyfriend in Virginia. Mary Anna decided go to Pepperdine University near Malibu. She took received a BS degree in social work. Nikki, Barbara and Norma went to a private school with Rob and Amy. When they graduated, they attended different universities in California. After the girls graduated college, they got married and had children. Jeanette had five grandchildren and three half-grandchildren.

Jeanette did not call or write Maria or the sisterhood since she moved out west. Their friendship seemed nonexistent.

Chapter 21

Ray owned a heating and air conditioning business for almost forty years. He was a very busy person. One afternoon, he came in his office and took some paperwork from his desk. At that moment, Ray stopped, dropped the paperwork, and fell to the floor. Ray's secretary, Dolly, heard him from his office. She came in and saw Ray lying on the floor. She checked his breath to make sure he was still alive. Dolly ran and called an ambulance. The medics came in the office and checked Ray's health. They took him to hospital. Dolly called Maria's office. Another person answered, and Dolly informed her that Ray was in hospital. The worker wrote down the note and gave the message to Maria. She was puzzled at the message.

Then it hit her hard that Ray was in the hospital for the first time ever. Maria left the office and drove to the hospital. She rushed to the front desk and asked the nurse for Ray's room number. The nurse looked up his last and told Maria that Ray was in room #18 on the first wing. She went to the room and found Ray there. Dr. Keller came in the room and saw Maria hugging Ray on the bed. He told Maria that he would inform her the next day of Ray's CAT scan results. Dr. Keller let Maria take Ray home and to rest in his own bed.

The next day, Maria and Ray were to see Dr. Keller, but Ray couldn't go because he didn't felt too good. He wanted to stay in bed. Maria went to see the doctor alone. She went to the lobby, and the nurse told her to have a seat and Dr. Keller. He came in late and told Maria to come with him to his office. He had Maria sit down before telling her Ray had a stroke in the right side of his brain, and that it was caused by stress from work. Ray would not be able to go back to work anymore. Maria was shocked that Ray had a stroke. She knew that Ray wanted to work the business all his life. Maria went home to Ray. She told her older son, Bobby, that she wanted him to take over his father's business.

Several years later, Maria and Bobby were still taking care of Ray at home. Maria moved Ray to another bedroom on the same floor. Ray's body became weak and he couldn't go to the bathroom or go outside by himself. Maria and Bobby agreed to take Ray to the hospital. A year later, a nurse called Bobby to tell him his father died at the hospital that morning. Bobby went to Maria's work and informed her that Ray passed away. Ray was buried at Fairview Cemetery. Maria's heart was broken; they had been married for almost 45 years. She would never remarry.

It was the summer of 1997. Culpeper had become more populated and more commercialized. Main Street had a lot of traffic and was now dirty.

Maria thought it was time to retire from the Beauty Salon, where she'd worked for 40 years. She went to a real estate agent and listed her business for $80,000. A week later, the realtor told Maria that two different owners wanted to buy her business. One owner offered to pay $115,000 for the business. She accepted. After settlement, the money was put in Maria's bank account. She paid off her debt and put some money in savings bonds for her grandchildren for college.

In the same year, Maria was alone in the house. It was hard to clean the whole house by herself. Ray and Maria had bought the house 42 years ago. She had planned on selling it, but Bobby wanted to buy it. He lived in a small apartment downtown. Bobby and his wife, Heather, wanted a house with a yard for their children. Bobby bought the house, and Maria looked for a house with one level. She found a one-level house that was being built and would be ready in a few months. Maria told Bobby he could move in the house while her new house was being built. She let Bobby and Heather use her furniture, too, because they didn't have enough.

She planned on buying new furniture for her new house.

Maria invited Vicky, Angel, DeeDee and Bonnie to her new house. Vicky drove her 1995 Buick Century through the street of new houses. They all had the same design, but different colors on the doors and windows. DeeDee sat in front reading a paper with Maria's address. Angel sat in back also looking for Maria's house. They saw a moving van with men carrying furniture into a house. They knew it was Maria's house. They parked on the street, came out of the car and looked for Maria somewhere around the house.

Maria came out the front door wearing comfortable, earthy clothes and hair completely white. She was 70 years old. She saw Angel, DeeDee and Vicky on their way to her door. They were glad Maria was there. DeeDee came over and hugged Maria, then Angel and Vicky hugged her too.

"Your house looks so nice," DeeDee said, shocked. "I'd like to see inside."

"Sure, you're welcome to come to my new house any time you'd like," Maria smiled.

They giggled and went in. They stood in awe at the foyer, which had a hardwood floor and chair rails on the wall. Vicky came in the living room and looked at the crown molding on the ceiling and a fireplace. DeeDee and Angel came in the living room and walked around.

"You're rich now," DeeDee giggled at Maria. "I can't wait until I retire and travel across the country with my Eddie. Maybe you can join us someday, ok?"

"Oh thanks," Maria smiled. "I'd love to join you and Eddie and visit other states."

Maria did not see Bonnie with them. "Where's Bonnie?" Maria asked.

"Vicky said that Bonnie had plans," Angel pointed.

"Oh, that's all right. Bonnie will visit later," Maria said, understanding.

They came back to the foyer; Maria told them to follow her to the master bedroom. Maria went in the bedroom first and showed Vicky, DeeDee and Angel her room. Angel came over to the window and looked outside.

"I would like to show you something," Maria said. "Come

with me."

She showed them her luxury bathroom. Maria jumped in the tub and was showing off. Vicky and DeeDee looked at each other and saw that Maria had a separate tub and shower.

"Wow!" said DeeDee, shocked. "How lucky you are to have such a luxurious bathroom. I need one for my house, but Chris would scream at me if I added anything new."

DeeDee laughed because she thought that was so funny. Angel came in the bathroom and was surprised to see a separate tub and shower. She walked around the bathroom; there were two sinks with a large mirror, white tiles on the floor and navy blue tiles on the wall.

"Who chose those tiles?" Angel asked Maria. "Were they here or did you get to choose them?"

"Me," Maria said, pointing her finger to her chest. "I liked these colors for the bathroom. Ray's favorite color was navy blue."

A man was looking for Maria. He came in the master bedroom and found Maria in the tub. Maria saw him wave and knew he wanted to ask her where to put the boxes and furniture. Maria told her friends she'd be right back. Maria got out of the tub and left the bathroom to follow the man. They came into the hall and he pointed to a box. The box contained old personal letters written between her and Jeanette. Maria didn't want to look through the old letters; she pointed the box toward the attic. The man nodded and climbed a ladder to the attic with the box under his arm.

Angel left the bathroom, followed by DeeDee and Vicky. Angel saw the box marked "Personal letters," which the man took to the attic. She suspected something was wrong with Maria. Angel walked to the kitchen and looked for Maria. DeeDee and Vicky looked at each other and followed Angel again. Angel came in the kitchen and saw Maria. She was drinking a glass of water. She was wondering why they were all staring at her.

"What's the matter with you?" Maria asked, concerned.

"Umm," Angel said, "never mind. I'd like you to show me around the house."

Maria smiled and showed them the backyard. She opened the French door and they walked outside. The backyard had one acre with a fence. DeeDee at the house next the door. Vicky came over to Maria and Angel.

"Look at the mountain," Vicky said, pointing. "You have such a beautiful view of it from the family room."

They agreed with each other person and looked at the mountain.

"Oh I forgot to ask you," Maria said to Vicky and Angel. "Do you want a drink? I have spring water and apple juice."

"I'd like some water please," Vicky said.

"Same for me, please?" Angel said.

DeeDee came over and Maria asked her what she'd like to drink. DeeDee told Maria that she wanted some apple juice. Maria went in the house and got some paper cups, the spring water, and apple juice and put them on the counter. Maria forgot to ask them if they wanted ice.

She went outside and asked them, "Does anyone want ice?"

"Yes please," they all said.

Maria came back inside again, took the cups filled them with ice from the water/ice dispenser. Then she poured the water and apple juice. She planned to take all the cups but couldn't hold them at the same time. She found a tray from a box, put the cups on the tray and brought them outside. Vicky, DeeDee and Angel were talking about the view. DeeDee saw Maria one her way over to them. Vicky and Angel looked at Maria and picked up their drinks. The moving man came in the kitchen looking for Maria, then came outside. DeeDee saw the man wave to her.

"The man wants to talk to you," DeeDee said, pointing to the man.

Maria went over to the man, and they went in the house. She needed to sign and form and pay them.

"Thank you very much," Maria said, "for your help in moving my things to my new house. I'm glad you guys didn't hurt yourselves moving the furniture and boxes here. Have a nice day. Bye."

The men smiled and walked through the hall to the front door. Maria checked each room to make sure everything was there.

"I should have asked them," Maria said, "to help me move the furniture to the right places, but it wasn't worth the extra money. So, can I ask you to help?"

145

Vicky, DeeDee and Angel didn't mind helping Maria move the furniture around the house. Maria came to her bedroom first, put the frame together, then put the mattress on top. They moved the boxes to the wall so there'd be more room to walk around. She showed them around the house some more. There were three bedrooms, two full bathrooms, a powder room, family room in the same area as the kitchen and a sunroom.

They talked about old times. Vicky looked at her watch and saw it was past seven o'clock in the evening.

"It's past by seven," Vicky said. "I think I better go home now and hope to see you again later, ok?"

Vicky stood up and hugged Maria. She offered her best wishes for living in her new home. Angel and DeeDee thought they had better go too. They went to Angel's car and waved to Maria at the front of her house. She waved at them while they drove away.

Maria came in the house and closed the door; she lay against the door and looked at herself in the mirror. She started to walk slowly to see if the man closed the attic. It was closed. She did not want to go to the attic and look through the box. She didn't to want to flashback to what had happened between herself and Jeanette. Maria walked past the attic to the family room and sat on the loveseat to look out the window at the mountain. She wondered how Jeanette was doing in California since she left Maria's house fifteen years ago. She had a hard time imaging if Jeanette changed to a new life without alcohol. Maria hoped that Jeanette was no longer an alcoholic, for her daughters' sake.

Chapter 22

The house was not finished yet; boxes were unopened and the furniture stood against the wall. Maria came in the living room first and started to unpack the boxes. She tried to move the furniture around the room. She put some vases on the end tables and coffee table and pictures on the wall. She planned to order new curtains and blinds for the windows. After two weeks, Maria was finally done unpacking. Maria put sleep sofas in the guest bedroom and office for her children. They lived in other states.

Maria mailed her friends and family her new address. She decided to mail them a card with an invitation for a housewarming.

Jeffery, his wife and their two sons arrived at Maria's house from Baltimore, Maryland. He drove a new Dodge Caravan for the four hours travel. The boys opened the van and ran to front the door. In the foyer, Maria saw the boys standing at the screen door. She opened the door and let in her grandsons.

The boys hugged their grandmother hard.

"David and William," Maria said excitedly, "you're such big boys! But I forget, how old are you?"

"Seven," David said.

"Nine," William said, "but I'll be ten next week."

Maria smiled and looked at the boys; she hadn't seen them in a year. David was about four feet and two inches tall with light brown, curly hair. He was a good boy, but sometimes had a hard time paying attention to his parents. William was five feet and four inches tall with dark brown, wavy hair. He loved to read books. Jeffery and his wife, Iris, came in the house. They dropped their luggage on the floor and stood in awe at the foyer. Maria came and hugged them.

"Your house is so beautiful!" Iris said.

"Mom," Jeffery said, upset, "I miss our old home where I grew up."

"I know," Maria nodded.

Maria planned to take their suitcases, but Jeffery took the heavy luggage for her. They went to the guestroom. Iris looked out the window at the mountain.

"Jeffery," Iris called his name, "come here. You can see the best view of the mountain from here."

Jeffery walked and looked out the window. He was glad to see the mountains since Baltimore had no mountain view.

"I used to look at the mountains many times," Jeffery said with smile. "I lived here whole my life, so it was boring to me." Jeffery was teasing Iris, so she slammed Jeffrey's stomach hard.

"Ouch! That hurt!" Jeffery laughed.

"Hey, be nice!" Iris said.

Iris knew that he loved to tease everyone. Jeffery pulled Iris' hand to leave the bedroom, and they saw their sons in another bedroom.

The phone started to ring. Jeffery tried to find it somewhere in the kitchen. Maria came in the kitchen and was puzzled at Jeffrey's behavior.

"I heard the phone ring," Jeffery said. "Where's the phone?"

Maria did not realize that she forgot to set a flash for the phone's ringer.

"The phone's near the window right there." Maria said, pointing to the wall.

Jeffery found the phone and answered it quickly. "Hello?" Jeffery asked.

"Hi Jeffery," Jobelle said on the other end. "I recognize your voice. It's been a long time since I've heard you. Bobby picked Helen and me pick up at Dulles Airport. We're staying at Bobby's place for a week and got here a few minutes ago."

Jeffery told Maria that Helen and Jobelle were at Bobby's house. Maria was glad that they had arrived safely. But she wondered if they brought their families.

"Did you and Helen come with the family?" Jeffery asked Jobelle on the phone.

"Oh, of course," Jobelle said, "we're bringing them over to see their grandmother. I guess I better go now so we can get to mom's new house. I can't wait to see it! See you later, bye."

Jobelle hung up the phone and told Helen to get ready to go. Helen went outside and called her three children into the house. Jobelle came downstairs and took her year-old twin girls out of the crib. She told her husband, Jason, to get the bag. Jason grabbed it and came upstairs to Bobby's van. Tom came out of the bathroom. Bobby went downstairs to Connie's bedroom. Connie was eighteen years old, down to the earth and became deaf when she was two years old due to a high fever. She was lying on her bed reading a romance. Bobby flicked the light switch to get Connie's attention.

"Ready to go now?" Bobby asked. "We're going to your grandmother's new house."

"Ok," Connie said, "let's go."

She jumped off from her bed and grabbed a large bag. Connie followed her father upstairs to go outside. Roland was five years younger than Connie. He was playing baseball with his cousins outside. Bobby told Roland to get ready to visit his grandmother. Roland and his cousins ran to the van.

"Are we leaving now to go to your mother's new house?" Tom asked his wife, Helen.

Helen nodded and grabbed her purse.

Jeffery told Maria that everyone was on their way to her house. Maria was so happy. In a few minutes, Bobby arrived at Maria's house. Helen and Jobelle came out of the van and gazed at the house. They looked at each other.

"Are you kidding me?" Helen asked. "That's her new house?"

Maria looked out the living room window and saw Bobby's van parking on the street. She ran outside and waved at Helen and Jobelle with their families. Bobby pointed at Maria who was standing outside waving to them. Helen and Jobelle heard Maria's voice and looked at her. It was a shock for them that she could afford to buy this new house.

Jobelle ran and hugged her mother, then Helen came over and hugged them. Iris looked for her mother-in-law in the house but saw Maria outside with her daughters. Iris ran and told Jeffrey and the boys that everyone was there. Jeffery jumped off the bed and ran through the hall to go outside and hug Helen and Jobelle. Iris and her sons came over and hugged too. They went out to eat at Pizza Hut.

The next day, Maria's sisterhood friends and friends from the salon came to her house for the housewarming. They gave Maria lots of gifts and some seeds for a garden in her back yard. They had a pot luck lunch, and everyone talked, laughed, helped open presents and cleaned up after the party ended at five o'clock. Maria's children and the sisterhood's family stayed at her house for dinner until the food was gone. The sisterhood washed the dishes and bowls, then put everything away. Maria's friends left, and after another hour, Helen and Jobelle went back to Bobby's house.

The first week of September, Maria hosted a party for the 50th Anniversary of O.W.L.S. Sorority from Gallaudet College. DeeDee and Vicky put the hot teapot on the coffee table. Angel brought Karen O'Hara in the house. Karen was over 75 years old; she was the sorority's advisor when they were first became a sisterhood of Phi Kappa Zeta a long time ago. Bonnie and Vicky came and hugged Karen, who was holding a bowl. DeeDee came in the living room and saw Karen standing in the foyer. She walked a little faster to Karen and hugged her. Angel told Karen to put the bowl at the kitchen.

"Where's the kitchen?" Karen asked Angel.

Angel pointed to the door. Karen walked through and noticed Maria at the sink. Karen put the bowl on the island and came over Maria. She looked at Karen and hugged her.

"I brought a bowl," Karen said. "It's on the island there. I made my favorite dish, chicken with rice and chives. I knew everyone will like it."

"Oh that sounds good," Maria said. "I want to try it myself later."

She turned back to the sink and washed dishes. Karen noticed Maria's eyes looked tired, like she hadn't been sleeping very well. Karen thought something might be wrong with Maria.

"Are you all right?" Karen asked, concerned.

"I'm fine, thanks," Maria said and continued to wash the dishes in the sink. Karen did not leave Maria alone. She looked at Karen and said, "You can go to the living room now, and I'll be there in a few minutes."

Maria pushed Karen to the living room. Karen stood close to the door. She was still worried something was wrong with Maria's health.

DeeDee and Angel looked at Karen near the door by herself. Angel came to Karen and patted her shoulder. She looked at Angel with a sad face.

"What's the matter with you?" Angel asked.

"Oh," Karen muttered. Angel pulled Karen's hand to the sofa and told Karen to sit there. "I noticed Maria's eyes. They just didn't look right to me."

Angel was baffled and looked at DeeDee and Vicky; they didn't know Maria's health history. Bonnie came in the living room with an alumni book from her sorority group. Angel, Karen, DeeDee and Vicky looked at Bonnie with worried faces.

"What's wrong?" Bonnie asked nervously. "You're going to scare me to death?"

Maria put a plate of strawberry shortcake on a tray, picked it up and walked through to the living room. They were admiring the strawberry short cake, when Maria's body weakened and she dropped the tray. The tray hit the coffee table and Maria's body fell towards the floor. They stood up from the sofa and came over to Maria. She lay on the floor and with her eyes shut.

Bonnie was shocked. "Better use your hand to feel Maria's heart. Is she all right?"

Angel checked Maria's chest with her hand; she looked at Bonnie.

"Is she still alive?" Bonnie asked.

Angel nodded. "Vicky, would you please call 911 right away?"

Vicky rushed to the kitchen and picked up the phone. She put it into the TDD and dialed 911. The red light started to flash a

151

ring for a few seconds, but later the ring stopped. She was puzzled and redialed again. But there was still a problem with the 911 service. They only hung up, because they didn't know how to use TDD. Vicky had given up her struggled with calling 911 services. She hung up the phone and went back to the living room. They looked at Vicky with her stricken face.

"I give up," Vicky complained. "I tried to call 911 a few times, but they kept hanging up the phone."

Bonnie was shocked and looked at Angel and DeeDee; they were speechless.

"I think we better take Maria to the hospital right away," Bonnie fretted.

"How can we take Maria?" Vicky asked.

"Come on! Just carry her body into my car!" Bonnie ordered.

Angel and DeeDee pulled Maria up by her shoulders. Bonnie lifted Maria's legs up. Vicky rushed and opened the front door. Bonnie walked backwards with her head turned toward the door. Angel and DeeDee would sometimes drop Maria on the floor, because her body was overweight. They carried Maria outside to Bonnie's car. Vicky tried to open the door but it was locked. She looked for the keys in Bonnie's purse, found it, and opened the door. Bonnie put Maria in the back seat. Angel and DeeDee laid Maria's arms on her stomach. Maria's width fit the wideness of the Grand Marquis, and she was 5'7" tall. Bonnie got into the front seat. Angel and DeeDee came in front with her, but Vicky couldn't fit in the front seat because it was so full.

"You better get Maria's purse," Bonnie told Vicky, "so you can find her keys and lock the house."

Vicky nodded and ran into the house and looked for Maria's purse the bedroom, but it was not there. She ran into the kitchen and looked for the purse, which she saw on the island. Vicky ran to the door and locked it.

Vicky got into the backseat with Maria. She had to lift Maria's head and lay it in her lap. They drove to the hospital right away.

When they arrived at the emergency room, DeeDee ran through the swinging doors and looked for a nurse. DeeDee found a nurse at the front desk and told her that she needed someone to help bring Maria to the emergency room. The nurse told another nurse to get a wheelchair and follow DeeDee to the car. Angel opened the back door and tried to get Maria out. The nurse said they were too old to pull Maria out of the car. She told them to wait a few minutes while she called some men to help. The men brought a stretcher and pulled Maria out of the car. They rushed her into the emergency room and checked her vitals. Bonnie parked her car and came into the hospital. The nurse asked if anyone brought Maria's purse. Vicky raised her hand and held up Maria's purse. She looked for Maria's insurance card and gave it to the nurse. Angel ran to the nurse and gave her Bobby's phone number at work. The nurse called Bobby and informed him that his mother was in the hospital.

Fifteen minutes later, Bobby and his wife, Heather, walked through the doors to the front desk. He looked for a nurse, but they were all busy on the phone or talking with the doctors. Heather spotted four deaf women sitting quietly.

"I see Maria's friends there," Heather said. "They look sad for your mom."

"Where are they?" Bobby asked.

"Right there," Heather pointed.

Bobby found the women in the waiting room. They were quiet. He came over to the women with Heather. Vicky saw Bobby on the way and patted DeeDee's lap. She looked at Vicky.

"What?" DeeDee asked.

Vicky pointed to Bobby. He was on his way to see them. Angel and Bonnie looked at Bobby and hugged him.

"I'm glad you're here for my mom," Bobby smiled. "Thank you for bringing her to the hospital. It's the first time anything like this has happened to her."

"Yes," Bonnie nodded. "It's a long story, but I think it would be best for us to tell you later, ok? I hope your mom will be all right."

Bobby hugged Bonnie. She saw and pointed to Dr. Millers. Dr. Millers was standing there waiting for Bobby.

"Are you Mr. Scott," Dr. Millers asked. "Your mother is all right now. We'll have her test results tomorrow. You may see your mother now. She's in room 11."

"Ok, thanks Dr. Millers," Bobby nodded.

He told the women that they could see Maria. They went to Maria's room and saw her lying on the bed. She had just awoken before they showed up in the room. Maria was dizzy from the medication. Bobby came over to Maria and held her hand.

"Are you ok?" Bobby asked. "I hope you'll be fine soon. Mom?"

"I'm fine, just tired," Maria said. "That's all I want to say, ok Bobby?"

Bobby was glad that she was all right. Maria looked at the women who stood near the bed.

"Thank you very much," Maria smiled, "for bringing me to the hospital and calling my son Bobby. I appreciated it."

They smiled at Maria. Maria's head became weak and she laid it back on the pillow.

"I'm sorry," Maria muttered, "the medicine makes me sleepy. Damn it."

She fell asleep. Bobby and Heather decided to leave and would pick up their mother and talk to Dr. Millers the next morning. Bonnie, Vicky, DeeDee and Angel left the room; they went back to Maria's house to clean up the mess. After they cleaned the living room, they each went home alone.

Chapter 23

Early in the morning, Bobby and Heather came into Maria's house and grabbed some clean clothes from the closet. They drove to the hospital. Bobby wondered what caused his mother's illness.

"Heather," Bobby asked, "what do you think made Mom black out and fall on the floor last night?"

"Well, we won't know until we talk to the doctor." Heather said.

Bobby nodded his head and kept driving to the hospital. He found a space and parked his car. They came out of the car and walked into the lobby. They went directly to Maria's room. Bobby pushed the door open and looked at Maria in bed. Maria saw Bobby.

"Are you all right now?" Bobby asked.

"Yes, I'm fine, thanks!" Maria opened her arms.

Bobby came over and hugged Maria. Heather showed Maria the clean clothes.

"Oh thanks, Heather," Maria said with smile. "I needed those badly."

Maria took her clothes and hugged Heather. The nurse came in the room with a tray for Maria's breakfast. Maria wanted Bobby to inform the nurse that she needed take a shower. He explained to the nurse what Maria said.

"Yes, she'll get a shower after breakfast," the nurse said.

Bobby told Maria what the nurse said. Maria nodded her head and opened her arms again. Bobby hugged and kissed Maria's cheek.

"Are you sure you're all right now?" Bobby asked. "You look fine to me, but we need to see Dr. Millers."

Maria nodded her head while the nurse pushed the wheelchair into the bathroom. Bobby and Heather left the room and waited for Maria to finish her shower.

About thirty minutes later, Maria and the nurse came to Bobby and Heather in the lobby.

"I feel better now," Maria said. "I feel refreshed, so let's go to Dr. Miller's office now."

The nurse pulled then pushed the wheeler chair. Bobby and Heather followed her into the elevator. The nurse pushed the button for the third floor. When the elevator opened, they walked through the hall to Dr. Miller's office. The nurse planned to push Maria to Dr. Miller's desk, but she pointed to the window. The nurse moved Maria close to the window. Bobby and Heather sat in front of the desk.

"Dr. Miller will be back in a few minutes," the nurse told Bobby. "I'll come back after you've finished talking with him, ok?"

The nurse waved at Maria and left the office. Maria looked out the window; she had a nice view of downtown. Bobby was somewhat worried about his mother's health. Dr. Miller came in the office and patted Maria's shoulder.

"How are you, Mrs. Scott?" Dr. Miller asked clearly.

"I'm fine," Maria said softly.

Dr. Miller shook hands with Bobby and Heather. He went to his desk and sat down. Dr. Miller looked at the folder at Maria's result.

"Well the test results show..." Dr. Miller tried to tell Bobby. "It's hard to explain."

Bobby was puzzled and looked at Heather, then looked back to Dr. Miller.

"What are you trying to tell me?" Bobby asked.

Dr. Miller shook his head and looked down at the folder again. Then he turned his head to look at Bobby.

"Your mother has got..." Dr. Miller muttered, "leukemia."

Heather was so shocked, she held her hand over her mouth.

She thought she was going to faint. Bobby did not understand what Dr. Miller was talking about. Maria was bewildered; she didn't understand what they were talking about, and she didn't want anything to be hidden from her.

"What's going on?!" Maria yelled at Bobby. "Please tell me what Dr. Miller said."

Bobby looked at Maria quickly; she noticed his eyes were teary. This hit her hard and confused her.

"Would you please tell me," Maria implored. "Just tell me, is it one word or more than one?"

Bobby looked at Dr. Miller. He did not say anything. Bobby looked at Heather, and she turned her head down slowly. Bobby looked back to Maria again and tried to explain what Dr. Miller said.

"Mom," Bobby said, "Dr. Miller told me that you have leukemia."

"What are you talking about?" Maria asked. "I have leukemia? Oh no! Are you sure that's what he said?"

Bobby nodded his head "yes". Maria was shocked.

"Would you ask him," Maria told Bobby, "if there's a cure?"

Dr. Miller blinked his eyes. "There is no cure for leukemia," Dr. Miller said. "It's so hard to cure because the white blood cells continuously increase."

"He said 'no'," Bobby told Maria.

Maria was upset and turned her head to look out the window. Bobby could not say anything.

"How long does she have to live?" Heather asked Dr. Miller.

"She could live for four or five more years," Dr. Miller said, "providing she take her medication. But I can't promise anything."

Dr. Miller gave some leukemia information to Bobby to read at home. Bobby came to Maria and patted her shoulder. She looked slowly at Bobby.

"I just accept it," Maria said. "I can go to heaven and see Ray and my mother too. You don't have to worry about me. I am doing fine, ok Bobby?"

It broke Bobby's heart to hear his mother say that. Maria held Bobby's hand, and he started to hug his mother. Heather started to cry but came over and hugged them. Dr. Miller was at his desk. He was just quiet and sad for them. Heather pushed the wheelchair to the hall. Dr. Miller stood up and called Bobby.

"Wait a minute!" Dr. Miller shouted.

Bobby and Heather stopped and looked back at Dr. Miller. Maria wondered why the wheelchair stopped and looked at Heather.

"I'll call the nurse for you," Dr. Miller said. "She'll take care of Maria for you."

He hung up the phone and told them the nurse would be there shortly. When the nurse arrived, she pushed the wheelchair to the elevator, and they went to the first floor. They left the building. Bobby got his car up and drove to the front of the building where Maria and Heather waited. Heather opened the door for Maria to get in front, but Maria wanted to sit in the backseat and let her mind be quiet. Heather closed Maria's door and sat in front. When Bobby pulled away, the nurse waved at them as they drove down the street.

Maria was quiet and looked outside while Bobby drove to her house. Heather looked back at Maria and tried to talk to her, but she wouldn't look at Heather. She looked at Bobby, who was sad and worried about his mother's health, and whether or not she'd be alive in two or three years. Bobby arrived at the house and parked near the garage. Heather and Bobby looked back at Maria, who still said nothing. Maria got out of the car and closed the door. She walked to the front door and waved to Bobby and Heather. They left Maria's house and drove away.

Maria unlocked the door and came in the foyer. She lay against the door and looked at the ceiling light with four clear bulbs. In her mind she thought, "Why did I have to get leukemia?" She walked to her bedroom, put the bag of dirty clothes and her purse on the dresser. She looked at her self in the large mirror. She looked sad and shocked. Maria sat on the bed, took her shoes off, tucked her feet in and pulled the covers over her body. She looked at the ceiling toward her window. She removed her glasses, put them on the nightstand and tried to sleep.

Chapter 24

Early Sunday morning, Maria awoke and looked at the sun coming in through the window. She thought that she should announce her health condition to her friends and members at church. She got out of bed and took a shower. Maria dried her body and put on a nice white dress. She went to the kitchen and poured herself a bowl of Special K cereal and milk. She took the bowl to the sunroom, sat down on the love seat and ate it. After she ate breakfast and cleaned up, she left to go to church. She was still trying to think how to tell the people at church.

At church, the preacher was lecturing the congregation. Vicky was bored with his lecture and stared out the window. What she saw was Maria was coming to church. Vicky looked at Angel on the other side of the bench. She tried to wave to Angel, but Angel was listening to the preacher. Vicky was frustrated she couldn't get Angel's attention, so she decided to look for something small to throw at her. Vicky found a small piece of paper and rolled it into a little ball to throw at Angel. Vicky looked back to make sure no one would notice her throwing something at Angel. Vicky threw the paper, but the paper went by Angel's face. Angel looked up and saw Vicky waving to her.

"Hey you," Angel said, dismayed, "it's not nice to throw paper at me! Oh grow up, woman!"

"It's Maria!" Vicky said.

Angel was surprised Vicky told her that Maria was there.

"Oh, Maria is here!" Angel told the preacher by mistake.

The preacher looked befuddled at what Angel told him.

"Maria is here," the preacher announced to the congregation. People there were surprised, ran over to the windows and looked for Maria in the parking lot. DeeDee followed them. Angel was embarrassed and looked at the preacher.

"I wasn't talking you," Angel said. "I was saying it to myself."

The preacher felt foolish and thought he should not have told everyone. Maria drove and found a parking spot at the end of the lot. She parked her car and walked to the church. A young boy saw Maria coming.

"Mrs. Johnson is coming in," a little boy said.

The people looked at Maria before she came in, ran back to their seats and sat quietly. The running congregation knocked DeeDee to the floor. Maria walked through the doors and looked at the preacher on stage. DeeDee stood up by herself; her dress was now dirty from being on the floor. Maria looked surprised to see DeeDee alone in the corner. Maria wondered what DeeDee was doing there.

"I'm looking for a hole," DeeDee said, "where the mice come in."

DeeDee looked for a hole at the base of the wall. The members of church started laughing so hard at DeeDee's sense of humor. Angel rolled her eyes up and felt embarrassed. Vicky thought DeeDee's behavior was foolish. Maria believed DeeDee was looking for a hole and decided to take DeeDee to the front bench.

"You have a seat there," Maria said.

DeeDee nodded her head and sat on the bench next to Angel. Maria smiled at Angel and went to the stage. DeeDee looked at Angel quickly, but Angel didn't know what Maria was doing. Maria climbed on stage.

"Can I speak with the congregation for a moment please?" Maria asked.

" Yes," the preacher nodded, "go ahead."

He left the lectern and let Maria have it. She came to the lectern and called an interpreter to come on stage. Maria felt nervous with what she was about to say. The people wondered about Maria's health.

"Good morning everyone," Maria said. "I would like to tell you that I was in the hospital last week. I thank my sisterhood for bringing me to hospital. Sadly, my doctor told me that I have leukemia. I'll be undergoing treatment and hope you'll pray for me to fight the disease. Thank you for your support."

Maria waved to the audience, left the stage and walked outside. The people rose up and looked at Maria walking out the front door. Angel and Vicky were shocked. DeeDee started to cry. Maria went outside and lay against the door. She looked at the sky, accepting her death. Maria started to go to her car. She felt bad for the people at church. They were shocked that she had leukemia. She got in the car and wiped tears from her eyes. She started the engine and left the church.

Chapter 25

A few days later, Maria saw Dr. Miller in his office. Dr. Miller brought out a small package with leukemia treatment for her. He put it on his desk and opened the box. Maria wondered what Dr. Miller was doing.

"What is that?" Maria pointed to the box.

"This is for you," Dr. Miller said. "It's chemotherapy to fight against acute forms of leukemia."

Maria nodded and felt uncomfortable with the treatment. She knew leukemia was very strong and could be killing the white blood cells in her body. She had to be on chemotherapy for a while to stop the loss of white cells in her body.

"First thing I want to try is Alpha-interferon," Dr. Miller explained, "to stop the spread of leukemia cells to your white cells."

He told Maria to take her shirt off. Dr. Miller gave her a shot in her shoulder. Then she put her shirt back on her. Dr. Miller gave Maria the chemotherapy schedule. She was to come into his office every Tuesday and Thursday.

During the year, Maria got a fever that made her very sick. Her body changed from weak to better then back to weak again. She stayed in her bedroom at home. She had suffered from the chemotherapy treatment for a long time. Angel, Bonnie, DeeDee and Vicky helped Maria by changing the sheets and feeding her during the day. Bobby and Heather took care of Maria every evening after work. Maria told Bobby that she wanted to stop treatment because she was too old. She just wanted to go to heaven to be with her husband, Ray. Bobby was upset by this, but after a while accepted Maria's wish.

Bobby paged Dr. Miller. Dr. Miller looked at the phone number on his pager and called Maria's house. Bobby heard the phone ring; he ran to the kitchen and quickly grabbed the phone.

"Hello?" Bobby said.

"This is Dr. Miller. Do you need me to come over Mrs. Scott's house right away?"

"Well, I'd like to talk to you about something," Bobby muttered. "My mom wants to stop chemotherapy."

Dr. Miller was surprised that Maria had given up the fight for her life.

"Ok," Dr. Miller said. "I need to get some paperwork ready before we can end the chemotherapy. You can come to my office. I'll need you and your mother to sign an official letter dictating her instructions. Ok?"

"That's fine," Bobby said sadly. "I'll be there as soon as you have everything ready. Thank you. Bye."

He hung up slowly, went to the sunroom and started to cry. He couldn't believe his mother could die at any time now.

Dr. Miller started to work on the forms to stop Maria's chemotherapy treatments. Early in the next morning, Dr. Miller called Bobby's office and informed him that the official letter would be left at the front desk in the lobby. Bobby left his work to pick up the letter at the hospital. When he arrived at the hospital, he rushed through the doors to the front desk. He told the nurse his mother's last name and she gave the letter to him. He got back in his car and drove to Maria's house.

In few minutes later, Bobby arrived at his mother's house. He stopped at the front door, though, because his body suddenly became weak. He had to sit on the step. Bobby had a hard time accepting his mother's wish to let her suffer the leukemia and die. He stood up quickly and held his breath before entering the house. He walked to Maria's bedroom, but she wasn't in bed. Bobby became worried and searched the house until he found her in the sitting room. Maria sat on the love seat with a cup of hot tea. She looked at Bobby and saw the letter in his hand. Maria looked up at Bobby's face.

"Is that the letter," Maria pointed to the letter, "Dr. Miller typed so I can stop treatment?"

Bobby nodded and showed the letter to Maria. She took it and opened the envelope. She pulled out the letter to read it. Bobby sat down on a chair and with his head hanging down, he started to cry. Maria noticed Bobby's body jerking like he had the hiccups. She looked at Bobby, who was crying about the letter. Maria knew that he did not want her to die. She felt sad for him and looked back at the letter. Maria stood up and came over to Bobby. She lifted Bobby's chin up; he opened his eyes to meet Maria's eyes.

"I know that you don't want me to go," Maria said. "It's hard to accept what I want to do. I don't want to see my sisterhood, and you and Heather, working so hard for me for nothing. I want to let go. Please try and understand my wishes, ok Bobby?"

Bobby nodded his head and closed his eyes shut with his head down. Maria kissed Bobby's head and walked to her office. She sat at her desk and found a pen. She signed her name at the bottom of the letter. Maria looked for Bobby, but he hadn't followed her into the office.

"Bobby," Maria called, "please come here now."

In the sunroom, Bobby lifted his head up slowly and heard Maria's voice from her office. Bobby stood up and walked through the kitchen to her office. Maria gave the pen to Bobby and pushed the letter to the end of the desk. Bobby stood by the door and refused to move at all. Finally, he grabbed the pen and signed his name on the letter. Bobby took the letter and left the office without looking back at Maria. He kept walking to his car and left right away. He tried to control his emotions during the drive to Dr. Miller's office.

In the end of spring, 1999, Maria became worse and weaker. She lost about twenty pounds and could not walk to the bathroom or kitchen by herself. Bobby took Maria to the hospital to be taken care of while she was sick so. Bobby took care of Maria's house for a while, but he couldn't take it. He decided to sell Maria's house and furniture. He called his sister and brother to take some furniture with them. Maria's sisterhood helped Bobby pack and clean up the house.

A few weeks later, Maria knew that she would be dying at any time. She told Bobby to call her lawyer, Robert Ryan, to come right away. Bobby called Robert Ryan and left a message. Around seven o'clock that evening, the room was full of people. Maria's children were there, as were Maria's sisterhood friends. Angel kept staring at Maria's face; her skin was a pale like cream and her lips were dry from the medicine. Maria lay on her side looking out the window. She kept quiet and watched the sun go down. Robert Ryan showed up in the room. Bobby walked over to Robert.

"Thank you for coming here," Bobby greeted. "My mother's on the bed. She wants to tell you something for her Will before she is gone."

Robert nodded his head and came over to Maria's bed. He sat on a chair, opened his briefcase on his lap and took out a pen and paper.

"I'm ready," Robert told Bobby. "Can you tell me what your mother wants?"

"Go ahead, mom, tell him what you need." Bobby told Maria.

Maria blinked her eyes shut for a second, then woke again. She had only her right hand with which she could communicate. It was difficult for Bobby to understand what Maria tried to say with only one hand for ASL.

"Only two things," Maria said slowly. "First thing, I want the 1964 Thunderbird Convertible to go back to Jeanette. When you find her somewhere in California, please give the car back to her."

Bobby wondered why Maria wanted to give the car back to Jeanette. He thought it would be nearly impossible to find her.

"How can I find Jeanette?" Bobby asked Maria.

"I'll figure out a way," Heather said.

Robert wrote on the paper what Maria said about gave the car. He looked at Bobby careful.

"Is that all Maria would like me to add?" Robert asked Bobby. Maria shook her head slowly.

"One more thing," Maria said. "I don't want my body buried in a grave. I want to be cremated and my ashes put in a vase. I want my ashes taken to the hill where I went my whole life. Please pour the ashes over the ground."

Maria moved her arm in an image of holding a vase with ashes inside and scattering them on the hill. Sadly her hand stopped and lay on top of the pitcher. Bobby waited for Maria to say something more. She didn't talk or move her arm down. Bobby looked at Robert and Heather; they didn't know what happened to Maria. Bobby waved at Maria's face, but her eyes did not turn to look at Bobby's hand. Bobby felt something was wrong and Maria's arm. Her arm fell down and dropped the pitcher to the floor. Bobby was confused at Maria's actions and wanted a nurse to come in right away. Jeffery felt scared about his mother and left the room. He walked down the hall and wondered if she was dead or alive. He started to cry. Jeffery went to a desk where two nurses sat with a computer. The nurses looked at Jeffery and suspected something was wrong with his mother.

"I need you to come now," Jeffery said anxiously.

A nurse followed Jeffery to the room. She lifted Maria's hand and held her wrist for a few seconds. She then closed Maria's eyes and looked at Bobby.

"Your mom passed away," the nurse said softly.

Chapter 26

It is 1945. Jeanette and Maria are teenagers running over the hill to play the merry-go-round game. Suddenly Maria is out of control and falling in a hole in the ground. She screams for help. Jeanette tries to catch Maria but it's too late because the ground is blocked from Jeanette. She can't get through. Jeanette starts to scream for help.

Jeanette woke with a shake in her body. She checked her face and thought it was real life, but it was only a dream. She went back to bed again and tried to sleep. A few minutes later, Jeanette decided to get out of bed. She went to the bathroom, turned on the light and looked in the mirror at herself. She had a scar on her left eyebrow from the past. She was 71 years old and had short white hair. She was overweight now, weighting over 165 pounds at a 5'1 height. Jeanette did not want to see Maria again, but the past was over now. Jeanette thought she should write a letter to Maria and tell her about her new life.

Jeanette put her glasses on and went upstairs to the storage room. She looked for an old brown box somewhere in the small room full of boxes. Jeanette looked for that box for an hour until she found it in the corner. She picked it up and blew the dust away. Jeanette brought it to her bedroom and put the box on the bed. She ripped the tape off and opened it slowly. Jeanette looked in the box and took out the letters wrapped in rubber bands. She flipped through the letters, most of which were from her friends and relatives, not Maria. Jeanette found a Christmas card from Maria. She looked at Maria's address on the upper left corner of the envelope.

"Thanks God," Jeanette said.

Jeanette left the storage room and turned the light off. She went to her office, turned on the computer and started to type a letter to Maria. When Jeanette finished writing, she printed the letter and signed it. She addressed the envelope and put it in her purse. She thought she better take a shower.

Jeanette rushed out of her house drove to the post office to drop the letter in the mailbox. Then she went to her small store in Venice. She parked her car in back of the store, walked in and went upstairs to the loft where her office was. Jeanette was nervous and hoped Maria would accept her apology.

In the morning, Maria's family and friends went to the church for Maria's memorial. The preacher talked about Maria's life. Karen O'Hara stood up and walked to the stage. She inhaled her breath and started to sing.

"Oh Lord," Karen sang, "can't be that Maria passed away in the moment. The angels took her to Heaven and a beautiful home there. I hope that she will have joy and meet people in Heaven. We look forward to seeing you again when the angels take us to Heaven."

The people started to cry over Karen's song. She left the stage and went back to her seat. The men came over to the coffin and carried it through the congregation to the front door. They went outside and walked downstairs toward the funeral car. One man opened the rear door, slid the coffin in and closed the door. The driver started to leave the church. Bobby and his family rode in a limousine. They followed the funeral car to the funeral home. At the funeral home, a man opened the coffin, took out Maria's body and laid it on a long, silver tray to be cremated. The man locked a door and started the fire. After an hour, her body was ash. The man opened the door and pulled out the silver tray; he swept the ashes into the vase and gave it to Bobby.

Bobby left the funeral home to drive to the hill. Everyone was already at the hill and waiting for Bobby. When Bobby arrived at the hill, he brought out the vase. He held the vase until the choir finished their song. Then Bobby opened the top of the vase and poured Maria's ashes over the ground.

The group of mourners went to Bobby's house for the wake, and to eat and drink. They were sitting and talking about their personal lives. Connie sat on the love seat. She was bored listening to all the old people and couldn't wait to go back to Gallaudet University the next day. She went downstairs to her bedroom and opened the curtains to let in some light. Connie looked at some books on the shelves, but found nothing to read. She gave up looking and went to bed.

The mail carrier had arrived. Connie knew Greg Parker since she was about three years old. Her grandmother used to talk to Mr. Parker and about funny things. Connie noticed he was looking at a letter like something was wrong. Connie decided to meet him outside. She came over Mr. Parker, and he smiled at Connie.

"Hey Connie," Mr. Parker said, "how are you doing? It's been a while."

"I'm fine," Connie said. "How about you?"

"Pretty good," he nodded and looked at the mail. Someone sent a letter to your grandmother here."

Connie looked puzzled and took the letter from him. She looked at the address in the left corner of the envelope and saw it came from a Jeanette. She looked at Mr. Parker.

"I'm not sure who Jeanette Collins is," Connie said. "Maybe my father will know who she is. I'll show this to my father this afternoon. Thanks and hope to see you again."

Connie waved at Mr. Parker and turned back to go in the house. She realized she forgot to tell Mr. Parker that her grandmother had passed away. Connie turned back to the mail carrier again.

"Mr. Parker," Connie muttered. "Did you know that my grandmother, Maria, passed away last Thursday evening?"

Mr. Parker was shocked to learn about Maria's death. "I'm sorry to hear about your grandmother's passing away," he said. "What was the cause of death?"

"It was leukemia," Connie answered.

Mr. Parker nodded and waved at Connie. She waved back and went back in. Connie came in the living room, but no one looked at her. She did not say anything and just went downstairs to her bedroom. She jumped into bed and planned to open the letter, but she could not do that because it was her grandmother's letter. Connie thought to wait until her father came to her. She'd let him open the letter. Her eyes were tired and she decided to take a catnap.

A few hours later, the house was empty. Bobby looked for in her bedroom. He went to her bedroom and woke her up.

"How are you today?" Bobby asked.

"I'm fine," Connie said. "I was going to just take a catnap, but I slept too long."

Bobby smiled and kissed Connie's cheek; he left the bedroom. Connie remembered the letter from Jeanette.

"Daddy, wait a minute," Connie yelled. "I got a letter that was for grandma."

Connie showed the letter to Bobby. He looked at the left corner of the envelope, but didn't know who Jeanette Collins was. Bobby ripped open the envelope and pulled out the letter. A small card had fallen to the floor. Bobby picked up the card; it was a business card from Jeanette's store. He read the letter. Bobby was surprised that it was from his mother's best friend, Jeanette. Now he remembered who she was.

"Do you know that person?" Connie asked.

"Yes, I do remember her," Bobby said. "She was your grandmother's best friend. They grew up together in. But..."

"But what?" Connie wondered.

"Well it's a long story," Bobby muttered. "Maria and Jeanette got in a bad fight over stupid personal things."

"When did that happen?" Connie asked.

"It was a long time ago, when you were about four years old," Bobby said, "perhaps about seventeen years ago. After that happened, Jeanette decided to move to California and enter the Betty Ford Center. I believed that she's been sober for a long time and has new life in California."

Bobby did not tell Connie the details of the fight, but he gave her the surface story between Jeanette and Maria. Connie nodded and wondered why her grandmother fought Jeanette.

"Did I ever meet Jeanette?" Connie wondered.

"Yes, but it was a long time ago," Bobby said. "You probably don't remember her. She was short and a chain smoker. She lived with your grandmother before moving out to California."

"Maybe I remember her," Connie figured, "but I'm not sure. Maybe if you'd showed me a picture of her, then I'd remember her."

"Jeanette lived with her four daughters," Bobby explained, "in your grandmother's basement."

"Yeah," Connie said, "I remember Jeanette had four girls. I only played with the last girl, but I didn't like her behavior towards me."

"It was Norma," Bobby said.

"Norma?" Connie said.

Bobby nodded and put the card and letter together into the envelope; he gave it back to Connie. He kissed her cheek, stood up and walked away from her bedroom. Connie held the letter and looked at him as he went upstairs. Connie read the letter about Jeanette's life in California and looked at the business card, which gave the address of Jeanette's art store in Venice. Connie tried to remember what Jeanette looked like when she was young. She had given up and put the letter into the envelope and walked to the window. She was thinking about flying to California to see Jeanette in the summer. Connie would have to wait until college was finished for summer vacation, then she'd fly with her boyfriend, Fred. She wanted to know what caused their friendship to end.

Chapter 27

The sun started to go down over the ocean. Jeanette stood outside on the porch and looked at the sunset. She wondered why Maria did not respond to her letter, which she wrote three weeks ago. Jeanette went inside the house, walked through the living room to go upstairs. She stopped in the hall and looked at the door of the storage room. Her heart started to beat fast for no reason. She went in the room, turned on the light and looked for a box marked "OLD FRIENDS". She found the box under an old desk, took it out and came to her office. She put the box on the desk and sat on her chair; she opened the lid to look inside. She picked up some old pictures to look through that she hadn't seen for a long time ago. Jeanette looked in the box again, took some other pictures out and a yearbook from Gallaudet College. She flipped through the yearbook and looked for her old friends. A picture flew from the yearbook to the floor. Jeanette picked the picture up. She was shocked that it was her and Maria in their first year of college.

That first day, Maria and Jeanette went to College Hall. They stopped in the lobby so Jeanette could look at her schedule of classes. Her classes were on the third floor.

"My first class is English," Jeanette said, rolling her eyes. "Nothing new to me."

Maria looked at her schedule; she thought that she was in the same class with Jeanette, but her class was in another room. She felt sad that they weren't together anymore.

"We're not in the same class," Maria muttered. "I guess it's

172

time for us to part now. I'm not used to going without you."

"Yeah," Jeanette nodded her head and hugged Maria. Maria started to cry. Jeanette blinked her eyes shut for a second, then opened them. "We have to get used to being apart during our college years, right? I think it's best if we go to our classes now. Talk with you later. Bye."

Jeanette ran upstairs to the third floor. Maria kept quiet and walked to her class.

The flash from the phone's ring startled Jeanette. She dropped the picture to the table, looked at the flashing light and walked to the living room.

The final exams were over. Students were excited that school was finished for summer and they could party with their friends. They were all moving out of the dorms. Connie and her boyfriend Fred moved their belongings into Fred's 1995 Subaru Outback. It was almost full, except for the two front seats for them to sit. They drove to Connie's house in four hours. Her young brother, Roland, was playing baseball outside with his friends. Roland heard a car coming and saw that it was Connie. He ran over to the car. Connie got out of the car and hugged Roland.

"Are you home now?" Roland asked. "How long will you stay here?"

"I'm off school for three months," Connie smiled, "but we plan on flying to California for a week, then come back home again. Is dad home now?"

Roland nodded his head and pointed to the house. Fred came to Connie.

"Take all your stuff," Fred said, "to keep it away from the sun."

"Thanks for your concern," Connie teased Fred, "they're not important to me."

Fred knew Connie did not like having her stomach tickled, so he tickled Connie's stomach. She screamed so loud and smacked his hands away. Fred laughed and ran to his car. Connie was pissed off at Fred.

"Hey you," Connie said, "don't ever tickle my stomach,

understand me?"

Fred laughed at Connie and opened the rear door. Connie rolled her eyes up. Fred took out a small box and gave it to Connie. She stood and waited for Fred to get another small box. Bobby was asleep in the living room; he awakened by the noise from the TV. He got thirsty and needed a drink of water from the kitchen. Bobby walked through the hall to kitchen; he saw Connie and her boyfriend outside. Bobby went outside and waved his hands to get Connie's attention. Connie saw her dad, put the box on the ground and ran and hugged him as hard as she could.

"How were your final exams?" Bobby asked.

"Fine, I passed everything," Connie answered.

Bobby smiled and hugged Connie again. Bobby saw Fred standing near the car. He waited for them. Bobby came over and shook Fred's hand.

"How was your day?" Bobby said.

"Fine, thanks," Fred said.

"Dad," Connie called. Bobby looked at her. "I would like to talk to you about our plans."

"Yes?" Bobby asked. "What are you planning?"

"Well," Connie muttered, "I'd like to meet Jeanette Collins in California. Is that all right with you?"

Bobby was surprised, but he did not say anything. "Ok," Bobby accepted. "I'd be more than happy to take you both to Dulles Airport, if you'd like."

"Yes," Connie smiled, "that'd be great. We leave next Monday morning at eight. We're flying American Airlines."

Bobby was glad that Connie wanted to meet Jeanette, but he knew that Jeanette had no idea that Maria passed away a few months ago. He looked at Fred, who waited to help Connie move her personal things.

"Do you want me to help take your things down to your room?" Bobby asked Connie.

"Yes," Connie agreed, "I'd love it if you'd get my things out of Fred's car. Thanks, dad!"

Connie hugged Bobby again and they walked toward Fred's car. Fred helped, too, and they moved everything into Connie's bedroom. After Fred's car was empty, Bobby ordered a large pizza with double cheese and pepperoni. Thirty minutes later, Connie's mother was dropped off at home by her friends. Heather waved goodbye to her friends while they drove away, and she came in the kitchen with some bags. She saw Connie sitting there. Heather put the bags down on the floor and hugged Connie.

"I'm so happy to see you again," Heather smiled.

"How was school?"

"Fine," Connie said, "I passed all my classes."

"Great to hear that!" Heather said happily.

Heather heard a flush from the bathroom. She looked at saw Fred coming out. He waved to Heather.

"Hi, I'm glad to see you again," Heather said. She went over and hugged Fred. Heather heard the front door bell ring.

"Who's at the front door?" Heather asked Bobby.

"It's Domino's pizza delivery," Bobby answered.

"Oh great, I'm starving!" Heather said.

Roland ran to the front door, and Bobby pulled his wallet out from his rear pocket.

"It's $14.55 with a free two liter bottle of diet coke," the delivery man said.

"Dad, I don't like diet coke!" Roland complained.

"Oh be quiet," Bobby said, giving twenty dollars to the deliveryman. "Stop being so picky. There's other soda in the refrigerator."

Bobby handed the diet coke to Roland, who took it to the kitchen. The deliver man laughed at Roland and gave the pizza to Bobby. The delivery man counted Bobby's change.

"No, you keep the change," Bobby said. "Thanks and be careful with driving. Bye."

"Thanks, I will," the deliver man said and ran to his car.

Bobby closed the door and carried the pizza to the kitchen. He put it on the table, while Heather brought out some plates and forks. Connie put ice in six glasses, and Heather poured diet coke in each glass, except Roland's. He wanted to drink a regular Pepsi. Fred put a fork and napkin on each side of the plates. They sat down and ate. They had a good time talking for an hour. After the pizza was gone, Connie carried the plates and glasses to the sink. Bobby threw the empty pizza box in a trashcan outside. When he came back inside, he walked to his bedroom. Connie saw Bobby carrying two old boxes that were all taped up. Bobby put the boxes on the table. Connie looked puzzled at seeing the boxes.

"What are those?" Connie asked. "Who do they belong to?"

"These were your grandmother's," Bobby said. "You can keep them, if you'd like."

"Oh," Connie exclaimed, "thanks Dad!"

She hugged her father and gave one box to Fred while she carried the other one downstairs. They went in Connie's bedroom, put the boxes on the dresser and cleared off the bed. Connie brought a box with her to the bed and put it next to Fred. She started to remove several layers of tape, then opened it. She looked inside and saw an old Gallaudet College yearbook from 1947, as well as many other pictures. Connie looked at Fred.

"It's an old yearbook from Gallaudet College," Connie said excitedly. "I'm so thrilled to see these old pictures to compare the past and present Gallaudet campus."

Connie took the yearbook and some pictures out of the box; she looked for her grandmother in the pictures. Fred looked at some pictures too. They kept looking through the yearbook and pictures for several hours. Bobby came in Connie's bedroom and looked at the pictures over their shoulders.

"Oh Dad," Connie said, surprised, "we really enjoy looking at my grandmother's old pictures."

"Good to hear that," Bobby smiled. "Guess what?"

"What?" Connie wondered.

"It's past midnight," Bobby said, pointing to his watch.

"Oh no," Connie said, shocked. "I didn't realize it was so late. I need to unpack some clothes!"

Connie put the pictures and yearbook in the box. Fred took the box back to the dresser. She looked for her suitcase and opened it on the bed. It was full of her clothes, which she took out and put away in the closet.

"I want you to get some of your clothes," Connie said, "and we'll put them together with my clothes in one suitcase. It'll be much easier for us to use one."

"I agree with you," Fred said.

Fred looked at his luggage and got some clothes for the trip.

Go to the Hill

Connie put his clothes and hers into a suitcase, closed it, and put it on the floor. She picked up her purse to make sure the two tickets were still there.

"We better go to sleep right away," Connie said.

Connie and Fred went to bed together, still wearing the same clothes.

Early in the morning, Bobby came in Connie's bedroom. He turned the light on to wake Connie up, but she wouldn't get up. Bobby decided to shake Connie; she had a hard time opening her eyes for a few seconds, then finally opened them up. Connie looked at the clock on the nightstand.

"Five o'clock in the morning?" Connie asked.

Are you forgetting your plans today?" Bobby asked.

"Oh, yeah," Connie smiled slightly. "That's right, thanks for waking me up."

Bobby laughed and left the room. Connie tried to wake Fred up, but it wasn't easy. She decided to push Fred hard. He fell off the bed and woke up.

"What are you doing to me?" Fred asked moodily. He stood up and walked to the bathroom. Connie was still laughing. She got out of bed and took clean clothes for their trip today. She went to the hall and saw Roland's sleepy head.

"Good morning, Roland," Connie said. "We're going on our trip today. I'll miss you."

Roland nodded his head; he heard Fred flush the toilet and leave the bathroom. Roland went to the bathroom. Fred went back to the bedroom, grabbed some clean clothes and a towel and went back to bathroom to wait for Roland to finish. Finally, Roland came out so Fred could take a shower. Connie rolled her eyes and went upstairs to use another bathroom. Heather cooked a large breakfast for five people. Bobby set up plates and glasses on the table. Roland came in the kitchen and sat down; a few minutes later Fred came in the kitchen and sat next to Roland. At last, Connie came in the kitchen with the luggage. She put the luggage and her bag near the door and came over to her mother while she cooked pancakes and bacon. Connie kissed her mother's cheek.

"Good morning, mom," Connie said, excited. "I'm ready to

go now."

"No," Heather said, "not yet. We'll have breakfast first. We need to leave by 6:30. We only have thirty minutes left. Ok?"

Connie nodded and sat down next to Fred. She poured grapefruit juice into her glass, drank the whole thing, then got more juice. Fred wanted more juice, so she poured some juice into his glass. Roland put his glass next to Fred's.

"Do you want more too?" Connie asked, pointing to the grapefruit juice.

"Yep, please," Roland answered with his sleepy head.

"You sure?" Connie wondered.

Connie poured juice into Roland's glasses. "Thanks," Roland said.

"I forgot to tell you something," Fred said. "Thanks for pouring me some grapefruit juice."

"That's ok," Connie said. She rubbed Fred's back. "I know you didn't like getting up so early this morning."

Fred smiled and looked at the plate; Connie knew that he was a shy person. Heather finished cooking and put a large plate of eggs, pancakes and bacon in the middle of the table to let everyone take it as they pleased.

"Honey," Heather called Bobby, "We better eat before leaving for Dulles soon."

Bobby was in the bathroom; he finished shaving and went to the bedroom to get a nice shirt. Bobby came in the kitchen and kissed Connie and Roland; he shook Fred's hand good morning.

Bobby sat down next to his wife and grabbed some eggs and pancakes and bacon. They all ate together. After breakfast was over, they rushed to put the dishes in the sink. Connie took the bag and let Fred take the suitcase. They went outside to Bobby's four-door Dodge Ram. Roland walked slowly because he was still so tired. Heather got her purse and came out of the house. Bobby unlocked the doors and let everyone in. Connie and Fred put their bas in the back of the truck, then sat in the back seat with Roland. Heather sat in the front seat. The last person in was Bobby; he was always calm and never felt rushed. Bobby started the engine and drove to Dulles Airport. It took about an hour from Culpeper.

When they arrived at Dulles, Bobby stopped by American

Airlines and let Connie and Fred out of the truck. He went to the rear door, opened it, and gave the luggage to Fred. Heather hugged and kissed Connie.

"Have a safe trip to California, ok?" Heather said, concerned.

"Ok," Connie said, "I'll be fine. Thanks, mom. Hey Roland, be a good boy for a week, ok?"

Connie hugged and kissed Roland too. Heather came to Fred and hugged him. Bobby hugged Connie hard.

"Connie," Bobby said, "I'd like you to tell Jeanette I said 'hello', ok? I'm sure she'll remember me from when I grew up with your grandmother. You and Fred have a safe trip. I hope everything will be worked out with Jeanette even though.... her old friend Maria already passed away."

Connie nodded her head. She knew it would be a shock for Jeanette to learn Maria was gone.

"Ok, Dad," Connie muttered, "I'll try my best to tell Jeanette about my grandmother passing away."

Connie hugged Bobby, Heather and Roland; they waved at Connie and Fred while they went through the doors. Bobby and Heather got back in the truck. Roland went in the back seat and fell asleep. Heather looked at Bobby.

"It's hard to believe," Heather said, "that Connie felt brave enough to meet Jeanette for the first time in a very long time."

"Yeah," Bobby said. "I guess it's time for Connie to tell Jeanette about her best friend Maria."

Bobby started the engine and left the airport.

Connie and Fred waited in line to check in. When they finally arrived at the desk and checked their luggage, Connie gave two tickets to the woman. She checked the computer and gave them their boarding passes for Gate 24. The woman told Connie and Fred that they would need to ride shuttle "D".

"Thanks," Connie said with ASL.

They walked to security, put their bags on the belt, and walked through the alarm system. They picked their things up and went to the shuttle. They sat and waited for other people to come in the shuttle. It started to go down and traveled to another the building.

The shuttle opened its doors and let people out. Connie and Fred rushed to find Gate 24. They found their gate and looked for two available seats. They sat near the window. Connie stood up and walked to the window. Fred wondered what was wrong with Connie. She turned to look at Fred, then she sat on the floor.

"What are you doing?" Fred asked.

"Well," Connie muttered, "it's hard to explain, but Jeanette's heart will be broken when she learns about my grandmother's death."

"I understand that," Fred nodded his head. "It will be difficult for Jeanette. I'm sure she'll understand."

The airline attendant announced it was time for boarding. People stood up, took their bags, and stood in line to give a woman their tickets. Connie and Fred followed people into the line. When it was their turn, she checked their tickets, ripped them and returned them to Connie. Connie and Fred boarded the plane and looked for their seats, which were almost at the end of the plane. Connie wanted to sit by the window, so Fred sat in the middle. Fred put the bags in the overhead compartments and sat next to Connie.

"I am positive about it," Connie sighed.

Fred smiled and held Connie's hand. Once the airplane was full, it started to leave the building. After waiting its turn for takeoff, the airplane finally started to move, going faster and taking off to the sky.

Chapter 28

The airplane traveled across the country for five hours. Connie was asleep, but Fred watched the movie. Connie woke up and looked out the window to see if they were landing in Los Angeles. She looked at Fred.

"Will we be there soon?" Connie asked.

"I don't know," Fred said. "I'll ask the stewardess if she knows."

Fred waved at the flight attendant, he took a napkin and pen, and asked how long until they arrived at Los Angeles. She read his note and wrote on the other side of the napkin. She gave it to Fred. He read the note to Connie.

"We'll be in Los Angeles in an hour."

"Thanks," Fred said clearly to the stewardess.

"I can't wait to get out of here," Connie said.

"Yeah, me too," Fred agreed.

About an hour later, the airplane started to descend. Connie and Fred looked at the Los Angeles area through the window. It was almost to arrive at LAX.

"Finally, we're there," Connie said, excited. "We'll have a good time together in L.A. for a week. First thing, we want to meet Jeanette, then we'll go travel around the Los Angeles area the rest of the week."

"Yes," Fred said. "We'll find Jeanette first and let her know that Maria is gone. I hope she'll take the news of her best friend's death all right."

The attendant checked each seat to make sure the tray was

closed and the passengers were buckled up for landing. Fred and Connie buckled their seat belts. Connie looked outside as the plane slowly arrived on land. People stood up and stretched their backs. They took their bags out of the storage compartment and waited for someone to open the door. A man opened it and let the people come out of the airplane. They walked through a tunnel to the building. Connie and Fred continued walking through a crowd of people through the large airport. They saw fast food restaurants and small stores, then Fred saw the sign "Baggage Claim" with an arrow pointing right. He told Connie to go on the right side. They walked and went down an escalator, and kept walking until they found the Flight 2624 baggage claim. The people waited for their luggage to show up. It took thirty minutes. A light finally flashed and the bags started rolling around. Fred and Connie looked for their blue suitcase. The blue suitcase showed up and Fred ran and grabbed the luggage.

"Good catch!" Connie laughed.

Connie and Fred went to Hertz Rental Car and asked for a mid-sized car for one week. After they signed some papers, they took the rental car. Connie looked at a map of the Los Angeles area and found Venice. It wasn't far from airport.

"We're so close to Venice," Connie said. "Go to Route 1 North. Keep going straight, then turn left on Venice Blvd. But I don't know if Jeanette's store is on the right or left side of Pacific Avenue."

"Don't worry about it," Fred said. "We'll find it."

Fred drove carefully on the road because the drivers were crazy and speeding. They found Venice Blvd., turned left and drove until they arrived at Pacific Ave. He found an available parking spot on the other side. Connie came out of the car first. She noticed Fred's legs were shaking. Connie knew that Fred was not used to driving on such a busy road, because he grew up in a small town in upstate New York.

"Are you all right?" Connie asked.

"Yeah," Fred muttered, "I'll get used to L.A. by he end of the week anyway."

Connie smiled and looked at the business card to find Jeanette's store. Connie decided to ask in any of the stores if they knew where Jeanette's store was located. Connie went in a restaurant and asked the host for directions to Jeanette's store. The host told them it was only a few blocks away from the restaurant. She went out front with Connie and Fred.

"Can you see a white building with light pink windows?" the woman asked, pointing to the building. "Just go past this building, go on the right and walk by a second building, then turn right again and look for a few cottages on the side."

"Cottages?" Connie asked, puzzled.

"Yes, that's where the business is," the woman nodded her head.

"Cool. Thanks!" Connie smiled.

Connie and Fred waved at the woman and walked to the cottages. There were three small cottages with different colors. Connie looked at the card for the number. It was number three.

"Three," Connie told Fred.

She looked for the number, and Fred noticed a large "3" painted in a hot green.

"I found it!" Fred said, pointing to the cottage.

"Good!" Connie said.

They walked to the cottage and came in the building. It was full of paintings on the walls, as well as different shaped pottery on the shelves. Connie saw a beautiful, jet green vase on a round table next to the front desk. A young woman with earthy clothes and a long brown pony tail went over to Connie. Fred patted Connie's back and pointed to the woman. Connie looked at her and read a badge that said "Kim".

"Can I help you?" Kim asked.

"Oh yes," Connie said. She showed Kim the business card with Jeanette's name on it.

"Is she here today?" Connie asked.

Kim nodded her head and told them to follow her. Kim waved at Jeanette who looked back at her.

"What?" Jeanette asked with her gesture.

Kim pointed to Connie and Fred. Jeanette looked at them.

"Are you Jeanette Collins?" Connie asked.

Jeanette was puzzled and nodded her head.

"Yes I am," Jeanette said with ASL. "How do you know me?

Do you want help with something?"

"I am Connie Scott," Connie introduced herself. "I am Maria's granddaughter. And this is my boyfriend Fred."

Jeanette was surprised felt like it was magic to be meeting Connie. She remembered Connie; she moved out to California when Connie was about four years old.

"Wow," Jeanette said. "You are such a beautiful woman now! How is your grandmother, Maria?"

"Thank you," Connie said. "My grandmother is fine, but..."

Jeanette turned her head up to the loft and told them to come with her upstairs. She missed Connie's last words explaining her grandmother went to Heaven. Connie looked at Fred's eyes; she did not finish talking.

"Come on!" Jeanette said, excitedly.

Connie and Fred followed Jeanette upstairs to the loft, where her office was. Jeanette told them to sit there and ran to a long table with pictures of Jeanette's children and grandchildren. She took some pictures to show Connie that she had grandchildren. Connie looked around the office; it was a cozy room with pinewood on the walls and a nice French window in the middle of the roof. Jeanette put her pictures on Connie's lap. Connie looked at the pictures of Jeanette's family, but she tried to tell Jeanette that she missed what Connie said. She looked at Fred for help.

"Cool it," Fred tried to calm her. "You'll be able to tell Jeanette about your grandmother's death."

Connie turned her head back to the pictures. Jeanette came to and sat down. Connie stood up and put the pictures on Jeanette's desk. Jeanette wondered why Connie's face looked so sad. She looked at Fred, but he didn't say anything. Jeanette looked back to Connie again.

"What's the matter with you?" Jeanette wondered.

"Ok," Connie muttered, "you missed my last words about my grandmother. She went to Heaven."

Jeanette was shocked.

"NO!" Jeanette yelled loudly.

The customers downstairs heard Jeanette's voice in the loft. Connie and Fred tried to calm Jeanette down. Connie did not realize that Jeanette was out of control with her emotions. Kim quickly came upstairs to the office. She looked at Jeanette standing between Connie and Fred; they held Jeanette's hands to calm her.

"Jeanette," Kim asked, "are you all right?"

"I'm fine," Jeanette said nodding her head. "I'm all right now, thank you, Kim."

Kim went downstairs to help the customers. Jeanette sat on the chair and told Connie that she wanted to go outside for some fresh air. Fred helped Jeanette go downstairs to the front door. Connie opened the door to let them all go outside. Connie closed the door shut. Jeanette pointed to the beach, indicating they could go there for a while. Jeanette held Connie's hand and they walked across the street to the beach together. Fred looked for an available table. He found one and let Jeanette sit there first, then Fred and Connie sat down. Connie looked at Jeanette's eyes touching hers.

"I am sorry," Connie signed, "to inform you about my grandmother's death."

"That's ok," Jeanette said, as she held Connie's hand. "It's just such a shock. I never expected it to happen."

Jeanette explained to Connie about her being an alcoholic for a long time after her husband was killed in Vietnam. Before things got any worse, a doctor ordered Jeanette to check into the Betty Ford Center for alcoholism. Now Jeanette had been sober for eighteen years and was successful in her life. They went back to Jeanette's store, and Connie and Fred walked around Broadway in Venice.

After five o'clock, Connie and Fred went back to see Jeanette at her store. They wanted to make sure was all right. They came in the store and looked up at the loft. Kim saw Connie and Fred looking up.

Kim came to Connie and asked, "Did you want to see Jeanette?"

"Yes," Connie replied. "I want see if Jeanette's all right."

"I'm sure that she's fine now," Kim said.

She knew Jeanette was in another room. Kim told Connie to wait while she got Jeanette. Kim found Jeanette and told her that Connie and Fred were waiting for her. Jeanette was surprised that Connie and Fred wanted to make sure she was all right. Jeanette told Kim she needed to finish packing something in a box to mail to a customer, but that she'd be out in a minute. Kim went back to Connie and Fred and told them Jeanette would be right out. Connie and Fred kept busy looking around at the paintings on the wall and the vases on the shelves. They waited for Jeanette to finish her task. Finally she was done and came over to Connie and Fred.

"I'm glad that you're still here," Jeanette smiled. "I think I'm going to fly east tonight. Would you mind dropping me off at the airport before ten this evening?"

Connie was surprised that Jeanette wanted to fly to Virginia at the last minute.

"I don't mind dropping you off as long as you tell me where." Fred said.

"Los Angeles International Airport," Jeanette replied, "just drop me off at United."

"No problem," Fred said.

Jeanette wanted Connie and Fred to follow her to her Malibu home. Jeanette cooked chicken with rice and French beans for their dinner that evening. While Connie and Fred ate dinner and put their dirty dishes in the dishwasher, Jeanette went to her bedroom upstairs and started to pack her clothes and personal things for her trip back east. She closed her suitcase on the floor and pulled it on its wheels down to the foyer. She put it near the door, walked to the kitchen and looked for Connie and Fred, but they weren't there. Jeanette thought they might be in the family room, because in there was a large window with a good ocean view. She went to the family room and saw them outside. Jeanette opened the side door to go outside and walked to Connie. She looked at Jeanette.

"It's such a beautiful view," Connie admired. "You're lucky you live here."

"Thanks," Jeanette smiled.

"Are you ready to go now?" Connie asked.

"Yes, I'm ready now," Jeanette replied. "I want to check the house before we leave, ok?"

"Sure thing," Connie said. "We'll take your luggage to our rental car and wait for you."

They went in the house and locked the side door. Jeanette turned the light off in family room. Connie and Fred went to the kitchen.

"Where's your luggage?" Fred asked.

"It's near the front door," Jeanette pointed to the foyer.

Fred and Connie went to the foyer, and Fred picked up the luggage. Connie opened the door to let Fred out. Fred put the suitcase in the trunk, and then he and Connie waited Jeanette to finish checking the house.

Jeanette made sure all the lights were out, except the one in her office, which she left on. She went outside and locked the front door, rushed and climbed in the rental car. Fred and Connie looked at Jeanette in the back seat.

"Is everything done now?" Connie asked.

"I guess it'll be all right," Jeanette replied.

"Let's go," Connie told to Fred.

Fred started the car and drove to the Los Angeles International Airport. There was bad traffic, so it took Fred an hour to drive there. He kept his eye on the road until they arrived at the airport. Connie thought they should park the car and go in to keep Jeanette company.

"Jeanette," Connie said, "we'd like to keep you company until you board your plane, ok?"

"Oh thanks!" Jeanette smiled.

Fred drove to departures and looked for United.

"Better go park there," Connie said, pointing to some parking.

Fred drove into the parking garage opposite United Airlines. He looked for parking but it was full, so he drove to the second floor. There was still no parking. Fred tried the third floor and found parking there. He parked close to the elevator. They got out of the car, grabbed Jeanette's luggage and went to the elevator, down to the main floor.

Jeanette warned Fred and Connie about L.A. drivers, and how the lanes for "departures only" were very crazy, especially in the evening. They crossed the street from the garage, being careful of traffic, to the airport.

"I think I go there," Jeanette said, pointing to a line for check-in, "to buy a ticket for the East Coast tonight."

Connie and Fred followed Jeanette to the line and waited for Jeanette to be called for service. The middle-aged couple left the counter. "Next," a woman called to them.

Connie told Jeanette to move up. Jeanette went to the attendant and put her luggage on the holder.

"I can't hear you." Jeanette pointed to her ear. Jeanette had made reservations earlier that day and pulled from her purse a piece of yellow paper with her reservation number written on it. Jeanette gave it to the woman. She checked the computer and found Jeanette's name on the list, then printed her round trip tickets for a return the next week. The woman wrote a note and gave it to Jeanette. They went through security to Gate D5 for Dulles Washington International. Jeanette sat next to the boarding entrance. Connie sat next to Jeanette and Fred stood up. Jeanette was tired from her busy day. She looked at Fred and Connie.

"I know this was all last minute," Jeanette said. "I haven't visited the East Coast since I left your grandmother's house. Can you believe it?"

"Wow, that's been a long time," Connie marveled.

A woman came over to Jeanette and told her the Seniors could board the plane first.

"Do you have your ticket with you?" the woman asked.

Jeanette nodded her head and showed the ticket to the woman. She took it and ripped the ticket before giving it back to Jeanette.

"Come with me," the woman smiled. "We can go in the airplane and find you a seat."

Jeanette and Connie stood up at the same time. Jeanette hugged Connie and Fred then went with the woman onto the airplane. But Jeanette forgot to tell Connie something. She ran back and came to Connie.

"I forgot to say something," Jeanette said. "Thank you very much for stopping by to see me. Thank you too, Fred."

"I'm so glad we were able to see you again after such a long time," Connie said softly.

"Yes," Jeanette smiled slightly. She took something from her jacket pocket and put it in Connie's hand.

"I never forgot that you looked like your father."

Connie was surprised Jeanette realized she and her father looked alike. She looked at her hand. It was fifty dollars. Connie looked at Jeanette quickly.

"Fifty dollars," Connie asked, "what's this for?"

"I don't have any change," Jeanette giggled. "It's to pay the parking. If there's any money left, then spend it with your cute boyfriend. I think I better go now. Bye!"

Jeanette hugged and kissed Connie's neck and Fred too.

"Thanks for the money," Connie said. "You have a safe trip. I love you."

Connie waved to Jeanette, who went with the woman down the tunnel to the airplane. Connie's eyes started to tear up. It felt so good to see Jeanette. Fred held Connie's shoulder; she moved her head to Fred's shoulder and cried.

"Are you ok?" Fred asked.

"Yes," Connie nodded her head slowly. "My heart is already breaking about Jeanette. But I'm glad that she's all right now anyway."

"Are you read to leave now?" Fred asked.

"Yes, I think so," Connie replied.

They walked through the crowd of people to the garage. They found their rental car. Fred unlocked the door and let Connie get in. He got in and drove to the booth to pay for parking. He gave the ticket to the man who told Fred the cost was $5 for the hour. Connie gave Fred the $50.

"I have five bucks in my wallet," Fred said. "Let's save the 50 for our week here, ok?"

Connie nodded and put the money back in her purse. Fred gave the man five dollars. They traveled through town when Connie suddenly remembered something she forgot to tell Jeanette.

"Oh no!" Connie slapped her head.

"What's wrong?" Fred asked, puzzled.

"I forgot to tell Jeanette," Connie signed, "that my grandmother wanted to give the 1964 Ford Thunderbird Convertible back to Jeanette. And Maria's ashes were thrown at the hill. I hope my father will tell her all that tomorrow."

"I'm sure he will," Fred said.

"I hope so," Connie thought.

They kept traveling to downtown L.A. and looked for a motel somewhere in the area.

The airplane flew up to the sky. A flight attendant came to Jeanette and asked her if she would like something to drink, but Jeanette didn't want anything. After a while, she changed her mind and asked for a cup of water to take her medicine. The woman poured water into a cup and gave Jeanette the cup and bottle of water. Jeanette thanked her. She took her medicine from her purse and took her pills with the water. She looked out the window, but it was too dark to see. She decided to close the window and fall to sleep.

Chapter 29

Overnight, some people slept on the seat, but others never felt comfortable enough to sleep on the seat. A little boy opened the blinds and saw the sunrise coming over the horizon; the sky turned light blue from dark. People started waking up and opening their small blinds to look outside. The stewardesses pushed a gray cart with coffee and juices first, followed by breakfast. The stewardess new Jeanette was deaf, so she rubbed Jeanette's shoulder. Jeanette woke up slowly and looked at the woman.

"Do you want something for breakfast?" the woman said with a gesture.

"Yes," Jeanette nodded her head.

"Fresh fruit or eggs?" The woman showed two different trays to Jeanette.

"Fresh fruit," Jeanette pointed. The stewardess removed the wrapper off the tray of a bowl of fruit and blueberry muffins. She put the tray next to Jeanette.

"Can I have some water, please?" Jeanette asked.

"I'll get it for you," the woman said.

She called another attendant to get a bottle of water, which they passed to Jeanette. She looked at her watch and saw it was past seven o'clock in the morning. After Jeanette was finished breakfast, an attendant collected the trays. Jeanette noticed people listening to an announcement that they would be arriving at Washington Dulles International Airport in a few minutes. Passengers started buckling their belts. Jeanette knew that they would arrive at any time. She looked outside the window, but

191

seemed unfamiliar with the area. She noticed mostly new buildings and highways. There was a construction boon since she left Virginia eighteen years ago. A few minutes later, Jeanette saw Dulles International Airport. She was confused because Dulles looked too big to her. Jeanette thought she'd never seen the airport before, but she knew that new buildings were added.

As the airplane descended, Jeanette kept looking outside. She was still shocked at all the change since she left. The airplane landed, and people stood up, took their bags out of the storage compartments and waited for the door to open. When it opened, people walked through the tunnel to the building. Jeanette followed the people to the Mobile Lounge Gate. She was amazed at the building's modern design. Jeanette continued to walk with the people and look around the halls; there were many new expensive stores and restaurants. Everyone went into the mobile lounge gate to take a shuttle to the Main Terminal. Jeanette couldn't remember riding a shuttle before.

When they arrived at the Main Terminal, the shuttle started to move up to connect with the building and let the people off to go to Baggage Claim. The long walk made Jeanette tired. She went downstairs and found her flight at the baggage claim. The suitcases were already there. Jeanette looked for her black suitcase, but couldn't find it anywhere. She finally grabbed a black suitcase when a man with a white jacket came over to Jeanette. He showed her a black suitcase with red tape.

"Excuse me, Madam," the man asked, "is this black suitcase yours?"

Jeanette looked at it and read the tag. It was hers.

"Yes, that's mine." Jeanette nodded her head.

She gave the other black suitcase to the man. He waved to Jeanette and went outside. Jeanette was kind of embarrassed because she took the wrong black suitcase. She decided to forget about it and look for National Car Rental on the same level. She found it and went to the counter to show a woman her reservation number for a car. She checked the computer and informed Jeanette she would be getting a large Dodge Intrepid for the week.

After Jeanette signed the paperwork, she told the woman that she didn't know how to get to Culpeper from Dulles. The woman took out a map and marked it with a yellow marker from Dulles to Culpeper and gave it to Jeanette. Jeanette rushed to catch the shuttle to the National rental cars. When Jeanette got off the shuttle, she walked into the office where someone showed Jeanette the car and said that the key was already inside. She opened the trunk, put her luggage away and closed it. Jeanette got in the car and drove onto Autopilot Drive. Jeanette looked for a sign for Route 28 South. She saw it and turned right, but she wasn't used to such aggressive drivers and thought she had better drive carefully here.

Jeanette got off I-66 west and onto Route 29 south. She was surprised at all the new buildings and stores now in the Culpeper area. She wasn't used to Culpeper because of all the changes, like new, wide roads, more buildings and new houses. It was no longer the same small town in which Jeanette grew up. Jeanette was trying to remember the road where Maria lived. She found the street and drove up it. She noticed the houses had new designs. There were second stories added, new brick exteriors and new trees and plants. She saw a house with two domes on the roof.

Jeanette drove slowly and looked for Bobby's house on the left side. She stopped by the third house and parked her rental car. She got out of the car and looked around the neighborhood. There were so many changes since Jeanette left eighteen years ago. Jeanette looked at the back of Bobby's house. There was a new screened in deck, and a new sidewalk leading to the deck. She walked toward the deck. There were two boys playing catch with their baseball gloves and ball. A boy saw the woman going to the house.

"Roland," the boy pointed to the woman, "look at that old woman going to your house."

Roland looked at the woman and ran over to Jeanette. She looked at Roland while he ran to her.

"Excuse me, Madam," Roland tried to call Jeanette.

Jeanette saw Roland running to her. Roland stopped and looked at Jeanette; he never saw her before.

"Do you want my father?" Roland asked.

Jeanette looked at Roland's face and recognized him from some pictures Connie showed.

"Are you Roland?" Jeanette asked. "Is your father Bobby

home?"

Roland didn't realize Jeanette was deaf.

"Are you deaf?" Roland asked. "Do you know my father?"

"Yes, I knew your father well," Jeanette replied.

Roland nodded his head and pulled Jeanette's hand toward the screened-in porch. Roland brought Jeanette in the kitchen and put his baseball glove on the table.

"Can you wait here?" Roland asked. "I'll find my father somewhere around this house. Right back, ok?"

"Ok, thanks." Jeanette smiled.

Roland came out of the kitchen and tried to call his father. Jeanette looked at the round table with an old cerulean blue plate on it. She remembered it was used for butter and had never forgotten the incident where she accidentally put her cigarette out into the butter. She looked at the kitchen, which had been renovated after Maria sold the house to her son, Bobby, seven years ago. Jeanette noticed the old oak wood cabinets and white tiles were changed to the new white vinyl cabinets and laminate floor. It was a brighter and cleaner looking kitchen. She noticed a picture of three people on the refrigerator. Jeanette walked over to the refrigerator and pulled the picture off. It was of Maria with her grandchildren, Connie and Roland. Jeanette hadn't seen what Maria looked like at Jeanette's age. Maria's hair was completely white and she was overweight.

Roland found Bobby in the basement fixing the bathroom sink with Heather. Roland came in the bathroom.

"Father," Roland said, "there's a deaf woman in the kitchen who says she knows you. I never met her before."

Bobby was puzzled and looked at Heather.

"Did she tell you her name?" Bobby asked.

"No, I forgot to ask," Roland said.

Bobby went upstairs into the kitchen and turned the light on. Jeanette screamed because the fluorescent lights were too bright when they reflected off the picture to her eyes. She dropped the picture to the floor and hid her hands from the light. Her voice scared Bobby, but he recognized it.

"Are you Jeanette?" Bobby asked, surprised.

Jeanette moved her hands away from her eyes and saw Bobby

standing next to Heather and Roland. Jeanette was surprised that Bobby's face looked almost the same as his father's, Ray. Bobby was older and gained weight. Heather was shocked that Jeanette showed up at their house right after Connie met her in California.

"Are you Bobby?" Jeanette wondered.

"Yes, that's me," Bobby nodded his head slowly.

Jeanette laughed and said she was glad to see Bobby after such a long time. She came over to Bobby and hugged him and Heather.

Chapter 30

Bobby told Jeanette that he added a new 6' x 6' screened-in porch so his father could relax outside. Bobby put an old fashioned lamp with chain to hang from the ceiling. It used to be in the old kitchen before the renovation. On one side of the porch was an old, white metal glider with two arms, like a sofa, which moved like a swing. There were three light green chairs on the other side. Jeanette sat on a chair near the corner. Bobby and Heather sat on the glider, and Roland sat on a small desk between the glider and brick wall. He played catch by himself with his baseball glove and ball. They listened to Jeanette tell her experiences from the past, when she left this house to move to California. It was hard for Jeanette to relive the hellish years of being an alcoholic - from when her husband Paul was killed in Vietnam until Maria beat her up. Jeanette felt out of control in her life and just had to move. She was a successful recovering alcoholic and quit smoking. She gained weight and was healthy.

Bobby and Heather told Jeanette about Ray and Maria's death. They described Ray's stroke from job stress, and how Bobby took over the business after he died. They told Jeanette that Maria retired, sold her business and bought a new house. They explained how shortly after that, Maria was diagnosed with leukemia.

Bobby said, "She fought for her life, but wanted to stop chemotherapy. She was ready to let go."

Jeanette wanted to visit Maria's grave and stood up to leave.

"I want to visit your mother's grave," Jeanette said. Bobby kept quiet and looked at Heather. Jeanette was puzzled at Bobby's behavior.

"Is something wrong?" Jeanette asked.

"You better tell her," Heather whispered to Bobby.

"Ok. My mom isn't in a grave," Bobby muttered.

Jeanette didn't quite believe him. "I want to know where your mother's grave is," Jeanette said seriously.

"My mother wanted her body cremated," Bobby explained. "Her ashes are scattered over the hill."

"What?" Jeanette wondered.

Roland waved at Jeanette; she looked at Roland's hand.

"Go to the hill," Roland said.

"What?" Jeanette was still baffled.

"My grandmother told me the story," Roland explained, "about how she used to go to the hill when she was little with another little girl. She never told me the girl's name, but told me they went to the hill for many years. That's why she wanted her ashes thrown over the hill."

It hit Jeanette's head like a hard rock. She flashed back to the past, when Maria and Jeanette were in a bad fight on the hill before Jeanette moved to west. Jeanette didn't want to go back to the hill, but she did want to see where Maria's ashes were scattered.

Jeanette pushed open the screen door and walked out. Bobby and Heather followed Jeanette outside to her rental car. Roland thought that he might go with Jeanette.

"Dad, can I join her?" Roland asked his father.

"I don't know. You can ask her," Bobby said.

Jeanette got in the car and closed the door shut. Roland ran to the car and waved at Jeanette. Jeanette looked at Roland and let opened the window.

"Can I join you?" Roland asked.

"Oh, that's nice of you to offer," Jeanette smiled, "but I prefer being alone at the hill. Thank you very much for asking me."

"Ok," Roland nodded his head.

He walked away from Jeanette. She watched Roland and knew that he wanted to join her to visit his grandmother. Jeanette looked at the old detached garage; the door was open about three feet and she noticed the back of a car with two round brake lights. She remembered she gave Maria that car before she moved to Northern

Virginia. Jeanette got out of the car.

"I know that car inside!" Jeanette pointed to the detached garage.

Roland looked back at her while she walked toward the garage. Bobby and Heather wondered what Jeanette was doing and followed Jeanette. Jeanette pulled the garage door open completely and looked at the old car under the car cover. She removed it from the car. Bobby and Heather came in the garage and looked at Jeanette. She was shocked that Maria had not sold this car. It was in very good shape. Jeanette came to the driver's side and looked at the mileage; it was still low.

She looked at Bobby quickly. "I didn't think this car would still be here," Jeanette said, surprised. "But it is! Bobby, what are you going to do with this car?"

Bobby did not say anything. Heather looked at Bobby and knew he didn't want to admit anything. Heather slapped Bobby's butt, making Bobby tell the truth about the car.

"Do you have something to tell me about this car?" Jeanette pointed to the car.

"Before she died, my mother told me," Bobby muttered, "that she wanted the car given back to you."

"What? Say it again?" Jeanette was confused.

"That car belongs to you now," Heather explained.

Jeanette was shocked. She didn't understand why Maria decided to give the car back to Jeanette. She walked around the car slowly and started to loudly weep. Jeanette thought it would better to leave the car with Bobby and Heather. She ran out the garage door to the rental car. Bobby and Heather followed Jeanette and tried to help her. Jeanette held her hands over her face because she didn't want them to see her face. Bobby pulled Jeanette to hug him. Heather rubbed Jeanette's back to calm her down. Jeanette finally put her hands down and looked at Bobby for a few seconds, then she laughed at him. Bobby looked at Heather and wondered what Jeanette found so funny.

"I'm all right now," Jeanette said, wiping the tears from her eyes. "I was shocked, that's all. I'm find now. Thanks, Bobby."

"Ok," Bobby said, still confused. "You scared me to death."

Jeanette started to laugh. Bobby and Heather laughed, too.

Roland didn't understand why they were all laughing. Jeanette stopped laughing and calmed her breathing down. She looked at Bobby slowly.

"Bobby," Jeanette said, "you remind me of your father and your daughter's personality. But that's good, so you don't have to be ashamed of yourself."

Jeanette started to laugh again. Bobby's face got a red at hearing his personality was the same as his father and daughter, Connie. Heather smiled and Jeanette stopped laughing again.

"I think I better go now," Jeanette said, trying to stop laughing. "I'll see you later, after I visit the hill, ok?"

Bobby nodded his head and opened the car door to let Jeanette in. He closed the door shut.

"Thanks." Jeanette said, blowing a kiss to Bobby.

Jeanette drove down the street and put her hand out the window to wave at Bobby, Heather and Roland. They waved back at Jeanette while she drove away.

Chapter 31

Jeanette still remembered how to get to the hill from Bobby's house, even thought a lot had changed. Jeanette drove for about twenty-five minutes, but it was not possible for the hill to be that far away. She thought she missed the road and turned back. She remembered the road was between an old house with a dull red barn and a small store with the rose in a large tire in front of the store. She thought the road was demolished for a new shopping center. She was upset that she couldn't find the road to the hill. Jeanette stopped by a 7-11 store and asked the clerk for directions to "the hill." He didn't understand her and thought that Jeanette was looking for the park. The man took a paper and pen and drew a map for Jeanette. It was directions on how to get to the park from the 7-11.

She got in the car and read the directions. She drove for about fifteen minutes until she saw a brown sign with a picture of a pine tree and table on the right side. Jeanette turned right and kept driving to the end of the road toward a parking lot. She looked and found an available parking near the picnic area. She parked her car there and came out of the car. Jeanette walked to the picnic area. She didn't remember that area with its new roads and picnic pavilion. She was disappointed with the government for ruining the environment. Jeanette decided to look for a path through the woods. She followed the path for an hour. It was hot and sunny outside, and she was no longer used to the humidity. She took off her thin jacket and held it on her arm. When the path ended, she continued to walk. Jeanette came up and down a hill and gave up looking for the hill. Her knees were sore from walking all day. She saw a tree over a hundred years old; it had plenty of shade. She decided to sit under the tree to avoid the sun. Jeanette walked under the branches and lay against the tree trunk. She was tired and took a nap for a while. When she awoke, she looked at the branches toward the hill. It looked familiar to her, like she had visited it before. Jeanette stood up and looked around the tree to see if it was the right one. She ran to the hill and looked back at the tree. It was the one she remembered. She looked up and started to walk up the hill. Jeanette looked at the hill where Maria's body ashes were scattered.

Jeanette was so thrilled to find the hill after eighteen years. She started to run slowly through the long grass that hadn't been cut for many years. She looked over the mountain. It was the same as before. Jeanette looked at the ground where they used to go for so many years.

In the summer of 1945, the weather was very nice and warm and sunny. Maria and Jeanette were teenagers playing "merry-go-round." They were rough and fast, and Sean kept filming the girls. They fell apart. Maria fell on the ground and shut her eyes; a few seconds later she opened them. She could see through the long grass up to the blue sky. Maria lifted her head up and was sad because the station wagon, as well as Sean and Jeanette, had disappeared. Maria stood up and ran to her blanket and books. It was gone. She looked around the hill. She did not expect to see Jeanette there. Maria was puzzled at Jeanette's body; Jeanette was over seventy years old and was wearing modern clothes. Maria wasn't used to seeing Jeanette dressed like that.

"Who are you? Where did you come from?" Maria asked, freaking out.

"I'm Jeanette Johnson," Jeanette said. "Do you remember me? We grew up together here."

"No," Maria said. "I don't understand what you're talking about. Where did you come from? I haven't seen those clothes before. They look so strange to me."

Jeanette looked at her clothes and knew that Maria was not in the future, when she had become old like Jeanette.

"Well," Jeanette explained, "I'm in the 21st century, and you're still in the early 20th century."

"What?" Maria asked, confused.

"You don't understand my point!" Jeanette screamed and turned her head down.

She was frustrated with Maria, because of their different ages. Jeanette tried explaining to Maria what they did in the past. She looked at Maria again. Jeanette was surprised that Maria was not a teenager any more; she was the same as Jeanette before she died. Jeanette wasn't used to seeing Maria that old. Maria had a full head of white hair, gained weight and was wearing comfortable clothes.

"I understand what you're talking about it." Maria said.

Jeanette was scared and nodded her head. Maria did not say anything about her fight with Jeanette.

"I knew that was wrong," Maria admitted. "I'm sorry. I didn't mean to fight with you. I knew both of us were wrong. I thought that we could forget about the past. Now we're back at the hill as friends, like old times."

Jeanette kept quiet and still nodded her head. Maria understood how Jeanette felt. Maria looked at the mountain.

"It's such a beautiful view," Maria raised her hand to the mountain.

Jeanette still nodded her head. Maria looked at Jeanette's eyes and knew Jeanette was afraid from the past.

"Please, would you like to talk to me?" Maria tried to be nice to Jeanette.

Jeanette had a hard telling if it was Maria, because she hadn't seen her for so long and was now talking to her soul.

"It's hard for me to talk," Jeanette muttered.

"Yes, what are you trying to say?" Maria asked.

"Can you forgive me for what happened in the past?" Jeanette was scared and looked at the ground.

Maria nodded her head and came over to Jeanette. Maria lifted Jeanette's chin to look in her eyes, which were full of tears.

"Yes, I forgive you, Jeanette," Maria said softly.

Jeanette sighed and hugged Maria. The soul became nothing and Jeanette fell to the ground and started to cry.

Go to the Hill

Jeanette slept on the hill for a few hours. When she awoke she saw it was almost seven in the evening. Jeanette got up and started to walk back to the parking lots. She went down the hill and looked at the old tree. Jeanette smiled. She was happy she made it to visit Maria's ashes on the hill before she went back to the West Coast.

Chapter 32

A quiet wind blew the trees and pines, moving them a little. The sun set and the weather became cooler. Jeanette kept walking on the path to the picnic area and sat on a bench. Her feet were sore from hiking all day. Jeanette saw it was now past eight o'clock. She rested a while then got up and walked to the car. She took out her directions and followed them back until she the 7-11 store on the right side. The drove to Culpeper and looked for a hotel downtown.

She found a Holiday Inn on Route 29 South. Jeanette parked her car near the lobby. Her feet were still sore, so she walked slowly to the lobby. Jeanette saw a woman at the front desk and saw her nametag said "Chrissie."

"Can I help you?" Chrissie asked.

"Paper and pen," Jeanette gestured.

"Sure!" Chrissie smiled. Chrissie took out a pad and pen and put it on the counter. Jeanette wrote a note and gave it to Chrissie. She read that Jeanette wanted a room for a week.

"Ok," Chrissie said. "I'll check the computer to see if we have a room available for the week. It'll only take a second, ok?"

Jeanette nodded her head. Chrissie an available room.

"Good, you got it in," Chrissie smiled.

Jeanette felt like she needed to take a nap.

"Cash or credit?" Chrissie asked.

"Credit," Jeanette said.

Jeanette took a credit card out of her wallet. Chrissie swiped the card and waited for approval. It was approved. Chrissie gave the card back to Jeanette and pulled a paper for her to sign from the printer. Jeanette signed her name, and Chrissie gave her a key for to a room.

"127," Chrissie pointed to the number on the tag. "It's on the first floor. Walk past the doors and turn left outside."

"Thanks," Jeanette said.

Jeanette left and went outside to her rental car. She grabbed her luggage and came back to the hotel. She looked for room "127", found it and unlocked the door to go in. She put her purse on the dresser and sat on the bed. She took off her shoes and lay down for a nap.

When Jeanette woke at 10:30 p.m., she was hungry. She decided to get something to eat for dinner. Her body was still used to West Coast time. She put her shoes back on, took her purse and left the room to go to the front desk. Jeanette looked for Chrissie, but she wasn't working that evening. A man was at the front desk. His name was Don, and he was about twenty years old; he was tall with a shaved head.

"Paper and pen," Jeanette asked with a gesture.

Don took out some paper and pen. Jeanette wrote that she wanted to know if there was a 24-hour restaurant nearby. Don nodded his head and wrote the name of a restaurant named Ola Mae's Diner on South Main Street, near Walters Street and Orange Road. Jeanette wasn't sure if she had eaten there before.

"Thanks" Jeanette said.

Jeanette walked toward her rental car and drove to South Main Street until she saw a sign for Ola Mae's Diner. She parked her car there and walked to the restaurant. She looked at the other stores on the street, but didn't recognize them. She came in the restaurant. It was a little crowded that evening. She saw an available stool at the bar. The host came to Jeanette. She pointed to the bar asking if she could eat there. The host said "sure" and let Jeanette sit there. The waitress at the bar gave Jeanette a menu and asked her what she wanted to drink. She wanted a glass of water with a slice of lemon. The waitress put the glass of water on the counter next to Jeanette. She read the menu and chose a chicken salad with fruit. Jeanette pointed to the menu and showed the waitress what she wanted to order. The waitress took her order gave it to the cook.

Jeanette looked around the dining room; there were many people talking to each other. Jeanette had forgotten that this was the same restaurant she came to with her friends a long time ago. A few minutes later, the waitress put a large bowl of chicken salad on the counter and napkin wrapped around a fork and knife. Jeanette took her medicine before she started eating her dinner.

Jeanette left the restaurant. She planned on going back to her car, but she changed her mind and decided to take a nice walk downtown. Main Street had a new design of lights and there were new traffic lights. It was bright enough to see the sidewalk and stores. Jeanette looked at a store where she used to personal things, but it was now a new store. She was disappointed. Jeanette looked back at the other side of stores. She remembered Maria's beauty shop used to be there. Jeanette walked and looked for the beauty shop. She found it on South East Street. She crossed the street and looked in the window. It was too dark to see clearly, but she could tell it had been redesigned.

Jeanette decided to go back north and look for the bar where she used to hang out every Friday with her sisterhood. Jeanette could not find the Bar; it was closed and had moved to another part of town. Jeanette felt tired and needed to go back to her rental car. She walked back to the parking lots near the restaurant. It took about twenty minutes to walk there.

Finally she made it back, got in the car and left for the hotel. Driving, she passed a blue sign of "H" and thought she'd go see her old job at the Culpeper Regional Hospital. She turned left on Sunset Lane and saw the hospital on the right side. It had the same old building, but new buildings were added on the other side. She had good memories of her work and coworkers while she was employed there so many years ago.

She left the hospital and drove to the hotel. Jeanette walked in her room, sat on the bed and took her shoes off. Her feet got sore again from the long walk downtown. Jeanette had to take it easy at her age. She started to walk slowly to the bathroom and took her medication; she took it with a cup of water. Jeanette looked at herself in the mirror. She couldn't believe how much the town had changed.

She changed into her nightclothes, turned the light off in the bathroom and walked to the bed. Jeanette pulled the blanket opened and lay down. She turned the light off and tried to fall asleep. She really wanted to see her old yellow house the next morning. She wondered if it was still there.

Chapter 33

In early the morning, a light fog was over the grass near the road. The sunrise started to light up the sky a little after five a.m. People were driving to Washington, DC to go to work. An hour later, the lights on the main street turned off automatically.

The sun came through the curtain and touched Jeanette's face. She woke up and tried to block the sun with her hand. Jeanette got out of bed and went to the window. She pulled the curtain open too see outside.

"What a beautiful day," Jeanette thought.

She took a shower, put on nice clothes and went to a café for a small breakfast of coffee, bagel and fresh fruits. She still remembered how to get the yellow house. Jeanette decided to leave the hotel right away. She went to the car and drove north on Route 29 and kept taking the roads that led to her old house. Jeanette found the dirt road and looked at the farm area, which now had some new houses. Jeanette passed the curve and drove slowly until she found the yellow house on the right side. Because there was no shoulder, she had to park her rental car on the dirt road. She came out the car and walked to the gate. She stood and looked at the yellow house. The yellow house was about a half-mile from the gate. The trees in the driveway had grown tall. She remembered when Paul and the three girls planted the year-old trees.

Jeanette felt like homesick and wished she could buy that house, but she knew that wasn't practical. Jeanette saw a couple of people come out of the house and look at her standing by the gate. She decided to leave the yellow house before they came over to her. She got back in the car and drove back to Route 3.

Jeanette decided to find the house where she grew up. She drove passed the downtown and looked for the house. She saw the house with two pines. She moved slowly and looked at the front of the house. She was surprised that it was still in good shape. Jeanette knew that the owner must have been taking very good care of the house. She felt good and was glad to see her childhood home. She looked across the street to see Culpeper High School. She surprised to see it was no longer a school. It was another business district. Jeanette figured the high school was moved to another part of town.

A Chapter for O.W.L.S. Sorority was at Bonnie's house. She had six women there, all in their 70s. DeeDee and Linda were talking about the past. Vicky sat on a white chair under the tree and drank some ice tea. Kathy, Angel and Bonnie were sharing their good memories of Gallaudet College.

"Do you remember that girl," Linda said, "I forget her name, but she was of medium height with red head hair."

"Oh yes, it was Lynn!" DeeDee answered.

"Yes, that's it," Linda laughed. "Lynn was so crazy! When some boys were standing at the door at Fowler Hall, she poured a bowl of hot water on them from her bedroom window."

They women were laughing so hard. Bonnie stood up.

"We were young girls," Bonnie laughed. "We were too wild and picked up boys during our freshmen year."

Bonnie walked to the table with a bowl of ginger and vanilla ice cream; she picked the up the spoon and poured some ginger into the cup. Karen saw a white car parking in the street.

"Who's that woman in the car?" Karen pointed.

The women looked back to the car while a woman came out and looked at them.

"I don't know who she is," Vicky pointed. "Better ask Bonnie, not me!"

Angel waved to Bonnie then pointed to the woman walking towards the party.

"She must have lost her mind on the road!" Bonnie said, puzzled.

She walked to the woman. As they got closer together, Bonnie recognized the woman's eyes. It was Jeanette.

"Are you Jeanette?" Bonnie asked.

Jeanette was surprised to see Bonnie, who was thin with white hair.

"Yes, that's me." Jeanette nodded.

Bonnie dropped the cup and hugged Jeanette. Bonnie was so happy to see Jeanette because it had been such a long time.

"Jeanette is here!" Bonnie called.

The women were shocked and surprised that Jeanette showed up at the party unexpected. They ran over to Jeanette and Bonnie. DeeDee, Vicky and Angel stopped and looked at Jeanette's face. They hugged Jeanette hard. Kathy didn't know who she was. Karen stood up and walked over to them.

Jeanette looked at Karen.

"Do you remember Karen O'Hara," Bonnie asked Jeanette. "She was our O.W.L.S. Sorority advisor at Gallaudet a long time ago."

Jeanette did not remember Karen's face because of her age, but she did remember that Karen helped Maria when Maria was stressed about her classes and the Sorority.

"You helped Maria, right?" Jeanette asked.

"Yes, that's right!" Karen smiled and hugged to Jeanette.

"What a surprise!" Vicky said excitedly.

"Yeah," Jeanette smiled. "I'm glad to see all of you here. It was a perfect time to get together again. What are you doing here today?"

"It's the Chapter Sorority party," Bonnie said.

"O.W.L.S.?" Jeanette wondered.

"Yes!" Bonnie laughed.

Jeanette was surprised that they were having a Sorority party at Bonnie's house. Bonnie asked Jeanette to find a place to sit and have some iced tea or ginger with ice cream. Jeanette pointed to the pitcher of iced tea. Bonnie poured a glass and gave it to Jeanette. She went and sat down on the chair. DeeDee and Angel sat near Jeanette.

"How long are you staying here?" DeeDee asked.

"For a week," Jeanette said. "I came here at the last minute.

Go to the Hill

Right after Connie visited my work in California and informed me Maria passed away. It hurts so bad that I didn't have a chance to see her before she died."

"Yes, I understand how you feel about Maria," Bonnie nodded.

"Are you all right now?" Angel asked. "I mean did you stop drinking. I forget where you went to get clean in California."

"The Betty Ford Center," Jeanette answered.

"That's it," Angel said. "Was it worth the trip?"

"Yes, of course," Jeanette explained. "It was rough the first year. After that, I started a new life with a new husband, Scott. But he passed away six years ago of natural causes."

"Oh that's sad," Angel said. "Same thing happened with my husband, Andy. He had a brain tumor. He suffered terribly until he died at the hospital two years ago."

Jeanette felt sorry to hear about Angel's husband's death from a tumor. Most of their husbands passed away a few years. They were catching up on news since Jeanette left Culpeper eighteen years ago. They were glad to see Jeanette again. Bonnie told Jeanette that she had reservations at Hazel River Inn Restaurant at five o'clock. Bonnie called the manger to add another chair for Jeanette. Jeanette was happy to join them for dinner. Bonnie smiled and hugged Jeanette and welcomed her back again.

They went to Hazel River Inn Restaurant in downtown Culpeper. They had a good time tasting wine and cheese until their table was ready. They ordered dinner and talked for four hours. The restaurant was closing, so they had to leave. Bonnie wanted them to go to 401 South Night Club on S. Main Street. They agreed with Bonnie's suggestion and went to the bar to talk more. A few hours later, Karen and Vicky were almost asleep at the Bar. Vicky told them that she wanted to go home soon. They left the bar and wen to their cars.

"I need someone to help me," Jeanette asked. "Is anyone willing to drive with me to Dulles Airport to drop off the rental car?"

"How will you get around without a car?" Bonnie asked.

Jeanette explained, "Bobby told me that before she died, Maria wanted to give back the 1964 Thunderbird."

"How sweet," Bobbie nodded. "I don't mind following you to

Dulles to drop off your rental car. Then I'll bring you back with me, ok?"

"Thanks, I appreciate that," Jeanette smiled and hugged Bonnie.

Angle, Vicky and DeeDee came to Jeanette.

"I'm so glad to see you again," Angel said. "Hope to see you tomorrow afternoon. Take care of yourself. I love you." Angel hugged Jeanette and walked to Bonnie's car.

Vicky came to Jeanette. "Thanks for visiting us again," Vicky said and hugged Jeanette. "See you later. I love you and good night. Bye." Vicky left Jeanette and walked to Bonnie's car.

DeeDee came to Jeanette. "Good to see you again," DeeDee said. "What a surprise. I hope we can get together again before you leave with your old car back across the country. Ok?"

"See you tomorrow," Jeanette said. "We'll get together again before I leave next Monday."

DeeDee smiled and hugged Jeanette, then went to Bonnie's car.

Karen came to Jeanette and didn't say much since she didn't know Jeanette as well. "Nice to see you again," Karen said. "We'll talk later. Take care of yourself and good night. Bye."

Karen hugged Jeanette, walked to her car and waved. Jeanette waved back to Karen. When Bonnie left, everyone in her car waved to Jeanette. She felt glad to see them after eighteen years. Jeanette got in the rental car and drove through town back to the hotel.

When Jeanette arrived at the hotel, she looked at the sky, but there weren't many stars. Jeanette was disappointed; she wanted to see the stars so badly. She walked through the lobby to her room. She came in the room and looked in the mirror. Jeanette couldn't believe she saw the sisterhood at Bonnie's house. She had a good time to spending time together with them all day.

Chapter 34

Bonnie wanted Jeanette to stay at her house for the rest of her visit, so Jeanette checked out of the hotel and drove to Bonnie's house. There was much less traffic after nine in the morning on Route 29. Jeanette went to Bonnie's house and stood in the kitchen. Something smelled good. She looked at the table and saw that Bonnie made French Toast. There was also half a grapefruit for breakfast. Bonnie put two glasses on the table and looked at Jeanette.

"Please sit here for a good breakfast," Bonnie smiled. Bonnie pulled out a chair for Jeanette to sit on. Jeanette had not started to eat her breakfast.

"What's the matter with you?" Bonnie asked.

"Well," Jeanette muttered, "I want to drop the rental car of at Dulles Airport right away."

"Don't worry about that," Bonnie said, rolling her eyes. "It's better for you to eat the French Toast before it gets cold."

After breakfast was done, Bonnie took the dishes to the sink. They left the house, and Bonnie followed Jeanette's rental car to the airport. It took about an hour, but when they got there, Jeanette parked the car and told Bonnie to wait for her. Jeanette went to the office and informed a man that she was returning the rental car early. He canceled a few days and refunded some money. She came out of the office and climbed in Bonnie's car. They headed back to Culpeper.

Before they arrived in Culpeper, Jeanette told Bonnie that she needed to get a new license plate at the DMV. Bonnie agreed to take Jeanette. They parked the car and walked into the DMV. Bonnie pointed Jeanette to an information desk that would give Jeanette a form to fill out for a new registration and tags for the 1964 Ford Thunderbird convertible. Jeanette paid for the new registration and license plate tags, and they left.

Jeanette asked Bonnie to drive to Bobby's house so she could pick up the car. Bonnie told Jeanette that she'd need a temporary insurance card before driving the car across the country next week. Jeanette thought she'd call her insurance company in California to find out what to do. When they arrived at Bonnie's house, Jeanette tried to walk right in, but it was locked. Bonnie laughed because Jeanette was so anxious to call her insurance agent. Bonnie unlocked the door and let Jeanette in.

Jeanette put her purse on the table and took out her wallet. She found her insurance card and called. She told the insurance agent in California that she got a car in Virginia she wanted to drive back The agent told Jeanette that she needed a temporary insurance card, which they'd get to her within 24 hours. Jeanette could not drive the Ford without the insurance. She gave them Bonnie's address to mail the car. She was upset that she had to wait 24 hours before she could get the car. Bonnie told Jeanette that it was fine. Bonnie would take Jeanette wherever she wanted to visit.

The weather became stormy and it started to rain heavily. The rain came in the window of the guestroom, where Jeanette was napping. She smelled the rain and woke up to look out the window. She hadn't seen such a heavy rainstorm in many years. She felt so thrilled to smell the rain.

Suddenly the window was shut. Jeanette was puzzled and saw Bonnie.

"The floor will get wet," Bonnie said, upset. "I don't want to ruin my hardwood floor."

Jeanette looked at the floor; a lot of water came in while she slept. Her socks got wet too.

"Bonnie," Jeanette spoke slowly, "I'm so sorry that I didn't close the window, but I didn't know it was supposed to rain."

"I forgot," Bonnie nodded her head, "that you thought you were still in California."

Jeanette and Bonnie started to laugh. Bonnie went to the hall and got a towel to wipe the floor dry. Jeanette helped Bonnie clean up. After the floor was dry, Bonnie thanked Jeanette and walked out of the bedroom. Jeanette watched Bonnie going downstairs. It was still raining outside. Jeanette wanted to open the window again, but knew Bonnie would get upset. Jeanette decided to go outside. She changed to dry socks, put on her shoes and went downstairs to the front door. Jeanette stepped onto the porch and walked outside. She stood raised her arms up. She opened her mouth to taste the rain, which she missed for such a long time.

Bonnie was in the living room when she saw the light flash from the ringing phone. She came to the kitchen and answered the phone on the TDD. It was Vicky. She wanted Bonnie and Jeanette to join her for dinner at her house at five that afternoon. After she got off the phone, Bonnie went upstairs to find Jeanette, but she wasn't there. Bonnie looked all over the house for Jeanette until she found her in the foyer. Bonnie looked at Jeanette, who was completely soaked from the rain outside.

"What are you doing?" Bonnie asked, puzzled.

"I miss my rain," Jeanette smiled.

"That's all right," Bonnie sighed. "Vicky called me recently, inviting us to dinner at her house at five o'clock."

"Great, I think I better change," Jeanette said, heading up the stairs.

Bonnie laughed at Jeanette in her wet clothes. Jeanette went to the bedroom, took off her clothes and hung them on the tub in bathroom. She put dry clothes on.

The rain became light and the sun broke through the clouds. Bonnie gave an umbrella to Jeanette.

"I don't need that," Jeanette complained.

"Ok," Bonnie said passively, "I'll take it with me in case it rains again."

They drove to Vicky's house in a half-hour. When they arrived, Jeanette was surprised that the house was the same color it was many years ago. Vicky saw them and came outside alone. Bonnie and Jeanette got out of the car, walked toward Vicky, and hugged each other.

"DeeDee and Angel will be here soon," Vicky said.

215

Vicky opened the door to let Bonnie and Jeanette in the house, but Bonnie wanted Jeanette to go in first. Jeanette walked in the foyer, and Vicky showed Jeanette the family room and kitchen. Both were remodeled and newly painted. She guided Jeanette to the dining room. The table and eight chairs, as well as the hutch, were the same since Vicky got married. Vicky saw DeeDee and Angel come in the kitchen. They hugged each other and started to cook together. The table was already set with plates, forks, spoons, knives and glasses. Vicky put a pound of ham with pineapples and cherries into the stove. It cooked for an hour. Angel and Bonnie made potatoes and beans. DeeDee and Jeanette made a large bowl of Jell-O with real fruit. They ate dinner and cleaned up the kitchen. They went to the family room and talked about old times at Gallaudet. Vicky's eyes became tired and she looked at her watch. It was passed midnight.

"Good morning everyone!" Vicky joked.

They didn't understand Vicky's joke until they checked their watches. Then they looked at each other, hugged and went home.

Federal Express came to Bonnie's house the next day. The delivery man had a package for Jeanette. He rang the doorbell, which flashed inside. Bonnie looked at the flashing light from the front door. She opened the door; the delivery man gave the package to Bonnie and pointed where she needed to sign. She closed the door and went upstairs to the bedroom. Jeanette was in the bathroom, so Bonnie put the package on the bed and left the room.

Jeanette came out of the bathroom. She walked to the window and looked outside for the Federal Express truck. She was upset that it hadn't arrived yet; she wanted the insurance card to travel back to the West Coast next Monday. Jeanette sat on the bed and put her hand down. At that moment, she felt something funny with her hand. She looked at her hand. It was the package from Federal Express! Jeanette ripped it open and took out the card. She ran downstairs to look for Bonnie in the family room. She showed the card to Bonnie.

"Great! Let's get the Thunderbird now!" Bonnie said excitedly.

"Yes! I'm ready now!" Jeanette cheered.

She acted like a child and ran upstairs to get her purse with the plate tags, then went downstairs. Bonnie laughed at Jeanette and went to the kitchen to find her own purse. She went outside and waited for Jeanette. Jeanette came out, and they drove off to Bobby's house.

When they arrived at Bobby's, Jeanette jumped out of the car and walked to the detached garage. She pulled the door open. Bonnie walked and looked at the car inside; she was surprised that it was in such good shape. Bonnie looked all around the car. "It's in good shape," Bonnie admired.

"Yeah, I know," Jeanette nodded.

A shadow came over the car. Bonnie and Jeanette looked up, but they couldn't see the person's face because the sun blocked it. Jeanette knew it must be Bobby.

"Hey Bobby," Jeanette said. "I need your help in changing the license plates, please."

"Sure, I'll get a screwdriver," Bobby said certainly.

Bobby went to the house and came back with a screwdriver. He changed the plates. Jeanette got in the car and Bonnie sat in the front seat. Jeanette started the engine. It sounded so smooth.

"I'll call the gas station," Bobby said. "They can tow your car there."

Jeanette looked at Bonnie because she didn't know what Bobby was talking about.

"Why?" Jeanette asked, puzzled.

"The inspection is passed due and it needs a new one." Bobby pointed to the yellow pad on the windshield. It was from five years ago.

"Oh, that explains it," Bonnie said. "Yes, you need to get this car inspected."

Jeanette didn't realize that the state of Virginia required all cars get inspected every year. Bobby went back to his house and called the gas station, requesting someone come and tow the car there. A mechanic drove to Bobby's house and picked Jeanette's car up; Jeanette and Bonnie rode with him to the gas station. It was close to Bobby's house. When they arrived at the station, the mechanic lowered the car down and drove it in the garage. Bonnie told Jeanette that it would probably cost $10 for the inspection. The mechanic checked the tires, lights and brakes completely. It passed inspection.

"Your car's done," the man said. "The price is $10.00, cash or card, either way you want to pay for it."

Jeanette gave $10 to the man. Jeanette and Bonnie got in the car and drove back to Bobby's house. Bonnie got out of the car and climbed into her own car. She followed Jeanette to her house.

When Jeanette and Bonnie arrived at the house, Jeanette parked the car on the street. Bonnie parked her car near the house. She came out the car and looked at Jeanette still sitting in the car. Bonnie walked close to Jeanette's car.

"What are you doing in the car?" Bonnie asked.

"My car needs a wash and to be cleaned inside," Jeanette said. "I'll be back in an hour or so. Ok?"

"Ok, see you later," Bonnie nodded her head.

Jeanette drove downtown to look for a car wash. After the car was shiny and clean inside and out, Jeanette went back to Bonnie's house and parked next to Bonnie's car. Jeanette looked at the Thunderbird. It was so handsome! She was glad that the car belonged to her again.

Chapter 35

On Sunday morning, the fog was drifted away from a pond to cover the land near the house. The sky was dull with blue and gray mixed together and a full moon. Bonnie came in Jeanette's bedroom. She woke Jeanette and asked her to join her for church. Jeanette didn't mind going with Bonnie. She took a shower and put on a nice dress. She went to the kitchen for a small breakfast of coffee and a muffin. Bonnie drove with Jeanette to church in the morning. Jeanette hadn't seen that church in so long.

When they arrived, Bonnie saw Angel's car and parked next to it. Jeanette got out of the car and walked with Bonnie towards the church. Bonnie told Jeanette that the church added a new building last year for extra rooms and a meeting room. They walked in the church toward the front bench to sit with Angel, Vicky, DeeDee and Karen. Jeanette recognized some members she knew before. Angel told Jeanette about the new members and the preacher. They stayed at church until noon. Bonnie told Jeanette that every Sunday after the church, they went to Jenner's Family Restaurant for a breakfast buffet. Jeanette wanted to go with her friends. They went to the restaurant on Main Street and met other hearing people from church. They ate together for an hour.

Bonnie and Jeanette went home. Jeanette told Bonnie that she wanted to visit Maria's body at the hill before she traveled back home the next day. Bonnie agreed with her. Jeanette went to the bedroom and changed to casual clothes and sneakers for hiking up the hill. She went to the kitchen and got some bottles of water. Bonnie came in the kitchen from the family room.

"Good luck getting there," Bonnie said. "Be careful while you're walking in the woods. See you later."

Bonnie hugged Jeanette and left her alone. Jeanette walked out of the house to her car, and drove to the park. When Jeanette got to the park, she kept driving until the end of the road. She wanted to continue driving through the woods, but it was too rough on her car. She parked her car, got out and hung the bottles of water on her shoulder. She put on a hat to block the sun and started to walk through the woods.

After an hour of walking, she remembered her way. She saw the old tree and the hill. She felt so good that she made it there. She walked up the hill and stopped a few minutes to catch her breath before the long hike. Then she walked to the middle of the hill, where she used to stop because it was the best place to view the mountain. Jeanette sat and lay on the ground to rest a while. She smelled the grass then drifted to sleep.

The clouds were moving to the west and it started to rain. Raindrops hit Jeanette's face; she woke up slowly and looked up at the cloud. It was dark gray. Jeanette was surprised that the sunny day suddenly turned rainy. She stood up and ran down the hill to the tree. She was out of breath from running. She looked at the branches swaying hard. She was scared a bad storm was coming. Jeanette wrapped her arms around the tree trunk and shut her eyes to protect herself. The rain slowly trickled off. Her eyes started to open and she looked at the sky. It was clear, and sun came through the clouds. Jeanette walked out from under the tree. Her clothes were wet and she started to laugh, thinking that was so funny. She went up the hill and saw a rainbow in the sky.

She screamed to Maria. "Thank you, Maria, for saving my life!" Jeanette shouted to the sky.

She opened her arms and let the wind blow on her face. She felt so full of joy in her life. She saw the sun going down the mountain. She would have to leave before dark. Jeanette rushed through the woods for another hour and arrived at the parking lot before dark. "Thank God!" she said. She got in the car and left the park. Jeanette rushed to Bonnie's house. Jeanette knew that Bonnie would be worried about her in the bad storm.

Bonnie stood on the porch, worried that Jeanette got stuck in the storm or lost in the woods. Bonnie bit her bottom lip and walked around the porch. She would call the police if Jeanette wasn't back soon. Bonnie went in the house when headlight beams hit her. She looked at the car was relieved to see it was Jeanette. Jeanette parked next to Bonnie's car and saw Bonnie walking over to her. Jeanette saw Bonnie's eyes and knew she must have been so worried.

"Are you all right," Bonnie asked anxiously. "I thought you were lost in the woods during the bad storm this afternoon."

"Yes, I was in the woods when it rained," Jeanette signed. "I got safely out of the park and feel all right now. Thank you very much for your concern."

Jeanette hugged Bonnie, and they went in the house together. Jeanette went upstairs to her bedroom, took off her wet clothes and put a robe on. She went to the bathroom and filled the big old tub with warm water. Bonnie came in the bedroom to look for Jeanette, but she wasn't there. Bonnie saw the bathroom light was on, so she went to the bathroom and flicked the light switch and she stood by the door. Jeanette stopped the water and walked over to Bonnie at the door.

"Yes, what is it?" Jeanette asked.

Bonnie said, "Bobby called me this afternoon and wanted to know if you'd like to stop by his house tomorrow for a farewell party."

"Oh! That's so nice of Bobby," Jeanette said, surprised. "I'd like to go there tomorrow morning!"

"Sounds good. We're supposed to be there by 10 a.m., ok?" Bonnie smiled.

Bonnie left the bathroom and let Jeanette take a bath. Jeanette turned the water on again and filled the tub. She removed her robe and got in the tub. It felt so good to relax. Jeanette looked at the window with a long lace curtain, through which she could see outside. She leaned her head back and put her arms on the tub. She napped a while. She was so glad to see Maria at the hill.

Chapter 36

Jeanette packed her clothes into her suitcase. Bonnie came in the bedroom and watched Jeanette pack. Bonnie came over and helped Jeanette put the suitcase on the floor. Jeanette looked at Bonnie's face and felt like she already missed her. Jeanette knew this was the last time she'd see Bonnie and the sisterhood. Jeanette hoped they would visit her in California. Bonnie hugged Jeanette hard. They started to cry. Bonnie didn't want to see Jeanette leave Culpeper at noon.

They went to Bobby's house. Jeanette saw her friends standing and talking outside. Vicky saw Bonnie and Jeanette on their way over.

"Bonnie and Jeanette are here now!" Vicky pointed.

Angel, DeeDee, and Karen looked at Bonnie and Jeanette. Vicky went over to Jeanette, followed by DeeDee and Angel.

Jeanette got out the car. Vicky hugged Jeanette, then DeeDee and Angel hugged her. It was hard for Jeanette to control her emotions and she started to cry. Bobby opened the screen door and waved at Jeanette.

"Please come here," Bobby said.

Jeanette walked with her sisterhood to the porch. Bobby held the screen door open for Jeanette to come in. Jeanette hugged Bobby. Heather came out of the kitchen to the porch and hugged Jeanette hard. She knew that Heather would miss her a lot. Heather remembered Jeanette when she was in Heather's wedding.

"I'll miss you!" Heather said.

"Yes, me too," Jeanette nodded and hugged Heather again.

Heather held Jeanette's hand and brought her to the kitchen. Jeanette smelled bacon, and the smell was making her hungry. She noticed there was a long rectangular table surrounded by eight chairs. She was surprised that Bobby put it in the kitchen.

"I remember that old table," Jeanette said, pointing to the table. "Why'd you keep the table?"

"I like it," Bobby giggled. "I use it for special occasions, like today you know."

"Yeah, it make sense," Jeanette agreed. "A round table would be too small for us."

Heather pulled out a chair for Jeanette, who sat down and moved closer to the table. Bobby put eggs, toast and bacon on a large platter then put it all on the table. Bobby told the women to have a seat. They sat near Jeanette. Heather and Bobby gave plates to the women. Vicky stood up and put some foods on two plates for Heather and Bobby. Angel pulled two chairs for them sit down.

"That's ok," Bobby laughed. "Heather and I will take care of ourselves."

"No, you and Heather need to rest for now and have a seat here," Angel pointed to the chairs.

Heather hit Bobby's arm with her elbow. "Let's sit down and let them do this for us," Heather whispered.

"Ok, fine with me," Bobby admitted.

They sat down and moved closer to the table. Vicky put the plates on the table and poured grapefruit juice into each glass. Vicky put the juice away and sat down her chair. Everyone was silent. Jeanette moved her eyes around to the people at the table. She looked at Bonnie.

"What are we doing now?" Jeanette asked.

Bonnie moved her head down and giggled; she thought Jeanette was so funny. Jeanette was puzzled and kicked Bonnie's leg.

"I don't mean to laugh at you," Bonnie laughed.

"What did I do?" Jeanette asked, confused.

DeeDee started to laugh from Bonnie, which prompted the others to start laughing.

"What are you laughing for?" Jeanette was confused again.

Bonnie tried to calm down and held her hand on Jeanette's hand.

"It's all right," Bonnie said softly. "I was laughing at you because your eyes were wide open. You were looking at us like you didn't know why we were so quiet. We were about to pray for your safe journey back home to the West Coast."

"Oh that explains ii!" Jeanette said.

Jeanette looked at the people around the table, wondering which one would like to pray.

"Who will pray?" Jeanette asked.

"Let me pray," Bonnie said, raising her hand.

Bonnie stood up. "Thank you seeing us," Bonnie said. "We thank God that we could see you for a week. We were so very happy to see you again. You have a safe trip back home. We love you. God bless you. In Jesus' Name, Amen."

Bonnie hugged Jeanette and sat back down. They started to eat their breakfast. Jeanette got full, stood up and walked in the kitchen. She wanted to look around the house. Jeanette asked Bobby if he'd mind it if she looked around. Bobby told Jeanette to look. She went downstairs to her former bedroom. It was now Connie's bedroom. Jeanette went to another bedroom where Norma used to sleep. At that moment, Jeanette flashed back to her fight with Norma. Jeanette decided to go upstairs and walk through the hall to the living room. She needed to forget the past.

Karen came in the living room and saw Jeanette alone near the window. Karen came over to Jeanette and touched her back. She looked at Karen slowly with tears in her eyes. She noticed at Jeanette's eye started to

"Are you all right?" Karen was concerned.

"I'm fine," Jeanette said, wiping a tear from her eye. "I was just thinking about the past. You know I was an alcoholic and had a bad attitude with everyone."

Jeanette sat on the sofa and started to cry. Karen sat next to Jeanette and hugged her. Vicky and DeeDee came in the living room and looked at Karen and Jeanette hugging on the sofa. Vicky and DeeDee looked at each other.

"What's wrong with Jeanette?" DeeDee asked Karen.

"Just bad memories from the past," Karen explained.

DeeDee understood. She was glad Jeanette was a recovering alcoholic for eighteen years. Jeanette stood up and went to the bathroom. She closed and locked the door. She walked to the sink and looked in the mirror. She couldn't believe she started to cry in front of Karen. She took her glasses off and put them on the sink. She turned the water run and washed her face, then dried her face with a hand towel. She put her glasses back on and went to the kitchen. Vicky and DeeDee saw Jeanette coming.

"Are you all right now?" DeeDee asked.

"I'm fine. Thanks," Jeanette said.

"Good," Vicky smiled. "We'd like to show you something."

Vicky pointed to a cake that said, "Farewell to Jeanette. Have a blast on the West Coast with the Thunderbird." On the cake was an exact drawing of her car. Jeanette's heart broke and she started to cry again. They gave Jeanette a gift. She gave them her address and told them to visit her any time.

Before noon, Jeanette went to the bathroom before leaving on her trip. Jeanette went outside and hugged each person. She got in the car and started the engine. Heather wanted to give something to Jeanette before she left.

Bobby, tell Jeanette to wait for me!" Heather yelled.

She went in the kitchen. Heather came back out and ran to Jeanette. Heather gave her the cerulean blue.

"Is that for me?" Jeanette asked surprised.

"Yes, my mother-in-law told me the story," Heather laughed.

Jeanette never forgot she accidentally put a cigarette out on the butter.

"That was so funny," Jeanette said as she gestured putting a cigarette on the plate. "I'll never forget that."

"Yes, that's exactly what Maria told me!" Heather laughed.

Heather hugged Jeanette in the car, then Bobby hugged her and kissed her cheek.

"You have a safe trip back west," Bobby said. "Please contact us if you have any problems on the road. Ok?"

"Yes, I'll call you anyway. Thanks, Bobby." Jeanette smiled.

Jeanette turned the wheel and backed out to the street. Angel, DeeDee, Vicky and Bonnie followed Jeanette's car. They waved to Jeanette while she drove down the street. Jeanette saw them in the rear view mirror and waved back. She felt sad and already missed them. Jeanette drove through downtown on Main Street.

She waved at everyone and every building until she got to Route 29 South. She wasn't used to two lanes each way and remembered a time when there was only one lane.

When Jeanette got close to Charlottesville, she decided to get gas before getting on I-64 west. She pulled off to a gas station and had a service man fill the tank. She walked around, shopping like a tourist for postcards and a map of Charlottesville and the Blue Ridge Mountains.

She saw a display of many different colored scarves hanging up. She thought it might be fun to wear a scarf in her convertible. She chose a red scarf; it almost matched her pink scarf that was lost somewhere on Route 29 many years ago when she drove to Maria's house. Jeanette walked to the cashier and asked for a pack of Marlboros. Jeanette put the scarf on the counter and pointed to the car that was being filled with gas. The woman knew what Jeanette was trying to say. She totaled the prices for the gas, scarf, and pack of cigarettes. She put it all in a bag and added a book of matches. Jeanette paid for it all then took the bag with her to the car. She moved her car from the gas pumps to the parking lot. She unlocked the top and pulled the convertible open. Jeanette took the scarf and cigarettes out of the bag. She covered her hair with the scarf, removed the plastic off the cigarette pack and threw the bag in trash. She got back in the car. She put a cigarette in her mouth and started to smoke. She coughed very hard because she hadn't smoked for such a long time. But she got used to it and started to drive the car. Jeanette pulled into the street then suddenly braked very hard. She saw a man watering some flowers and trying to get her attention. He waved at her as she was leaving the gas station. She stopped and looked at the man standing there. Jeanette pointed to her ears to show she was deaf. The man nodded his head and put the hose on the ground. He came over to the car.

"Are you Jeanette Dreyfuss?" the man asked.

Jeanette was surprised that he knew her name and looked at his face to see if she could remember him. His face was wrinkled from chain-smoking, and she didn't recognize him. He pointed to the glove compartment. Jeanette looked puzzled and opened the glove compartment. She took some paperwork out and unfolded it. He pointed to his name at the bottom of the form. Jeanette looked at him quickly.

"Are you Mr. Andy Wells?" Jeanette asked, shocked.

"Yes, that's me!" Andy laughed.

She could not believe that Andy still lived in town.

"How did you know it was me?" Jeanette asked.

"I saw you in the parking lot," Andy explained. "You were wearing a scarf and smoking a cigarette. I knew it had to be you."

"You caught me!" Jeanette laughed.

"I don't believe it," Andy said, shocked. "That car still runs great and is in good shape. How did you take such good care of this car?"

"It's a long story," Jeanette giggled.

"Well, it was nice to see you again. Bye," Andy waved.

Jeanette waved at Andy and drove down the street. She saw a sign for I-64 West. She drove onto the highway and started to increase her speed to more than 65 miles an hour. She kept smoking the cigarette, but didn't like it, so she threw the cigarette away. Her scarf was tight on her head. She tried to loosen it, but then the scarf went flying away from her head. Jeanette looked in the rear view mirror and saw her scarf fly off somewhere on the highway. She laughed and didn't care about losing the scarf. She looked at the cerulean blue plate on the seat. She moved the plate to her stomach and held it while she drove on the highway.

Jeanette was glad that her best friend, Maria, never sold the 1964 Convertible Thunderbird. Now this car belonged to Jeanette.